ANACOSTIA FLATS

BY
MICHAEL J. RAWL

PublishAmerica
Baltimore

First printing

ISBN: 1-4137-9778-4
PUBLISHED BY PUBLISHAMERICA, LLLP
www.publishamerica.com
Baltimore

Printed in the United States of America

To Mary and Jean

———————————◆———————————

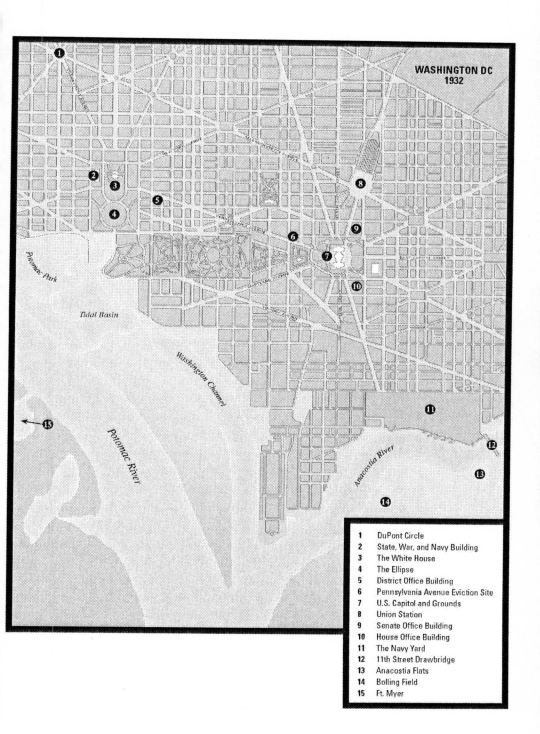

WASHINGTON DC
1932

Potomac Park

Tidal Basin

Washington Channel

Potomac River

Anacostia River

1	DuPont Circle
2	State, War, and Navy Building
3	The White House
4	The Ellipse
5	District Office Building
6	Pennsylvania Avenue Eviction Site
7	U.S. Capitol and Grounds
8	Union Station
9	Senate Office Building
10	House Office Building
11	The Navy Yard
12	11th Street Drawbridge
13	Anacostia Flats
14	Bolling Field
15	Ft. Myer

ANACOSTIA
FLATS

CHAPTER ONE

The Witness

Washington, DC—1931

The witness sat patiently behind a long oak conference table. A black metal microphone was on the polished surface before him.

The house conference room was not crowded. After six days of testimony by bankers and insurance actuaries the committee members were bored. They talked amongst themselves, read newspapers, stretched out on the hard benches, and reclined in their chairs. Their demeanor could be excused—this was an issue that they had been debating for nearly eight years.

At first glance the witness looked like any of the country's other 16 million out-of-work men—slight and haggard, his cheeks deeply lined and stubbly with growth, his curly black hair going thin. The man's face was remarkable only for his sad, overly large brown eyes.

The witness was wearing a plain white cotton shirt with a row of service medals affixed to it. His brown patched trousers were held up by dirty suspenders and under the table he clutched a shapeless brown hat in his lap.

Representative James A. Frear asked for his name and address and reminded him to speak into the microphone.

The witness leaned forward and said in a raspy voice, "Joe Angelo from Camden, New Jersey."

"What is your business?" Frear asked.

"Nothing. I am nothing but a bum," Angelo said. At this a few of the committee members stirred.

"By that I mean, sir, I have not worked for a year and a half," the witness said. "There is no work in my home town."

Frear asked where that was. Angelo told him Camden, New Jersey, 180 miles away.

"My comrade and I hiked here from nine o'clock Sunday morning, all by shoe leather. We come to show you people that we need our bonus. We wouldn't want it if we didn't need it."

The committee members began to put down their newspapers. Several moved to their seats above the witness table. Frear invited Angelo to tell them about himself.

"I'll tell you," Angelo said. "I have got a little home back there that I built with my own hands after I came home from France. Now I expect to lose that little place. Last week I went to our town committee and they gave me four dollars for rations. That is to keep my wife and child and myself and clothe us; also I cannot put no coal in my cellar."

Angelo went on to entertain the committee with his story of how as an underweight teen he had impressed the draft board by doing a handspring on the examination table. He said that when he returned home from the war his father had re-married a fat woman from next door and so he was on his own.

"All I ask of you, brothers, is to help us," Angelo said. "We helped you—now you help us. My partner here has a wife and five children and he is just the same as I am."

Angelo forged ahead. "We didn't go into the World War for the money," he said. "We went into it for our country. Back here in the ammunition factories they said, 'If you don't raise our pay, we're going to strike.' The soldiers didn't do that. We were Americans, for a dollar a day."

Elderly Congressman Henry Thomas Rainey leaned forward. "You are wearing some medal," he said. "What is it?"

Angelo fingered the medal pinned to his shirt.

"I carry the highest medal in America for enlisted men," Angelo said, "the Distinguished Service Cross."

"And what is that for?" Rainey asked.

"That is for saving Colonel Patton," Angelo said.

* * *

By the fall of 1931, America was entering the third winter of its Great Depression.

For more than two years the experience of the typical American family had been relentlessly similar. First the husband's wages were dropped to as low as five cents per hour. Then his working days were cut back from five to three, then two. Finally came the layoff with its final insult—a deduction from the last check of one day's pay for local relief.

After people lost their jobs they frequented the local employment center to see whether any work notices had been written on the chalkboard. After a few unproductive weeks a husband and wife often started a home business to cut hair, wash windows, or bake bread. The problem was that no one else had any money to pay them.

When they were unable to meet their monthly rent, families moved to smaller apartments or back into the homes of their aging parents.

Americans in 1931 had no credit cards, loan companies, food stamps, or unemployment income to fall back on. When their savings accounts were exhausted—at the start of the Depression the average family had $339 in savings—and with no other income available, husbands swallowed their pride and, like Joe Angelo, stood in line at City Hall for stipends of one or two dollars per week.

Despite such widespread hardship, there was often a high social cost for going on the "dole." In some towns the children of those on welfare were not allowed to attend school. Some welfare families were even barred from voting or going to church.

By the winter of 1931 the primarily male breadwinners for 35% of America's population—123 million people—were unemployed. Many wives trained only for homemaking were forced to look for outside work.

Normal life seemed to lie suspended. Factories lay empty and silent, banks and schools were closed. In large cities thousands of downcast people stood in line for hours to receive a loaf of bread.

Two million people were on the road, moving from town to town in search of work or subsistence. Many of these lonely travelers were husbands who had abandoned their families rather than watch them slowly starve. One-half million of those traveling were children.

Many cities posted armed guards at the city limits to turn these roaming hordes away. The guards were often members of American Legion posts—local business owners who wore Legion caps and carried baseball bats with which to protect their interests.

In the eyes of some, democracy appeared to have stopped working. There was a rumor of pending revolution in the air. Chapters of the Communist Party appeared in major cities, their leaders urging violent reform.

In Washington, D.C., Patrick Hurley, the Secretary of the War Department, began to deploy his limited Army troops to urban areas. Tall and robust, red-haired and square-jawed, Hurley was a man among men. His memory was encyclopedic, his ambition boundless. To those who knew him best Patrick Hurley was also complex and ill-tempered. His ascendency from abject poverty to the Hoover cabinet was the stuff of American legend.

As difficult as times were, many first-generation immigrants remembered well the even worse deprivations that they had suffered in Ireland, Germany, Italy, Russia, and Poland. Their survival instincts were well-honed.

Among the most disillusioned in America's small towns were the veterans who fifteen years earlier had fought for America in the Great War. Now in their late 30s and early 40s, these men had until recently been the middle-class stalwarts of their communities, working on small farms and at local businesses. Now they gathered each night at the local Veterans of Foreign Wars hall to drink watered-down beer and muster their dwindling resolve.

The call to serve in the war had come suddenly. From every community four million young men in their teens and early 20s were enlisted via the draft that was passed into law with the lobbying help of an army major named Douglas MacArthur. MacArthur then created and led the first division in World War I, called the "Rainbow" because it included men from 26 different states.

Seemingly overnight over one million Americans were sent overseas to fight for a cause that most did not understand. When they landed in France many did not even know where they were. They simply did as they were told—march, sleep, and shoot.

In 1932 patriotism still ran deep among the country's veterans but they were bewildered and angry over the bonus situation. After the Great War Congress had appropriated $3.5 billion to reward the veterans. Although this "bonus" money was not payable until 1945, it was clearly owed and they needed it now as never before. How could the country they had protected turn its back on them?

* * *

Portland, Oregon—April 9, 1932

Many of Portland's 30,000 unemployed men gathered each day in a downtown area known as the plaza squares. That spring had brought a new round of challenges to local families. It was not unusual to see people whose utilities were cut off cooking in their backyards, adding weeds to their soups. Mothers and their children carried sticks to the town dump to sort through fresh garbage and they went begging door-to-door in the better neighborhoods. It was chic for wealthy families to leave cartons of leftovers from their meals at their backdoor steps each night.

On this sunny, crisp day in Portland, a large powerful man in a red-checkered shirt stood on a wooden bench to address a crowd of about 200 men. He was George Alman, an unemployed lumberjack and a veteran of the Great War.

Alman's activism was inspired by the weekly CBS radio broadcasts of Father Charles Coughlin, an activist Roman Catholic priest from Detroit who was listened to by one-third of the country. Angered over congressional stalling on the veterans' bonus bill, Coughlin urged the nation's veterans to take matters into their own hands.

It is time, Coughlin raged, *for direct action. It is clear that the people you have elected are not going to act on the bonus. You must go there and confront them yourselves.* Coughlin emphasized that lobbying through the elitist American Legion had not worked. The Legion, which was formed after World War I for Army officers, simply wasn't concerned about the plight of the less fortunate enlisted men who had outnumbered WWI officers thirty to one.

Other speakers followed. Many at the plaza squares that day identified with an unemployed cannery worker named Walter W. Waters. His brief speech had been carefully rehearsed for days as

Waters walked the streets of Portland. Waters spoke of how poverty destroyed self-esteem and ambition and told how he and his small family had suffered through a grim meal of fried potatoes the preceding Christmas.

Rather than send 300 more petitions to Washington, let's send 300 men, Waters urged. The crowd cheered. It was Walter Waters' first speech.

* * *

Born in 1898 of old American stock, Walter Waters was raised in Idaho. Seeking adventure, he joined the Idaho National Guard in 1916. The next year America entered the Great War and Waters found himself sent to France in one of the first overseas units.

Waters and his fellow soldiers faced a bitterly cold winter and an even bleaker war situation. The French were exhausted and held together by pride and a few fanatical generals. In Great Britain only six weeks of food remained for the entire country due to the German submarine blockade. The United Kingdom had literally run out of young men to send to the war.

The job faced by Waters and 14,000 other early troops was to build docks, warehouses, and railroad lines, all in extremely cold and wet conditions, while the U.S. drafted, trained, and sent an entire army overseas.

Fortunately the German armed forces were also depleted. They had pulled back in the strategic Hindenberg Retreat, leaving fouled water wells and a wasteland of devastated countryside criss-crossed by 466 miles of snaking trenches. This retreat gave the Americans the time they needed to mass.

Within the year, Private Waters was sent into duty on the front line with the 146th field artillery. He served well, was promoted to sergeant, and made a medic.

During this time weapons of mass destruction were introduced onto the battlefield. Mustard gas, machine guns, large artillery for long-range shelling, airplanes with synchronized machine guns, and armored tanks all made their first appearance alongside traditional cavalry and infantry. Much of the new weaponry was experimental and when deployed it killed men on both sides.

The French battlefield was a wet, gray Salvador Dali landscape of defoliated trees, six-foot deep trenches, barbed wire, gaping shell holes, twisted and burned equipment, and the body parts of horses and men. Thick gray mud pulled soldiers' boots off. The gagging stench of thousands of men, living and dead, was all-pervasive.

Waters' brigade transported iron-wheeled artillery by mule and manpower along narrow French roads, usually in the black of night. They set up their positions based upon information from advance scouts, then shelled the German lines mercilessly in preparation for infantry attacks.

As a medic, Waters treated the burned and maimed soldiers in relatively primitive operating conditions. The medics of World War I did not have penicillin to destroy bacteria, sulfa to control infection, or blood transfusions to prevent shock. The mortality rate among the wounded was extremely high.

Upon his return home after four years of continuous military service, Waters suffered a breakdown and checked himself into a private hospital for a number of months. After he was released, Waters could not hold a job and he made an unusual decision.

"Eager to begin completely anew," he wrote, "I broke all family and personal ties and left Idaho." Waters took the assumed name of "Bill Kincaid" and traveled to the state of Washington where in 1926 he found work as a fruit harvester.

There he met a spunky young woman named Wilma. A local girl, Wilma was attracted to the world-weary "Kincaid." Though slight of stature, Waters had presence. With his bushy eyebrows, wavy blonde hair, and intense blue eyes, he resembled a movie star. His voice was deep and confident.

Wilma and "Bill" were married soon after they met. They moved to Portland where he worked at a canning factory. Wilma reportedly gave birth to two daughters and found a job demonstrating clothing in a department store window. They bought a car and rented a nice apartment.

By December of 1931 their modestly comfortable life was a thing of the past. The Great Depression had reached the West Coast and there was no work to be had. The $1,000 that the Kincaids had set aside was long gone. In order to apply for benefits, Waters began to use his real name again.

His pretend life was over, but another life that he could not possibly have imagined was about to begin.

* * *

In the days following Waters' speech, a core group of Portland men met to discuss his idea. Soon the decision was made to send a delegation of veterans to Washington. A local promoter named Chester Hazen was chosen as commander-in-chief, primarily because he owned a car and had once been heard on a local radio show. Hazen's job would be to drive ahead of the men to raise money and arrange for places for them to stay. George Alman would lead the marchers.

Within a few days, 250 men with $30 among them had signed up for the journey to the nation's capital. It was not a hard sell—they had nothing else to do.

CHAPTER TWO

Springtime in Washington

Washington, D.C., April 4, 1932

Spring was often the best time of year in the nation's capital. It offered a few precious weeks before the insects and oppressive humidity rose out of the wetlands along the Potomac. On April 4 the sky was a cerulean blue behind the gleaming white profile of the U.S. Capitol building.

President Herbert Hoover stared out the side window of the Packard as his driver negotiated the traffic circle below the Capitol and turned onto Pennsylvania Avenue, back toward the White House. Hoover's broad forehead was furrowed, his thick lips pursed.

The president had just addressed the members of the U.S. Senate where he told them in no uncertain terms that they must stay the course. The free market system would work. Hoover, who had great integrity, expected the same of U.S. business.

The president was confident that his Reconstruction Finance Act, finally passed after three long years, would move hundreds of millions of dollars to the failing banks, railroads, utilities, and large corporations. This money would then trickle down to create hundreds of thousands of new jobs. In the meantime America's elected representatives had to ignore pleas for relief from their constituents. Relief must be provided locally. Like a family, American had to live on what she earned.

The president knew that the Democrats were gaining power and trying to rally the public against him for the fall election—and of all the half-baked ideas being promoted by the Democratic-controlled House, the most dangerous was that of providing $2.3 billion in long-promised stipends to the veterans who had served in a war ended fifteen years before. Veterans were already being paid $1 billion per year in various benefits, accounting for about one quarter of the entire federal budget.

For one thing, the Treasury did not even have the funds to distribute. But even if it had, putting that much money into the hands of the common man—the same amount that Hoover's RFA was about to give to his rich business friends—would destroy the self-determination and the moral fabric of the American people. If Congress yielded to the temptation to print what Hoover called "fiat currency" and created a budget deficit, such action would destroy the foundation of America and the will of its people.

There was no reason for the president to compromise on this issue, for Herbert Hoover was not even a politician. The first elected office that he ever held was the presidency. Hoover's primary strengths— careful, lengthy planning and testing followed by detailed administration—were exactly the wrong set of skills for the times.

Hoover leaned back in his seat. When they arrived at the White House, perhaps his Irish cook Catherine would have a nice cup of tea ready for him.

* * *

Most things of importance in 1932—money, business, national policy, elected positions, even the nation's news—were essentially controlled by 600 corporations.

Wright Patman, a liberal congressman from Texas, claimed that this power was concentrated in just 200 wealthy Protestant men whose families ruled America's assets through seats on interlocking corporate boards and a pyramid of holding companies.

Many of those families are familiar commercial names today. They included the Mellons, duPonts, Rockefellers, Fords, Carnegies, Firestones, and Morgans. Their influence on law and policy was pervasive.

During 1929-1931, J.P. Morgan, one of the wealthiest men in the country, paid no taxes at all. Even when taxes seemed unavoidable the very wealthy were granted "abatements." Herbert Hoover's new Treasury Secretary Ogden Mills used this tactic to avoid paying $6 million in taxes on his father's estate.

Cracks, however, were starting to show. In 1930, the first year of the Depression, the once hapless Democrats gained an unexpected single-seat control of the House of Representatives.

The Democrats were using this slight majority to press for a wide range of imaginative and costly legislative proposals to boost the economy. The veterans' bonus bill HR 1, sponsored by the 44-year-old Patman, seemed to be the leading candidate for passage. If it succeeded, God only knew what might follow.

People received information in 1932 through either newspapers (editions were published throughout the day) or the relatively new medium of radio. One person, usually a Republican, typically owned both media outlets in over 80% of American towns. Thus for more than two years Americans had been subjected to the same relentless promise from Herbert Hoover that "things would be better soon."

The bonus had been thought up under President Woodrow Wilson as a way to make up the difference in pay that soldiers would have earned had they stayed home, versus what they were paid overseas. Rather than reward them upon their return from the war, the bonus was created as an annuity, to be funded with a set amount each year then payable in 1945 when the veterans would be middle-aged.

The annuity approach did not bother the veterans before the Depression, but now the tattered bonus paper that more than one million unemployed veterans carried was often the only thing of value that remained in their wallets.

Bonuses for soldiers were not unusual; in fact, they dated back to the days of Caesar. In the United States from the American Revolution through the Civil War, rewards usually in the form of land had been granted after each conflict to soldiers in recognition of their service. Now the veterans of World War I wanted theirs.

* * *

Portland Oregon—May, 1932

The odyssey of the Oregon veterans in search of their bonuses almost failed in the Portland rail yard.

Wth so many homeless people on the roads, railroads were taking a much stronger stance against vagabond travelers. During 1932, Southern Pacific ejected 683,000 vagrants from their trains. Union Pacific officials in Portland refused to cooperate with the veterans. One or two unpaid riders could perhaps be overlooked, but 250 were out of the question.

After two days of stalemate during which the veterans camped in the rail yard and scrounged food from sympathetic townspeople, George Alman announced that the men would climb onto the tops of the next boxcars that left the station.

"Go ahead," the stationmaster said. "There's a tunnel near here that will scrape you off."

"Put on some empties then," Alman said, "or let the tunnel do its scrapin'."

Eighty of the men climbed on top of cars on the next train that stopped at the station and the station master finally capitulated. He arranged for several empty stock cars to be hooked onto the late afternoon freight. "That's the best I can do," he told Alman.

When the men climbed into their new quarters they found that the cattle cars had not been cleaned out.

"Hell, I had many a worse ride in France," one veteran said, "and I didn't even know where I was going."

The men bailed out the dirty straw, unfolded blankets, and settled down for the long haul to Pocatello, Idaho.

It was 6 p.m. on May 12, 1932. The bonus march had begun.

* * *

In Washington, business proceeded as usual. As Congress approached its summer recess even Wright Patman admitted that the chances for HR-1 did not look good. The bill had not been reported out of the Ways and Means Committee, and without the support of the powerful American Legion lobby, the bonus appeared dead for another year.

The young congressman was not discouraged, however. He had just won an important victory for the Democrats through his other major legislation—a motion to impeach Treasury Secretary Andrew Mellon for benefiting himself and his friends through his cabinet post.

Andrew Mellon was an emaciated, white-haired figure with a long mustache and a deceptively timid demeanor. He had served as Secretary of the Treasury for successive Republican administrations since 1921. Andrew Mellon did not simply represent wealth. As the owner of the Aluminum Company of America, Mellon National Bank, Gulf Oil, and a majority shareholder of U.S. Steel, he *was* wealth.

During twelve years at the country's financial helm, Mellon reduced by 60% the federal taxes paid by those who earned $300,000 or more per year. He also rebated $6 billion in taxes to the very wealthy, including nearly $60 million to himself and his companies.

Wright Patman called Mellon "the worst enemy of the wage earners, farmers, and veterans" and the people of America largely agreed. A popular ditty of 1932 went: "Mellon pulled the whistle, Hoover rang the bell, Wall Street gave the signal and the country went to hell."

An avid collector, Mellon accumulated so much valuable artwork in his Massachusetts Avenue luxury apartment that, when he died in 1937, his donated collection formed the nucleus of what became the National Gallery of Art.

Patman put the dour Mellon and his dozen attorneys through two weeks of evidentiary testimony before the Judiciary Committee. Now he was overjoyed to learn that Herbert Hoover had accepted Mellon's resignation and had assigned him as U.S. Ambassador to Great Britain.

Hoover was secretly relieved at this opportunity to replace Mellon who had become an embarrassment due to his blatantly illegal dealings. Hoover was determined that what had happened to President Harding would not happen to his administration.

The timing of Mellon's ouster was ironic. For more than ten years he had been Washington's most outspoken opponent of paying any type of veterans' bonus.

* * *

Of all the places to live during the United States' Great Depression, Washington, D.C. was one of the best.

Some 73,000 of the 500,000 people who resided in the Nation's capital were federal employees who worked at secure jobs that paid an average of $3,600 a year. That was enough to buy a small house, pay the bills, and go to an occasional baseball game.

Several hundreds of thousands more earned comfortable wages lobbying, writing about, waiting upon, and providing housing, goods, and services to government officials. More than 10,000 people alone worked on elaborate building projects that symbolically glorified the expanding Washington bureaucracy.

While some 18,000 residents of the District were unemployed, they were mostly poor blacks who had lived in impoverished conditions in Washington alleyways since the Civil War. The Depression brought no change to the lifestyles of most Washington people of color.

The elite in Washington, D.C. were the embassy personnel and elected officials. The average salary for a U.S. congressman in 1932 was $10,000, two and one-half times that of the average American worker. Members of Congress enjoyed large offices; parking, postage and telephones; free family medical care; inexpensive meals in fine private dining rooms; and an office payroll of $5,000 that elected officials could use to hire relatives, friends, and mistresses. During the Depression, one-quarter of the nation's congressmen had relatives on the payroll and it was estimated that fewer than 10% of those did any real work.

The Republican Party had been in firm control of Congress for nearly thirteen years, during which congressional seats were typically awarded to the wealthy and well-connected, and 90% of congressmen were re-elected each term.

Now severe economic conditions had created an atmosphere of change. Fueled by the growing Democratic revival, a liberal movement in the House of Representatives was running counter to the ancient, hard-headed conservative block in the Senate. As a result nothing got done in the 72nd Congress except bitter in-fighting on the floors of both chambers. President Hoover hated this Congress and the feeling was mutual.

Comfortably isolated from the hardships experienced in all other parts of the country, the "fat cats" in Washington, D.C. were prime for a rude awakening.

In five cattle cars from Portland, Oregon, that awakening was on its way.

CHAPTER THREE

The Secretary of War

There was good reason why the position today called "Secretary of Defense" was known in 1932 as the "Secretary of War."

War was a tangible experience for Americans, many of whose grandfathers or fathers had fought in the Civil War. A number of men still living then had served in Cuba against Spain and in Mexico against Pancho Villa's raiders.

Then in 1917, four million Americans were drafted and a quarter of those sent overseas to serve in the "War to End All Wars." When the survivors returned after prevailing over the German army through sheer brutal force, the signs of war were everywhere: the armless man who lived next door, the blind veteran who sat in the sun in front of Town Hall, the soldier without a nose who stayed in a dark room in the back of his mother's house.

These constant reminders of the human and fiscal costs of war helped fuel a national fixation on peace. Congress debated vigorously over how to avoid future entanglement, and budgets for the military were cut substantially as America retreated behind its ocean barrier.

The Secretary of War watched with concern as America's principal military force, the U.S. Army, lost its vitality. Army weaponry was outmoded, its training lax, and military officers had even been told by President Hoover not to wear their uniforms while on duty in the nation's capital so as not to draw attention to their presence.

* * *

Across the continent another small military force was having problems of its own. The Oregon veterans' advance man Walter Hazen was nowhere to be found.

In one town after another the marchers were told that Hazen had been there collecting money, but no arrangements had been made to feed or shelter them.

Fortunately, word of their trek preceded them and the veterans were well received by enthusiastic crowds wherever the Union Pacific stopped. At one stop there were picnic tables laden with food awaiting them and they were allowed to camp in the town park. At another they were encouraged to form a parade and collect money from the townspeople.

The veterans caught up with Hazen in Pocatello, Idaho, where they confronted him. Hazen claimed that he had been unable to raise any funds. The veterans insisted on a search of his car and Hazen drew a handgun. A struggle ensued, during which he was disarmed, arrested by the local police, and charged with larceny.

Without money or any real organization, the veterans' spirits flagged and they began to argue among themselves. Quiet-mannered George Alman could not control the men. Despite his orders, roving bands went into Pocatello to panhandle and then refused to share their spoils.

Walter Waters watched as one man after another tried his hand at speech-making. At last he took his turn, standing atop a boxcar in the dusty, swirling Idaho wind of his youth. The day was cold and most of the veterans huddled in dismal groups around small campfires in the rail yard.

Waters had a bugler sound for attention and then he shouted down to the men, "If we don't go to Washington as an organized group of gentlemen and decent citizens, we won't go at all… (and if we stay here) you'll end up in some western jail.

"We need organization, just like in the Army," he continued. "We need a transportation committee and a supply officer. We can't go begging in every town we come to." The men started to get to their feet and nod to one another.

That afternoon Waters outlined a military structure that would keep the men focused and under control. Within a few more days he was elected commander.

Three days later they arrived in Council Bluffs, Iowa—Herbert Hoover's home town—where they were met by the mayor and police chief. Waters was given a key to the city and arrangements were made for the Wabash Railway to carry them across Missouri to St. Louis. At the first division stop the veterans found six crates of eggs, several shipping cans of milk, and boxes of bread and doughnuts left for them by local farm families.

Other veterans had joined the Oregon contingent along the way. The group was now up to 400 men.

* * *

Awaiting the veterans in Washington was a man who, because of his background, one might think would be supportive of the veterans. Instead he would become their greatest enemy.

Patrick Hurley was born in Texas. His father Pierce was always in trouble and, in 1882, on the run from the law, he took his wife and seven children across the state line into the wilds of pre-Oklahoma Indian Territory. There they lived a dismal existence as squatters on Choctaw Indian land.

One of the few bright spots in Patrick's youth was his beloved mother who instilled in him a strict moral code. Another was his friendship with Choctaw Chief Ben Franklin Smallwood. Smallwood taught the boy how to read and enthralled him with tales of a mystical city called Washington, D.C.

When farming failed, Pierce Hurley turned to coal mining. At age 11 Patrick worked the air bellows 10 hours a day, one hundred feet below the surface. Aboveground the Hurleys shared a four-room shack with another family.

The high-tempered Pierce Hurley drank and fought constantly. He often challenged Patrick to act like a man and once sent him with a loaded gun after a boy who had insulted him. Patrick shot at the boy but intentionally missed.

The year that Patrick turned thirteen, his family disintegrated. First his mother died in childbirth, then Pierce Hurley was disabled when his horse stumbled and fell upon him. Next Patrick's cherished baby sister Monica tried to tug a loaded shotgun off a bed by its barrel and it discharged, killing her.

Following this tragedy Patrick's older brother deserted the family and his older sister went into a convent. Patrick tried to support his three younger siblings for another year but then he left as well.

While working on a ranch in the Creek Nation, young Hurley was befriended by an older, bashful Cherokee cowhand named Will Rogers who took Patrick under his wing. The two traveled across New Mexico, then parted when Rogers took a herd of cattle on to William Randolph Hearst's 83,000-acre ranch in San Luis Obispo, California.

At age eighteen Pat Hurley met Dr. J. H. Scott, president of the Baptist Indian University. Scott was impressed by the boy's prodigious memory and persuaded Hurley to enroll in exchange for caring for the school's horses. Five years later, in 1905, Patrick Hurley graduated first in his class.

Believing he was an Indian, Yale University offered Hurley a scholarship only to withdraw it when he showed up. Undeterred, Hurley moved to Chief Smallwood's magical city of Washington, D.C. where he drove a hack cab at night in order to study law in the daytime at National University. A lesson from Roman history that he learned there stayed with him his whole life: one or two great men can affect all of mankind.

Armed with his law degree, the brazen young man secured an appointment with President Theodore Roosevelt and demanded a job. Smiling, Teddy told Hurley to "Go back home and get people to talk about you." And so he did.

Fortunes were being made in Oklahoma from land deals and oil and gas leases. Hurley was made national attorney for the Choctaw Indian Nation and soon became wealthy. He built a large house on the bluff of the Arkansas River and was considered one of Tulsa's leading citizens—brave, outspoken and quick to action. His only fault was a red-hot temper. Pat Hurley could be provoked easily to the point of losing self-control.

When the United States entered the first World War in 1917, Pat Hurley was quick to enlist. He was sent overseas as part of an artillery brigade but never saw battle. On his return to the states, he resumed his courtship of a beautiful young woman he had met at the Hunt Club Ball in Washington, D.C. Hurley pursued her to a horse show where he announced, "I am going to marry you!"

"Why I don't even know you!" Ruth Wilson exclaimed. Ruth was tall, blonde, and sublimely polished from her life on Philadelphia's Main Line. She was a remarkable pianist and her social skills were impeccable. Her background was the exact opposite of Hurley's. Yet three months later Patrick Hurley climbed aboard Admiral Henry B. Wilson's flag ship on the Hudson River to ask permission to wed his daughter.

The newlyweds returned to Tulsa where Hurley became involved in state politics. He served as head of "Republicans for Hoover" in Oklahoma in 1928 and at the national convention helped secure the votes that led to Herbert Hoover's nomination over Kansas Senator Charles Curtis, who Hoover then chose for his vice presidential nominee.

When Hoover formed his administration, Pat Hurley was offered several positions. He enthusiastically chose to serve as an assistant secretary in the War Department under Secretary James Good, who had raised massive amounts of money for Hoover's campaign from midwestern utility companies. In the spring of 1929, Pat Hurley moved to Washington, D.C. where he lived alone for several months until Ruth and their three children joined him.

A few months later James Good was struck with appendicitis. Unfortunately Good was one of those unusual people whose internal anatomy was reversed. When the doctors began to operate they could not locate his appendix and the unlucky War Secretary succumbed to perdontinitis.

Upon Good's death the handsome, energetic young attorney Patrick Hurley was advanced to the position of Secretary of War. Hurley was immediately swept into Washington's social scene thanks to his outgoing nature, beautiful wife, and important new position as a member of President Hoover's cabinet.

At last Pat Hurley was where he felt he belonged. He worked hard to become one of Hoover's closest aides (the other was millionaire Treasury Secretary Ogden Mills who succeeded Mellon in 1932), which allowed him to control access to the president and dispense political favors.

Because Herbert Hoover had great disdain for his elderly vice president Charles Curtis, for Pat Hurley the vice presidency in the election of 1932 did not seem like too big a reach.

Taken from "*Pat Hurley,*" *The Story of an American,* by Parker La Moore, Brewer, Warren & Putnam, New York, 1932.

*Patrick J. Hurley, the Secretary of War
in President Herbert Hoover's cabinet*

* * *

The State, War, and Navy building was a massive structure beside the White House, its portals draped with large flags. Today the wedding-cake style edifice is known as the Executive Office building.

One of Patrick Hurley's first tasks in the summer of 1930 was to appoint a new Army Chief of Staff to replace the retiring Charles Summerall.

Hurley recommended to Hoover that they appoint an officer whose exploits during the first World War were legendary: Major General Douglas MacArthur.

Hurley had briefly seen the famous soldier two times and he had been mightily impressed. The first sighting occurred on the Mexican border after MacArthur returned from a bloody mission during which he had shot and killed seven of Pancho Villa's men. The second was after one of MacArthur's many heroic combat episodes in France.

Despite his outstanding war record and his subsequent assignment as the commander of West Point, for the past several years Douglas MacArthur had been exiled to the Philippines by his superior, General John J. Pershing.

The bantam Pershing resented "Mac's" battlefield exploits during the Great War. Pershing felt that they caused him, the commander of the American Expeditionary Force, to be considered an "armchair general." (Pershing had earned a daring reputation of his own during the Indian Wars.)

After the war's end, MacArthur married the super-rich divorcee Louise Cromwell Brooks, with whom Pershing had carried on a torrid affair in France. While Pershing was not jealous of Brooks, he had hoped that she might marry his aide, Colonel John Queckemeyer. Pershing had lost his wife and two daughters in a tragic San Francisco fire and he treated Quackemeyer like a son.

The final straw was MacArthur's actions at West Point where he replaced many outmoded pre-Civil War practices with modern training techniques. Pershing and other military traditionalists were furious at the aloof MacArthur for trying to modernize their beloved academy.

Even though commanders at West Point traditionally served two-year terms, Douglas MacArthur was re-assigned by Pershing to the Philippines after just 12 months.

Although MacArthur enjoyed the islands and the Filipino people, Louise was miserable at their new posting. She spent most of her time with other disenchanted expatriates and reportedly had an affair. After three years, MacArthur's mother begged Pershing to let Douglas return since her other son Arthur, a promising naval officer, had recently died from a burst appendix. Pershing granted her request.

Upon their return Louise asked her wealthy stepfather Edward Stotesbury, a partner in J.P. Morgan and major Replubication donor, to use his influence to have MacArthur promoted from brigadier general to major general status. This made him at age 45 the youngest major general in the Army.

MacArthur was next appointed, to his dismay, to serve on the court-martial panel for General Billy Mitchell. He then headed the 1928 U.S. Olympic team in Sweden during which time his marriage to Louise came to an end.

In addition to angering Pershing, the major general managed to upset Herbert Hoover by turning down the president's offer to make him U.S. Chief Engineer with the specific objective of taming the flooding Mississippi River.

Instead MacArthur played up to the large ego of the new Secretary of War. After Patrick Hurley presented a memo to Congress in 1930 concerning Philippine independence, MacArthur sent him a gushing letter, calling Hurley's memo:

"...the most comprehensive and statesmanlike paper that has ever been presented with reference to this complex and perplexing problem. At one stroke it has clarified issues which have perplexed and embarrassed statesmen for the last 30 years."

MacArthur concluded: "I am sure that the United States intends even greater things for you in the future."

After receiving this letter Patrick Hurley—who just recently had criticized the newly divorced MacArthur as "a man who cannot hold his woman"—began to see the major general in a different light.

When Hurley put MacArthur's name forward for Army Chief of Staff, he faced a president who was still smarting over Mac's rejection of his pet engineering appointment, as well as the objections of Pershing, still the country's top military man thanks to his uniquely conferred title "General of the Armies." (Pershing commanded the largest, most luxurious office at the War Department and its biggest pension, even though his primary function was to raise money for the construction of Washington's National Cathedral.)

Hoover suggested that Hurley put forward another candidate. Hurley insisted that he had found his man. The argument went back and forth until Pershing grudgingly allowed "one of my boys" to be given the top Army job. Douglas MacArthur was named Army Chief of Staff in August 1930.

As a result, Patrick Hurley and Douglas MacArthur were the two senior men in the United States military when the veterans came to town in the spring of 1932. As the first marchers drifted in along Wisconsin Avenue from the Maryland state line like dim wraiths from his impoverished youth, Patrick Hurley hated them on sight.

CHAPTER FOUR

The Battle of the B&O

Although he worked diligently at his military career for nearly twenty years, Major Dwight David Eisenhower had not yet been given the responsibility that he craved, mainly because of the plodding nature of peacetime advancement. He was, in his words, "in a rut."

It was Eisenhower's misfortune to have entered active service after the dreaded "hump" was formed by the thousands of senior officers who were commissioned on August 15, 1917, to serve in World War I. Twelve years after the war ended, 1,200 of those officers were still in the service and they formed a living block to promotion for anyone who enlisted after them. Without a war, promotions came very slowly.

An outstanding football player before he suffered a busted knee, "Ike" was valued by the military for his coaching skills. The Eisenhowers lived in modest comfort during his various assignments thanks to the occasional financial support of his wife's family. However, at age 42 the ambitious career officer knew that he was capable of doing more.

To his regret, Eisenhower had not participated in the Great War. His first assignment was to train green new second lieutenants at Ft. Leavenworth, Kansas. Among his early recruits was a young man named Francis Scott Key Fitzgerald who, to Ike's amusement, spent every spare hour penning a novel, *The Romantic Egotist*.

From Leavenworth, Eisenhower was sent to command Camp Colt where the Army was devising strategies for tank warfare. At his disposal were three midget tanks on loan from Britain where they had been designed by a promising young military officer named Winston Churchill. Before Ike could be free of Camp Colt the war ended.

Eisenhower was next assigned to the new tank corps at Ft. George Meade, Maryland, where he and Mamie shared rough barracks with a colorful colonel named George Patton and his wife Bea.

Patton and Eisenhower became close friends. Both men were fascinated by military history, shared great ambition, and had quick tempers. They spent much of their free time together playing poker and developing theories about tank warfare—theories that would be of value to Patton in years to come.

Eisenhower then spent three important years under General Fox Conner in Panama. Conner personally schooled the younger man in military history and tactics, and he gave Eisenhower advice that would propel him to the next level in his career: "Attach yourself to someone with power and learn all you can from him."

In 1928 Eisenhower was assigned to Washington, D.C., a prime post for career officers. There he assisted General John Pershing in the meticulous preparation of his WWI memoirs and he attended the War College. Some 7,102 of the Army's 12,133 officers were, like Eisenhower, on non-military assignments with nothing to do but await another war, even as Congress continued to attack the Army's budget.

* * *

Veterans from an earlier war continued on their way to Washington. When they reached St. Louis the veterans were received not by waving citizens but by policemen waiting on the railroad platform, armed with riot guns and billy clubs.

Waters read the situation quickly and passed the word among his men to form ranks, show military bearing, and display discipline.

When the train slowed to a stop, Waters and his newly appointed captains were the first to disembark. Under the threatening glares of the armed police, the veterans' bugler sounded assembly and the ragged army climbed down from the boxcars and formed perfect military lines in the railroad yard.

Impressed by the veterans' discipline, the police allowed them to spend the night in the Wabash boxcars that they had ridden in across Missouri. In two days the Battle of the B&O would begin.

* * *

Returned to Washington after two years in Paris with Pershing's Battle Monuments Commmission, Dwight Eisenhower was at last given an assignment that let him showcase his organizational skills. He was to analyze the country's need for military resource should another war occur, reporting to the new Army Chief of Staff Douglas MacArthur. (The report never made it to President Hoover—members of his staff sent it back with a note: "The government has no intention of thinking of a future war.")

Although he had been an average student at West Point, Ike's real talent lay in writing. This new assignment was important and enjoyable, largely because Patrick Hurley and MacArthur got along so well. Both believed themselves to be men of destiny.

They shared Victorian values and spoke for hours about the lessons of Roman times. Hurley basked in the flattery that was regularly applied by his chief of staff and both men appreciated the attention of the Washington press corps, being acutely aware of the need to polish and protect their images.

Hurley and MacArthur also shared a commitment to strengthen America's military. In Major Dwight Eisenhower they discovered a loyal and detail-oriented aide who would effectively carry out their directives.

Eisenhower worked diligently at his new assignment, sensing that it represented his best chance so far to rise within the Army. He was very busy and his tireless efforts made him appear to others as cold and unfriendly. He privately described his duties as "slavish." MacArthur placed Ike in a cubicle next to his office from where he could be summoned at a moment's notice.

Military life had conditioned Eisenhower to show only cheerful respect to his superiors. Still he was entitled to his private thoughts. In a diary entry of June 14, 1932, Eisenhower wrote of Patrick Hurley:

"About 49 years old. Affable but rather petulant, courteous but unappreciative of good work on the part of subordinates. His interests seem almost wholly political—and he has sufficient wealth to take full advantage of every opportunity offered along this line… Keen on favorable publicity and always solicitous of members of the press, no matter what the occasion. Meticulous as to details of dress and personal appearance—sometimes characterized by the unfriendly sections of the press as a "dandy," Fop," etc. I do not believe he will go any higher in the political world, although he is very ambitious…he is not big enough…unquestionably he has decided that his one chance of political advancement is as a henchman to Pres. Hoover. Consequently, in public utterances he is slavish in his support of the Pres. He is jealous and unstable."

Eisenhower was quick to make up his mind about Patrick Hurley but it would take him longer to understand the sort of man he was dealing with in Major General Douglas MacArthur.

* * *

The first notice of the veterans' march to Washington, D.C. appeared as a small article in the *Washington Star* on May 22.

The week before the president had shocked the nation by stating, "There are no hungry men in America." In response, the AP wire service ran a photograph of Herbert Hoover on the White House lawn feeding one of his three dogs, a Belgian shepherd named King Tut. "Hoover's dog eats while millions starve," the caption read.

(King Tut spent each night patrolling the White House fence. The public came to know him as "the dog who worried himself to death.")

President Hoover did his best to appear positive and in charge in order to reassure the general public. He retired each night at 10:00 p.m. and arose every morning at 7:00. Most days he went directly to the west lawn to engage in a robust toss of the medicine ball with his closest cronies, including Patrick Hurley. The press dubbed this group the "medicine ball cabinet."

In private Hoover was often morose, largely because of his treatment by the press.

A mining engineer celebrated as a hero for his relief efforts during the Great War, Hoover was elected on the promise of new governing techniques and "a chicken in every pot." Hoover did nothing to cause the Depression that began so suddenly just seven months into his administration. He had even warned about its possibility while serving under Calvin Coolidge. Still the entire country blamed him for it.

In private Hoover could be relaxed, witty, and graceful, but to the public he came across as remote, dull, and uncaring. A joke making the rounds had Hoover approach the Secretary of the Treasury for a nickel in order to buy a soft drink. "Here's a dime," the secretary said. "Treat all your friends."

Another rumor claimed that Hoover was instinctively disliked by dogs. One evening the president and his wife visited the Hurleys for dinner at their Leesburg, Virginia, estate. As the president climbed the stone front steps to the large brick manor house, dressed in a cut waistcoat and striped trousers, the Hurley's yapping terrier Scotty rushed forward and urinated on Herbert Hoover's spats.

Ruth Hurley shrieked and her servant Sam Pinckney dropped to his knees to blot the stained spats but Hoover stopped them with a raised hand.

"Don't worry about it, Ruth," he said. "Everyone else is doing it."

* * *

Patrick Hurley received a letter from his friend John Nichlos, a utilities executive in Chickasaw, Oklahoma. The letter proposed an idea for the Hoover Administration to consider. Restaurants in Chickasaw were scraping the leftover food (called swill) from diners' plates into five-gallon cartons labeled "meat," "bread," or "vegetables." Poor people could chop firewood and do other chores in return for dipping into the containers.

"We expect a little trouble now and then from those not worthy of the support, but otherwise things are going well," Nichlos wrote.

Hurley thought the idea had merit and forwarded it to Colonel Arthur Woods, who had been appointed by President Hoover to monitor state and local relief efforts.

Although this particular idea was rejected, Woods did bring a number of suggestions for national relief to the president, all of which were vetoed. Hoover was adamant in his belief that relief was a local, not national, responsibility.

After Woods resigned in frustration in 1931, Hoover convinced a reluctant Walter S. Gifford, President of American Telephone and Telegraph, to serve in his place. Gifford was subsequently called to appear before Congress in January 1932 to update the members on national relief efforts.

Gifford astonished the congressmen by telling them that he knew nothing about state relief efforts or even how many people were unemployed. He did offer up an advertising campaign for the fall that promised "the thrill of a great spiritual experience" for those who gave to charity.

"I hope you are not criticizing me for looking at life optimistically," Gifford complained to an incredulous Senator Robert La Follette, Jr.

Senator Edward Costigan asked Gifford to provide the reports on which he based his optimism.

"I have none, Senator," Gifford replied.

* * *

By May 22, although Walter Waters and his 400 men had travelled two-thirds of the way to their objective, they found themselves stymied in the St. Louis rail yard. After resting for two days, Waters' transportation committee decided that the best route to Washington was via the Baltimore and Ohio Railroad whose trains departed from a junction two miles away in East St. Louis.

Waters arranged with a local veteran who owned a small truck to shuttle the men's supplies to the East rail yard. The commander then led the veterans, escorted by several motorcycle police, on a two-mile march over a toll bridge across the Mississippi. The toll keeper watched silently, not daring to demand money for their passage.

In East St. Louis they were met by an old man dressed in ancient military garb. He sported a white walrus mustache and a helmet featuring a two-foot feather plume. There were long cavalry spurs on the heels of his polished knee-length boots and a four-foot saber dragged along the ground from a scabbard on his waist. His insignia was that of an adjutant general in the Missouri National Guard.

The old reservist introduced himself to Waters as General Carlos Black and complimented him on how well the veterans were organized. But Black could not allow them to remain in St. Louis. Missouri Governor Louis Emersen had received strict instructions from the Commissioners of the District of Columbia to turn them back, citing interstate transit laws.

"Your time is up," Black told the veterans, adding that his job was to "split up" the bonus army.

Black's orders were reinforced by a B&O Railroad detective named Young who refused to allow them transportation. Young said that he was acting at the direct order of B&O President Daniel Willard who was responding himself to a request from Washington. The railroad executive complied even though he privately sympathized with the veterans. Willard told a friend that he, personally, would steal before he would starve.

The next morning the veterans massed near the eastbound track. When the first train was about to leave, Waters blew a whistle and the men swarmed onto the cars. The engineer refused to move. B&O and the veterans were at a stalemate.

The next day the veterans, a number of them former railroad employees, engaged in more creative passive resistance. Some applied soap to the steel rails so that the giant metal wheels of the B&O trains would only spin. Others decoupled cars and disassembled brake air hoses.

Willard appealed for local help but General Black's National Guard and the Missouri state police refused to get involved, calling it a railroad dispute. Detective Young brought in 150 hardened railroad bulls to stand guard, and Willard sent a B&O vice president to make it clear again to Waters that the veterans could not ride for free.

The confrontation entered a third day. A 30-car refrigerated train was delayed and the food that it carried began to spoil. The "Battle of the B&O," as the newsmen called it, was making headlines. An RKO Movietone film clip of the standoff was being shown in theaters across the country. The matter quickly became a national embarrassment for both the B&O Railroad and the Hoover Administration.

For the first time in his life Walter Waters was interviewed by the press. He said, "We are going to Washington to get our bonus payments and we will stay there until 1945 if that is what it takes." His quote was quickly put before the District of Columbia commissioners, who had sent the telegrams urging resistance to Emerson and Willard.

By trying to stop the veterans with force, the commissioners only brought them closer together. The "Battle of the B&O" forced Waters and his officers to establish a command structure that lasted throughout the weeks to come, with Waters at the top as "commander-in-chief," a title used by the American Legion and other veterans' groups.

Next in line came a series of captains, lieutenants, and sergeants who led companies of 40 men each. Closest to Waters was his own personal staff led by Doak Carter, a beefy former railroad detective, and Mickey Dolan as his personal bodyguard. Dolan was a former prizefighter who Waters had seen box in the stockyards at Portland.

For the next two months the slightly built Waters was almost always accompanied by Carter, his sour expression never changing, or by the black Irishman Mickey Dolan. Often watching nearby was the deposed commander George Alman, his jealous fury barely contained.

* * *

Awaiting the veterans in Washington, D.C. was not just a stalemated Congress and a wary War Department but also an entrenched societal structure, one that had fully embraced the Hurleys and Douglas MacArthur and that would serve almost as a combination audience and Greek chorus to them during the Bonus March episode.

At the top of this pyramid sat three powerful women: Cissy Patterson, publisher of the *Washington Herald*; the heiress Evalyn Walsh McLean, the current possessor of the Hope Diamond; and Alice Roosevelt Longworth, who by 1932 was well on her way to becoming "the other Washington monument." While not a classic beauty, the young woman was very photogenic with a sensuous mouth, blond hair, and oddly shaped blue eyes that changed shade according to her mercurial moods.

Alice, the daughter of Teddy Roosevelt, had known nothing but privilege her entire life. At age 17 she was dubbed "Princess Alice" and her wild behavior often brought her more newspaper coverage than was given to her popular father. A trust fund from her late mother's family, the Lees, allowed her to be independent.

One evening a mentally ill man from Long Island, armed with a gun and claiming to be engaged to Alice, forced his way onto the White House grounds. After the intruder was disarmed by Secret Service officers, Teddy Roosevelt said, "Of course the man is insane. He wants to marry Alice."

Alice rejected her cousin Franklin Roosevelt as a potential suitor by calling him a "feather duster," but attracted the attention of Nicholas Longworth, a rich and debonair congressman from Cincinnati, Ohio.

The young couple married in a lavish ceremony at the White House where Douglas MacArthur was part of the honor guard, and honeymooned briefly at John McLean's 80-acre estate, Friendship.

They then embarked on a cruise to Cuba so that Alice could see San Juan Hill, which disappointed her. They returned to Washington, D.C. where Nick had bought a large house at 2009 Massachusetts Avenue. There Nick and Alice went their separate ways as both engaged in numerous affairs—Nick with Cissy Patterson and Alice with Senator William Borah, among others.

When Alice's cousin Franklin came to town as Secretary of the Navy and married her other cousin Eleanor, Alice encouraged Franklin in his own affair with an impoverished young Washington beauty named Lucy Mercer.

These odd complications, competitions, and incestuous dramas characterized Washington society during the Depression years. Even 52-year-old Army chief Douglas MacArthur had a young Eurasian mistress named Dimples stashed away in the Chastleton Hotel. Nothing in the straightforward, hard-working backgrounds of the veterans or the pampered histories of the wealthy could prepare either group for their coming confrontation.

* * *

Police Superintendent Pelham D. Glassford pulled his blue Harley-Davidson motorcycle to a stop in front of his bohemian Georgetown townhouse, which he had fondly named the "Borneo Embassy." Glassford tilted back his brimmed hat and wearily rubbed his eyes.

It had been a long and tiring day for the superintendent of the District's 1,452-man police department, starting with an emergency 8:00 a.m. meeting with two of the three commissioners who ran the District of Columbia.

Attending this particular meeting were the Commission Chairman Dr. Luther Reichelderfer, a dapper retired physician with an imperious manner, and Major General Herbert S. Crosby who like Glassford was a decorated World War I hero. The subject of discussion was the journey of the Oregon veterans to Washington. Railroad officials in St. Louis seemed unable to deal with them and the negative publicity was hurting the president.

Glassford had already handled two civil marches during his brief career as superintendent, both of which lasted for several days. One was a group of Communists and the other unemployed men led by Father James Cox. Both had stayed a day or so.

Crosby told him that several other groups of veterans were headed to Washington as well. One from Utah was being held up by the B&O at the commissioner's request in Chicago. Another 200 veterans had recently left Johnson City, Tennessee, and 600 more had just been driven out of a railroad yard by police in New Orleans.

Acting on behalf of the commissioners, Glassford had earlier sent telegrams to Governors Albert Ritchie of Maryland and Gifford Pinchot of Pennsylvania to request that they not transport the Oregon veterans into the District. Now he showed Crosby the reply that he had just received from Ritchie. It read: "I know of nothing I can do to discourage their visit to Washington."

* * *

Before the veterans arrived, Pelham Glassford's primary duty had been police reform. In the city where the nation's laws were made, interpreted, and judicially enforced, police corruption had reigned for nearly 20 years throughout four different administrations.

The city had long been managed at the pleasure of the country's top elected officials. The District's three elected commissioners reported to the president and regulations were made as often for social or bureaucratic reasons as for legal ones. Enforcement was doled out according to the importance of the offender. Washington, D.C. was much like a small island empire.

In return for benign treatment, elected officials turned a blind eye to police transgressions. Bribery was the accepted currency and fortunes were made from bootlegging, drugs, prostitution, and shady condemnations to free up land for the fast-expanding federal bureaucracy.

To his credit, President Hoover came into office determined to change all of this.

His house cleaning began with the appointment of three new law and order commissioners. The job of reforming the police department was assigned to Herbert Crosby who quickly appointed his former WWI and West Point comrade Pelham "Happy" Glassford to get the job done.

* * *

Not all transgressions in Washington went unnoticed. In 1932 a pair of anonymous authors published a sequel to their earlier book *Washington Merry-Go-Round*, which had skewered the Hoover Administration. In this second volume, Patrick and Ruth Hurley were held up to ridicule for reportedly practicing their entrances to parties in front of a full-length mirror.

A furious Hurley convinced President Hoover to assign J. Edgar Hoover the job of discovering the authors' identities. The Bureau of Investigations director reported that the books had been written by a *Christian Science Monitor* reporter named Bob Allen and the *Baltimore Sun* Washington correspondent, Drew Pearson. Pearson had been Cissy Patterson's son-in-law and got most of his inside information from her friends.

Hurley insisted that Hoover dismiss Pearson's father who had recently been appointed governor to the Virgin Islands. Hoover, noting that Pearson was a fellow Quaker, refused. The president simply said that he would never speak to Drew Pearson again, and he never did.

Hurley then used his influence with Ruth's brother, who happened to be the business manager at the *Baltimore Sun*, to have Pearson fired. Later that year the Secretary of War came across the tall, balding Pearson during a party at a home on Massachusetts Avenue (today the location of the Cosmos Club). Thirty years later Pearson recalled the incident in his memoirs:

> Hurley accosted me in one of the most disagreeable scenes I have had in a semi-public place—and since then I have had many. His language was unprintable and finally I suggested that we retire to the basement where I could properly answer. He turned on his heel and left.

Inadvertently Patrick Hurley launched the career of Drew Pearson, for within the year Pearson and Allen began the infamous "Washington Merry-Go-Round" column that was, in time, syndicated by United Features to newspapers across the country.

For thirty-seven years Pearson produced eight columns a week (one for weeklies) as well as a Sunday night radio broadcast, all designed to spear bloated and corrupt Washington bureaucrats.

Pearson's puncturing of phonies and hypocrites earned him a reputation as the incorruptible hero of the common man. This reputation did not come cheaply. By 1949 Pearson could name a half-dozen people who had committed suicide because of his columns. Hundreds more had lost their jobs and careers and many of those ended up in jail. Pearson's work, always ugly and often inaccurate, helped to establish the modern journalist as "watchdog."

Drew Pearson never forgot an enemy. He was a festering thorn in the sides of Douglas MacArthur and Patrick Hurley for the rest of their lives.

* * *

Pelham Glassford, on the other hand, was a great favorite with the press—but then "Happy" Glassford always had been popular.

During his military career Glassford was made the youngest brigadier general of World War I. While commander of the 103rd field artillery, he would take his two-cylinder motorcycle out at night on reconnaissance to help direct the next day's shelling.

A talented artist, Glassford sketched the 103rd's famous insignia of a frightened dachshund in flight with an artillery shell embedded in its behind. His bravery and a wound suffered in battle earned him the Distinguished Service Cross.

After the war, Glassford spent several years with the Army in Washington and then, like Walter Waters, he undertook a journey of self-discovery, taking off across the country on his motorcycle. First the former general worked as a barker, electrician, and sign painter in a traveling circus. Next he spent a year as a reporter for the *San Francisco Examiner*, an experience that helped him deal with the press during his assignment in Washington.

The 47-year-old Glassford then moved to Arizona to help run the family horse ranch. After his father died suddenly, a depressed Glassford went to Washington, D.C. to organize an Armistice Day celebration being mounted by the new Veterans of Foreign Wars organization.

Glassford visited the District Office to make traffic arrangements for the event where he was reunited with Herbert H. Crosby, a major general he had known in France.

Crosby, one of three commissioners who ran the District of Columbia, had recently been appointed to find a new chief of police for the corrupt District force and soon began to recruit Glassford. Glassford accepted the position in November 1931 at a salary of $7,313 (thereby giving up an Army pension of $3,920) because it sounded like "fun and action."

While his easy manner and modesty quickly won over many on the police force, Glassford also earned the enmity of several career officers who had been passed over for the superintendent's job. As Glassford readily admitted, his only prior police experience was being arrested for running a red light on his motorcycle.

Glassford enjoyed living in Washington among so many of his former colleagues. He was particularly fond of Douglas MacArthur under whom he had served as a plebe at West Point. MacArthur in turn felt that he could rely upon Glassford no matter what he asked of him— a mistake that would later prove costly to the Hoover Administration.

During his years of travel, Glassford left behind a wife and three children on the West Coast. By the summer of 1932, Glassford was divorced and the 6'3" tall handsome general became well known for parking his Pierce Roadster convertible in front of attractive blonde women's homes late into the night.

Glassford's watercolors also became quite sought after. Not surprisingly the superintendent soon became a favorite of Cissy Patterson.

* * *

The Oregon veterans continued their stand-off in St. Louis even though Walter Waters unexpectedly resigned as commander after he was threatened with arrest. He suggested to the B&O police that they arrest "everyone" rather than him. An angry George Alman confronted Waters who said that he had a wife and children to think of and did not want to go to jail.

"I'm through," the commander said as he gathered his gear.

Even as Waters was leaving, the veterans learned that B&O workers had moved boxcars one by one to Caseyville, seven miles away, where they planned to assemble an eastbound train. When a large engine left the rail yard, the men chased after it, some running along the tracks in pursuit and others taken in cars by sympathetic local citizens and newsmen.

The veterans arrived in Caseyville in time to intercept the train and climb on top of its boxcars. As they sat there in the hot morning sun, another train carrying five companies of National Guardsmen sped past in the opposite direction toward East St. Louis.

Frustrated by the situation, Sheriff Muncie of St. Louis rounded up 50 cars and trucks from private owners in which to shuttle the 400 men to the Indiana line. There at Washington, Indiana, they found Walter Waters working with the Indiana National Guard to arrange for similar transportation across that state to Ohio. Waters explained that his resignation had been a "ploy" to force the St. Louis officials' hand and he was soon re-installed as commander-in-chief.

The veterans were only 600 miles from Washington and it appeared that no one wanted them to tarry.

* * *

Pelham Glassford met early in the morning with his old friend Douglas MacArthur at the State, War, and Navy building.

MacArthur paced up and down the length of his office at he listened closely to Glassford's outpouring. A large number of veterans were on their way to Washington and Patrick Hurley had flatly rejected the superintendent's plan to house them at Ft. Hunt, an unused Army post outside the District. Nor would Hurley allow the Army to provide them with tents and rolling kitchens.

"We have no legal way to deny their presence here," Glassford said. "So long as they are well-behaved they will be protected by the constitutional rights of assembly and petition."

Glassford said that he could either "fight or feed" the ex-soldiers and he chose to feed them. He told MacArthur how he planned to organize the veterans into units with their own officers and military police. He would personally raise money to feed them, and after the vote on the bonus bill had taken place, they would be quickly escorted from the District.

When Glassford finished, MacArthur stopped pacing and looked at him. "You are absolutely right," the Army chief said. "I hope and pray that you will be able to carry the plan through successfully."

But the wily MacArthur was not depending solely upon Happy Glassford. On May 25 he authorized his most trusted aide, Major George Van Horn Moseley, Deputy Army Chief of Staff, to "go ahead with all necessary arrangements to meet any possible emergency."

* * *

The progress of the veterans was followed closely at the national headquarters of the Communist Party of the U.S. in New York City.

For more than two years the Communist strategy had been to use America's unemployed men to stir revolt. They led street demonstrations and disrupted evictions. Their greatest success was a march by 3,000 laid-off workers in Detroit where police hired by Ford Motor Company killed four people and wounded fifty.

Although they opened offices in New York City, Chicago, and Cleveland, the Communists' effort to grow the party in America met with little success. In 1930 there were 3,000 members of the U.S. Communist Party. By May 1932, in the heart of the Depression, after two years of furious agitation and recruitment, the party had grown to only 12,000.

Now the biggest opportunity of all was unfolding, but it was out of their control. Party leader Emanuel Levin was called onto the carpet by his superior, Secretary Earl Browder. A stocky, bushy-browed man with no chin, Levin always had excuses, never results. His favorite activity was sending press clippings to Stalin.

Browder demanded to know why they did not have a leadership role in this march of veterans. There was, after all, a communist veterans group already in existence known as the "Workers Ex-Servicemen League" (or "weasels" as most vets derisively called them). It was WESL who should be leading this march, not this Waters from Oregon.

Emanuel Levin was dispatched to Washington to open a WESL office at 905 Eye Street. Sent to assist him was the Communists' presidential candidate for the upcoming election, James Ford, an African-American.

This was too big an opportunity to miss. Just like St. Petersburg in 1905, the revolution could be starting

CHAPTER FIVE

The Blind Opponent

One of the leading congressional opponents to the "bonus bill" was an outspoken blind senator from Oklahoma named Thomas Pryor Gore.

The senator was sightless as the result of two boyhood injuries. One occurred when he and other boys were throwing nails at a cow and Gore was struck by one in the left eye. The second happened when a playmate's toy gun failed to fire a spring-loaded wooden spike. Gore foolishly looked down the barrel with his remaining good eye just as the spring released.

Despite his handicap, a determined Tom Gore earned his law degree, became married, and was elected to national office.

Gore served in the U.S. Senate for twenty years before losing his seat in 1920 because he opposed the Great War. Gore worked with a young Patrick Hurley on Oklahoma Indian matters from time to time and was swept back into office for a final six years as part of the Democratic resurgence that began in 1930.

The blind senator lived with his wife Tot at Eden, a comfortable three-acre estate located on the verge of Rock Creek Park. Their Tudor-style house on Broad Branch Road was a sprawling gray stone structure that one approached by a curved front drive. A large fountain stood at the top of the drive. In the attic were thousands of dusty books, magazines, and old unread copies of *The Congressional Record*.

The Gores' daughter Nina was a sensuous young woman with high cheekbones and large brown eyes. Nina married Gene Vidal, a well-known aviator of the day.

Vidal was a former West Point football star and olympic athlete. At the time of their marriage he served as assistant football coach at West Point under Commander Douglas MacArthur.

MacArthur had a reputation for being aloof while commander of West Point. However, he was well acquainted with the vivacious Nina who ignored his constant reminders and regularly parked her roadster in MacArthur's assigned space.

Gene and Nina had one child, a precocious little boy named after his father who was born at the West Point hospital in 1925. Upon returning to Washington in 1929, the small Vidal family took up residence with the Gores, as much for convenience as financial necessity. The food that was prepared by Tot's full-time Eastern Shore cook was marvelous, and Nina's parents provided round-the-clock care for young Gene, now age four, while his parents indulged in a nearly constant binge of parties and hard drinking.

Little Gene grew up at Eden. When he was not spending hours going through the old books and newspapers in "Dah's" attic, the boy often accompanied his blind grandfather in the senator's chauffeur-driven car to his office at the U.S. Capitol. Members of Congress grew used to seeing young Gene sit beneath Gore's desk in the Senate Chamber, where he wore only shorts and read his favorite Tarzan books.

The Vidals' marriage was not a happy one. The sexually adventurous Nina felt that she had married too soon and she embarked on a series of affairs, the most serious of which was with the wealthy publisher Jock Whitney. Coincidentally, Gene Vidal was having a simultaneous affair with Whitney's athletic wife Liz. He was also romancing his co-worker, the aviatrix Amelia Earhart.

Gene Vidal wanted to become the Henry Ford of aviation. He formed an airmail company called the Ludington Line and he hoped to land a lucrative air mail contract with the federal government. It went instead to a rival airline in whose employ was Herbert Hoover, Jr.

* * *

Washington, D.C. became a magnet for veterans from across the nation. Even as the Oregon men were being shuttled by truck across the Midwest, small early contingents from other states began to journey to the nation's capital.

Among the first to arrive were six men from Lancaster, Pennsylvania. After a day-long drive, the veterans brought their overloaded pick-up truck to a stop in front of the U.S. Capitol.

None of them had been to Washington before. The sight of a gigantic American flag rippling above the gleaming white dome caused them to pile out of the truck and stand staring in awe.

Warned that a large force of veterans was on its way with an unknown agenda, two U.S. Capitol security guards huddled beside a window in an upper level. The guards looked down in apprehension at the knot of men gathered below them. Did they have guns or bombs? The guards stiffened as the men moved slowly toward the Capitol.

Staring upward at the billowing flag, the men from Pennsylvania removed their hats with their left hands, then raised their right hands and placed them over their hearts.

* * *

Zanesville, Ohio—May 24, 1932

In this picturesque Ohio town, Walter Waters had the first indication of how his small army was perceived by official Washington.

As Waters and Doak Carter supervised the unloading of a 35-truck convoy at the Zanesville city park, a Western Union delivery boy ran up and handed the BEF commander a yellow envelope. Waters tore it open and found a message from Representative Wright Patman. It read:

> Please reach Washington before men to confer with officials in regard to program here.

Soon after, an official-looking black sedan pulled up beside the trucks. A solidly built man in a brown suit climbed out of the car and was pointed toward Waters.

The man introduced himself as Mr. Buck of the United States Secret Service. He said that he had questions for the veterans' leader and asked Waters to follow him to a nearby hotel.

In a room at the Zanesville Hotel, Waters was questioned closely by Buck, who had been sent from the Treasury office in Cincinnati to intercept him. "Who are these men?" Buck asked. Waters replied that each man was a veteran and that they carried their discharge papers.

Buck wanted to know why they were going to Washington. Waters explained that their sole purpose was to achieve passage of the bonus legislation.

"Is there anyone in your outfit you can't trust?" the Secret Service agent asked.

Water said that while some men disagreed with the structure and discipline that he had imposed, all of the veterans could be trusted.

"Well, we've had your crowd under surveillance for some time, and we'll keep you there," Buck said. "Personally, you have a clean sheet with us."

Waters showed Buck the telegram from Wright Patman and a shadow passed over the Treasury agent's face—understandably, since the president of France and two leaders in Japan had been assassinated only weeks before.

"Please," Buck said, "don't leave your men, even for an hour. Our job is to protect Mr. Hoover, and remember, it only takes one man to do the damage. It would be dangerous for you to leave the men out of your control...you've got to stay to see that strict discipline is kept."

Waters walked from the hotel to the Western Union office to wire his reply to Patman. *Impossible to leave the men*, he wrote.

Now that the final stage of their journey was just ahead, the spirit of the marchers was high. After spending the night in the Zanesville park, trucks sent by Governor Gifford Pinchot of Pennsylvania picked them up at the Ohio line with word that they would be given just five hours to move through the Keystone State.

The Portland veterans reached Cumberland, Maryland, late on May 28. They were just a half-day's drive from Washington. Cumberland officials let them sleep on the rasin-covered floor of the same roller skating rink where a small contingent of the Washington-bound Communist protesters had stayed the winter before.

Waters and his men were now nearly 500 in number. They had traveled 3,000 miles in 18 days and inspired fresh hope in millions of people across the country that, at last, some type of action was being taken. During the final days of their journey the roads were lined with well-wishers cheering them on.

The men grinned and waved at a young girl who held up a red-lettered poster stating "Give 'em Hell!" Another said: "We're Counting on You." As he saw these signs, it dawned on Walter Waters that more than just 500 men were depending on him.

That night Waters wired ahead to arrange meetings with Wright Patman and Pelham Glassford. He borrowed money from a local veteran and took an overnight train to Washington.

* * *

Herbert Hoover was an intelligent, wealthy engineer whose only prior federal experience before being elected president had been service as the Secretary of Commerce under Harding and Coolidge.

In fairness perhaps nothing could have prepared Hoover for the challenges he faced with the Great Depression. Yet it was the way in which Hoover failed to adapt and deal with those challenges that characterized his presidency.

While a young boy Herbert Hoover caused a fire in his father's backyard factory that nearly burned down their small Iowa town. Rather than admit what he had done, little Herbert kept silent. Only 50 years later did he tell anyone what had actually happened. Some observers of the president attributed his indecisiveness in times of crisis to this early successful lesson to duck. Others believed that Hoover's dispassionate, introverted personality resulted from being orphaned at age eight. A boyhood friend recalled that he had never heard Herbert Hoover laugh.

No one denied that President Hoover was a hard and committed worker. Other than his morning medicine ball throw and an occasional trip with Lou Henry to the camp they had built on the Rapidan River in the Blue Ridge Mountains (to escape the Washington heat that Hoover hated), the president had no hobbies.

As a young man in the Harding Administration, Hoover had been an excellent bridge player. But that was before the jocular president insisted that Hoover accompany him on a cruise to Alaska as his bridge partner. The men played cards, smoked cigars, and drank whiskey every day from sunrise to midnight in a closed stateroom. When he could, Hoover escaped to the upper deck to gasp for fresh air.

On the return voyage, Warren Harding fell ill from congestive heart failure, contracted pneumonia, and died in San Francisco. (Some uncharitable gossips suggested that his wife, the "Duchess," poisoned him in revenge for his many affairs.)

Herbert Hoover never played bridge again in his life.

* * *

Even at age 38, Wright Patman was still boyish looking and—as Waters could tell from his rapid eye movements, the shifting of his straw hat from hand to hand, and the perspiration staining his shirt at 8:00 a.m.—the congressman was very nervous.

First Patman praised Waters for the character and conduct of his men. Patman said that he received reports from people along the veterans' route regarding their discipline. "The men are veterans," Waters replied. "They know how to conduct themselves."

Patman told Waters that he had been a machine gunner in the Army during the war and then served as commander of his local American Legion post in Texarkana, Texas. Waters nodded.

The second-term congressman then confessed that he was terribly concerned about the veterans coming to Washington. He told Waters "your very presence here has inspired great concern, even fear" among people in Washington including Patman's colleagues in the House of Representatives.

Waters assured Patman that they were not radicals and did not intend to cause harm. The congressman said that he understood but others in Washington did not. In order to protect Patman's future as a champion of the common man, it was essential that he not be implicated with having inspired or encouraged the veterans' march to Washington.

Patman looked at Waters beseechingly, practically wringing the straw hat in his hands. He appeared very much like the farm boy from Switch, Texas, whom he had once been.

"I will make sure that everyone knows you had no part in urging us to come," Waters told the anxious congressman.

* * *

With the Depression in its fourth year, there were ominous signs that the military budget might soon be pruned.

Missouri Democrat Ross Collins had recently been made chairman of the War Department Appropriations Committee. Collins disliked MacArthur and he was prying into every corner of the War Department, including Patrick Hurley's use of the Army Air Corps to fly him around the country for what Collins saw as activities related to the upcoming election.

Hurley had converted a pasture at his Leesburg estate into a private landing field where reporters could not monitor his comings and goings. He also put two carefully chosen pilots at his beck and call whose duties often went beyond flying.

Most recently Collins had proposed slashing 2,000 of the Army's 12,000 officers as part of a $24.5 million reduction in the War Department budget. MacArthur took this as a personal affront and howled that such a cut would leave the already depleted Army "prostrate," even though officers were the last thing that the Army needed.

An angry Hurley rushed off to challenge the House Military Affairs Committee in a performance that even MacArthur admitted did more harm than good. What was needed was a chance to remind the country why the military was important—a chance to flex its muscle in a national crisis.

* * *

Walter Waters, the unintended architect of that crisis, was worrying about how to best deal with a big-city police superintendent when the conference room door opened promptly at 9:00 a.m. and Pelham Glassford strode in.

Waters jumped to his feet and held back an impulse to salute. He had never met a former brigadier general of the Army.

Glassford clasped Waters' hand firmly and said how glad he was to meet him. Like Wright Patman, he told Waters that he had heard only fine things about him and his men. Everyone, it seemed, had the same message for Waters—stay well behaved and things will be fine.

Glassford towered in a friendly way over the slender Waters who was just under six feet. The police chief's face was open and pleasant and his expression radiated concern.

Glassford then asked for coffee to be served and the two men sat across from one another. The general said he understood that Waters had served in the 146th Field Artillery. He himself had been in the 103rd. Waters began to relax as he realized that Glassford was treating him as an equal.

Then Glassford told Waters that a vacant department store at 8th and I Streets had been secured as a temporary shelter for the veterans. He had made arrangements for a meal to be served on their arrival.

Waters said that the men had probably left Cumberland and should be at the District line by afternoon. Glassford reassured him that he had spoken with Governor Ritchie, who agreed to have his Maryland National Guard trucks proceed into the District rather than unload the men at the state line. Waters expressed his gratitude.

The superintendent narrowed his gaze and asked Waters if he could have his cooperation while the veterans were in Washington.

Waters said that he could but that the veterans did not intend to withdraw before they had lobbied the bonus legislation through Congress.

Glassford understood. He told Waters that he looked tired and suggested that he take a nap in the shady courthouse park across the way. "I'll see that you are called," he said.

As Waters stood up Glassford asked, "By the way, how many veterans will come here, do you think?"

Waters said that whenever they stopped in the last few days he received a flood of telegrams. He estimated that there could be 20,000 more men in Washington within the next two weeks.

Glassford raised his eyebrows and smiled. He clearly did not believe Waters' estimate.

* * *

Eden, Rock Creek Park—May 30, 1932

Senator Thomas Gore sat in the sun at his dining room table and was served his regular breakfast, a peeled boiled egg with toast. His wife Tot sat across from him and his grandson Gene was happily engaged on the floor under the dining table with his favorite book, *The Emerald City of Oz*.

Gene had recently discovered the Oz books and over the next six years he would read all 37 of them. Just like Dorothy, Gene was essentially parentless, living with a kindly older couple who very much resembled Uncle Henry and Aunt Em of Kansas. The books transported him from the real world of an alcoholic mother and an absent father to a fantasy world where children were in charge.

As she did each morning, Tot read to the blind senator from Cissy Patterson's *Washington Herald*. The front page story on May 30 described the arrival of the Bonus Marchers, accompanied by a photograph of a dozen thin and ragged men as they disembarked from a truck.

"Ah," the senator said. "So the boners are here at last."

Beneath the dining room table young Gene envisioned marching skeletons and shivered.

* * *

J. Edgar Hoover got his start in the intelligence field during WWI when he was hired by the Alien Service Bureau in the Department of Justice. He was made head of the General Intelligence Division, which rooted out radical groups and Communists.

The 37-year-old J. Edgar Hoover had recently been appointed to the top spot at the nation's Bureau of Intelligence in March 1932 by Herbert Hoover (no relation). Thin and just 5'7" tall, the new BI Director was just starting to acquire the paunch and bulldog-like appearance for which he would later become caricatured.

J. Edgar Hoover was manic about control and therefore concerned over reports that many hundreds, perhaps thousands, of veterans were headed to Washington. Largely due to its stable federal payroll, the nation's capital was spared from the civil unrest that hit other major cities.

In Detroit and New York City, bread was being taken in broad daylight off delivery trucks and bands of children were sent out by their parents to steal food. In High Point, North Carolina, when they were turned away from a local movie theater, a group of unemployed men shut down the city's electrical plant. In Patrick Hurley's home state of Oklahoma, a mob of 300 men and women raided local grocery stores.

At the request of the Bureau of Investigation, local newspapers did not report these stories so as not to encourage widespread riots.

Now war-hardened veterans were on their way to the nation's capital.

* * *

Pelham Glassford saw in Walter Waters a man he could work with. The next morning he brought two men to the temporary veterans' barracks and introduced them to Waters as the leaders of the York and Lancaster, Pennsylvania, delegations.

"Waters has things pretty well organized," Glassford said. "Why don't you consider signing up under his command?" One of the men told Waters that the Oregon marchers were the reason they were there.

Glassford informed Waters that he had received donations in the mail. About three hundred dollars in spontaneous gifts from donors across the country had arrived in the form of checks, money orders, and cash.

When he met with the early arrivals two days earlier, Glassford said that he had been asked to serve as secretary treasurer of the informal group. Waters concurred with the choice. He said that the handling of money was a touchy issue with the men.

The issue of a name for the group came up. When they were sent to France, the veterans had been called the "American Expeditionary Force." Waters said that some of his men were calling themselves the "Bonus Expeditionary Force," or just the "BEF."

Glassford nodded his approval.

* * *

When Herbert Hoover campaigned against Al Smith for president, the *Tulsa World* ran a cartoon on its front page that showed two trains racing down parallel tracks. Hoover's face was on the front of one train and Al Smith's was on the other.

Young Wilson Hurley saw this and thought that the winner of the election would be decided by which train won its race across the country. Unknown to him, his father would soon be off to Washington himself as Hoover's assistant Secretary of War. Wilson, his mother, and two other siblings would not join him for months.

Soon after he arrived in Washington, Pat Hurley bought a luxurious townhouse at 160 Belmont Road, NW, from the outgoing Vice President Charles Dawes. While he was separated from his family, Hurley stayed up late each night, reading.

Ever since his childhood, Pat Hurley had loved to learn from books. He always had piles of them stacked around his bed. Hurley's favorite topic, renewed by his new assignment, was Roman history.

"My father wanted to drive them out from the first moment the bonus marchers came to town," Wilson Hurley recalled. "I remember him saying to guests that there was no place in a democracy for people to come and threaten Congress in order to get bills passed their way.

> "The whole thing was a matter of principal. He would compare it to the decline and destruction of Rome—the dictatorship under Marius, the corruption of democracy under Pompey and Caesar, and eventually the collapse. My father thought all of that was about to occur in Washington and he thought that the Communists were behind it."

Of the many lessons that Pat Hurley took from his reading, one that was most meaningful to him was the imperative of loyalty to the state. No matter what the cost, the state must persevere. There was no greater personal honor than to make such a sacrifice.

* * *

Herbert Hoover toweled himself after a vigorous game of medicine ball on the south lawn of the White House. The game was played by tossing a heavy leather ball back and forth over an eight-foot-high net. Patrick Hurley, his brawny War Secretary, had been especially aggressive that morning. He had almost knocked over Hoover's pet reporter, the silver-haired Mark Sullivan.

The men stood in their striped athletic garb in the White House kitchen. They sipped fruit juice and chatted. It was 7:50 a.m. and the day was already hot.

Hoover mentioned to Supreme Court Justice Harlan Stone that he had been petitioned by the arriving veterans to meet with them. The president was affronted by the idea. He had already made his position on the bonus clear to the American people. (Hoover's speech in Detroit had been rudely interrupted by a legionnaire who yelled, "We want a beer!")

Hoover did not know what more the veterans could want. His administration had built eight hospitals for veterans across the country and allowed them to borrow more than $1 billion from their bonuses. They had even created a Veterans Administration under Frank Hines—it was Hines they should be speaking with, not Hoover.

"The veterans should have been stopped at the city line," Hurley said ominously. "They should never have been allowed to enter Washington."

* * *

But the veterans continued to come and it soon became clear that a more permanent encampment would have to be found. One early June morning Glassford ushered Waters, Doak Carter, and a member of their new BEF Committee, Harold Foulkrod, into his yellow roadster and drove them down South Capitol Street then left onto Virginia Avenue, headed toward the Anacostia River.

It was a bright day and the superintendent had the top down as they sped past well-kept row houses and small wooden stores. After a few minutes Glassford turned right onto 11th Street, a two-lane cobblestone road that paralleled the high stone wall of the Navy Yard on their right. The roadster rattled across the planks of a 300-yard long, one-lane drawbridge that extended over the still, greasy waters of the Anacostia River.

Once across, Glassford drove onto a shoulder of the road and parked the automobile. Waters and the other men climbed out and followed Glassford through a hedge onto a large rectangular field of 50 acres. The far back of the field sloped up to a high ridge, beyond which lay the small town of Anacostia. The men saw dozens of "subsistence" garden plots near the river.

Glassford spread his arms wide. This was their new home. Welcome to Anacostia Flats.

* * *

Even though the Hoover Administration refused to formally acknowledge the BEF, its War Department still had to deal with the veterans. Douglas MacArthur assigned Major Dwight Eisenhower the job of liaison with the District commissioners.

This gave Eisenhower a rare chance to relax. When he could, Ike walked two blocks down Pennsylvania Avenue to the District building where he sat for an hour or so in the press room, hoping to pick up tidbits of useful news from the reporters. Drew Pearson recalled seeing Eisenhower there, tipped back in his chair and reading a Western paperback.

* * *

Anacostia Flats already had a long and unusual military history.

For nearly 50 years, families in the nearby town were subjected to the frequent booming noise of Navy cannons firing 32-pound shells at their fields. Anacostia Flats was the designated "target" for the U.S. Navy's experimental battery.

These exercises began after a gun called the "Peacemaker" exploded on the USS *Princeton* in 1844. Onboard the Navy's first steam-powered frigate that day were President John Tyler, his fiancée, and a number of guests and officials invited for a pleasure trip along the Potomac to Mount Vernon.

As they passed Ft. Washington, President Tyler ordered the new gun fired in salute. The cannon blew apart and killed eight people, including two cabinet officers and the father of his young fiancée. Soon thereafter the experimental battery was created to field test all large guns before they were put into use.

The legendary Navy Yard Commander John Dahlgren paid residents of Anacostia one-quarter of the cost of each shell to retrieve the used cannonballs. Since some shots fell short along the flats, the resourceful farmers strapped boards to their feet and walked across the muddy shoals to dig out the cannonballs.

President Abraham Lincoln was a friend of Dahlgren's and he often visited the commander's front porch where they would watch the shelling and the diligent shot gatherers.

After the veterans assembled on Anacostia Flats, it was not unusual for them to dig up cannonballs.

* * *

Ever the military strategist, Pelham Glassford chose a site that was perfect for containing the veterans.

Anacostia Flats was fronted by the polluted Anacostia River over which the narrow 11th Street drawbridge controlled passage into the city. To its south the Flats were bordered by an immense drainage pipe that led from the town to the river; and to the north by a high rise of land where armed troops could be placed. There was another ten-foot-high ridge of ground at the far back of the Flats over which could be seen the menacing red brick insane asylum of St. Elizabeth's.

Nearby in Anacostia, the 11th Police Precinct was commanded by a friend of Glassford's, Captain P. James Marks. Beyond the town lay Bolling Field, the home of the new Army Air Force, and across the drawbridge was the Navy Yard and the heavily manned Marine barracks.

Glassford detailed these advantages in a memo to the District commissioners in which he wrote: "Although no disorders have occurred, the plan of the police department is to assemble all disaffected groups at Anacostia Park and should emergency arise to hold the Eleventh Street Bridge against a riotous invasion across the Anacostia River." He further noted that he planned to split the veterans into two groups: "bonafide veterans who have elected a commander" and others "believed under communist control."

Glassford secured permission to use Anacostia Flats as a temporary camp from the director of the U.S. Parks Service, Ulysses S. Grant III, the grandson of the general. Since Grant reported to Patrick Hurley, the choice was clearly officially approved.

(Grant and MacArthur attended West Point in the same class. They competed all through their years at the academy. In their final class standings, MacArthur was first and Grant second. To the chagrin of MacArthur's mother, Academy administrators chose Grant to model for the statue of a cadet rather than her son. But now, to Pinky MacArthur's delight, her son's career had shot far beyond that of his former classmate. Douglas MacArthur was chief of the Army while Grant was toiling at the construction of a memorial highway above the bluffs of the Potomac River.)

Anacostia Flats was bottomland. When it rained the land did not drain toward the river and the Flats became a mudhole. When it was dry, a constant foot-high cloud of dust and swarming mosquitos floated just above the ground. In Washington's merciless summer heat, temperatures in the bowl-shaped Flats rose as high as 110 degrees. It was a terrible place to put 10,000 people. But Anacostia Flats was not chosen for human comfort. It was chosen for military confinement.

Most likely unknown to Pelham Glassford, the very site that he chose for the Bonus Army encampment had an oddly parallel history. In the summer of 1632 the original Natochtank Indians, who had lived in wooden huts at that location for over 3,000 years, were driven away by an invading force of white settlers who seized their land. In an eerie precedent to what would befall the Bonus Army 300 years later, the wooden huts of the Natochtanks were burned to the ground.

CHAPTER SIX

Welcome to Anacostia Flats

Nearly 1,000 veterans preceded the Portland men to Washington.

On May 31, Walter Waters was either appointed by Glassford or, by his account, leaders from various contingents formally elected him as commander-in-chief of the newly christened BEF. An executive committee of seven men was established whose first task was to create the main camp at Anacostia Flats.

Pelham Glassford asked the owners of wrecking companies working on various federal projects to provide used lumber for a barracks, but this plan to construct housing was soon abandoned due to the sheer number of veterans who arrived each day.

Just finding food and preparing two meals each day became a major challenge. The police superintendent scoured restaurants and farmers' coops for contributions. He arranged for the storage of donated goods from nearby towns to be kept in a commissary at 473 G. Street, NW. Glassford asked Congress to appropriate $75,000 for food for the veterans but his request was denied. Another appeal for blankets and tents from Secretary of War Hurley was turned down because "the federal government (cannot) recognize the invasion."

Glassford convinced a friend in the Washington National Guard to provide equipment for a large-scale military kitchen at Anacostia Flats that he staffed with veterans who had served as cooks during the war. When funds ran low for supplies, Glassford wrote a check for $773 from his own pocket.

Asked about the check by the commissioners, Glassford replied that these were "his own boys" and he had to take care of them. His loyalty was appreciated by many of the men in Glassford's police department, the vast majority of whom were also veterans.

Finally overwhelmed by the number of new arrivals, Glassford simply told arriving veterans to forage for shelter materials. They fanned out across Southwest Washington and into the nearby Anacostia City dump where they appropriated boards, sheets of metal, bricks, old auto bodies, crates, coffins, bedsprings—whatever could be used to create temporary homes. Even long weeds along the Anacostia River were harvested to weave into thatch for roofs and for bedding..

Almost every shack and hovel on Anacostia Flats had a flag flying over it. After Glassford sent him a scolding telegram, hundreds of brown National Guard tents were contributed by a reluctant Patrick Hurley and a tent city was created for men who brought their families. This was dubbed the "country club" section of Anacostia Flats.

Sanitation soon became an issue. Doak Carter was assigned a crew to build a rudimentary latrine system that drained into the already polluted Anacostia River. This, plus a mandatory twice-daily muster of veterans who were ill, helped Camp Marks stay relatively disease-free. Walter Waters later remarked privately that a typhoid epidemic had probably been avoided only because the veterans had been inoculated during their wartime service.

In just two weeks Anacostia Flats resembled the dozens of other "Hoovervilles" that had sprung up across the country, with two important exceptions. This one was in the president's backyard…and it was huge.

After their temporary homes were built the veterans were able to lie back in the grass at the river's edge and enjoy the sights. Across the Anacostia River and beyond the Navy Yard was a panoramic view of the city of Washington. On sunny days the white dome of the U.S. Capitol and the slender needle of the Washington monument were silhouetted against sharp blue skies. At night a light often shone in the Capitol dome, signaling that Congress was in session.

The veterans were visited frequently by P.J. Marks, captain of the nearby 11th Police Precinct in Anacostia. Marks realized the need to keep members of the growing Bonus Army as friendly neighbors and so he arranged for water lines to be installed, provided building materials and food, and instructed his officers to be helpful.

The veterans were impressed by his kindness and voted to name the Anacostia Flats encampment "Camp Marks." This simple gesture eventually led to the camp's destruction. It might have even changed the course of world history.

* * *

Any idea of quickly moving the veterans out of the capital was soon put aside, but Glassford continued to remind Waters that the men were in Washington by the grace of the president and the District commissioners. One incident of bad behavior could result in the BEF's eviction. The key to it all was military discipline.

Each new arrival was sent to a processing station at Anacostia Flats where his discharge papers were reviewed; name, address and next of kin recorded; rules of the camp made clear (no drinking, gambling, fighting or panhandling); and a BEF membership card issued. Each veteran's signature was carefully compared to that on his discharge papers. If a man had no papers he was sent to the Veterans' Administration to obtain proof of his service.

Every man was then given a BEF membership card to wear on a chain around his neck. This was the secret to controlling the veterans—it was also the ration card that allowed them to be served breakfast and dinner and sometimes lunch if there was enough food.

The final enrollment requirement was to stand before the sign-in table and take the BEF oath of allegiance:

"Upon my word of honor, and in the presence of these witnesses, I promise and swear to uphold the Constitution of the United States to the best of my ability."

Taking the oath impressed newcomers with the need for purpose and order and it helped identify those few veterans who considered themselves "Reds" and thus refused to be sworn in.

When they were discovered, Communists were quickly ushered out of camp. The fortunate ones found their way to a building that Pelham Glassford had arranged for them at 13th and B Streets, SW. The less fortunate were roughed up by BEF security police and removed by truck to the Maryland state line.

During the eight weeks of the BEF episode, no more than 300 "Reds," about 1% of the total number of men involved, were identified by officials as being in Washington at any one time. Their commander John Pace estimated that only twenty-five or thirty of his recruits could be counted on to help carry out missions.

Once accepted into camp, veterans were assigned to areas that had been designated for their home states. There were five sectors within Camp Marks, each with its own "main street." Most nights, weather permitting, bonfires were built at the head of the streets where the veterans and their families would sit, playing banjos and guitars and reminiscing.

Glassford came to the camp almost every day. He rode his blue motorcycle slowly along the dusty lanes, stopping often to speak with the men. The superintendent was struck by the similarity of their stories. These were not vagabonds but solid middle-class Americans whose jobs, homes, and lives had been torn from them.

Most were from smaller towns and they came from every state in the union. Ashamed to stand in bread lines or accept local relief, they had journeyed to Washington instead. Other than two large Polish and Italian contingents, most of the veterans were of British, Scottish, or Irish descent.

The men brought with them a broad cross-section of skills. Many were farmers and laborers while others had worked as dentists, barbers, teachers, reporters, and small businessmen. One was an attorney who had graduated from Cornell. Most were married.

Of particular interest to Glassford was the fact that 65% of the men at Anacostia Flats had been in combat, while only 25% of those drafted were actually sent overseas.

Walter Waters also met most of the new enlistees personally during the first several weeks. He stood on the roof of a car to welcome newcomers and remind them of why they were there, what was being done for them and to ask them to be well-behaved.

After the third week, men started to summon their wives and children to Camp Marks. By the time Washington began to swelter in its famous July heat there were more than 300 children in residence at Anacostia Flats.

* * *

The BEF was just one more worry that Patrick Hurley had to shoulder for the Hoover Administration. Another involved a convoluted transaction replete with political intrigue.

Taken from The Bonus March and the New Deal, John Henry Bartlett; M.A. Donohue and Company, Chicago, 1937.

Walter W. Waters speaks to new arrivals at Camp Marks.

Ned McLean, the owner of the *Washington Post*, was desperate for money. He wanted to leave his wife, the heiress Evalyn Walsh McLean, and take his mistress, Rose Davies Van Cleve, to Paris. There, in a triumph of backwards thinking, the alcoholic McLean planned to marry Rose then petition the U.S. courts to grant him a divorce.

By 1931 McLean had squandered the enormous fortune left to him by his father John. All that remained were the *Post* and his horse ranch near Leesburg, Virginia. (Their suburban estate Friendship belonged to Evalyn, inherited from her father.) Ned McLean decided to put the *Washington Post* on the market, which quickly attracted the interest of William Randolph Hearst.

When President Hoover learned that Hearst planned to purchase the *Post* he was horrified. Hearst, who had just pledged his support to the Democrats in the November election, already owned two Washington dailies, the *Times* and Cissy Patterson's *Herald.* With the *Post* Hearst would control news coverage provided by half of the District's six papers and be able to crucify Hoover on his own home ground.

Hoover could not contact McLean directly. The man, a former consort of Warren Harding, was a foul drunkard who would have his bodyguard hold people he disliked on the ground while McLean urinated on them. Once McLean had even urinated in a White House fireplace during a Harding Administration social event. Hoover sent Patrick Hurley as his emissary.

There followed a series of late-night meetings at Friendship between Hurley and McLean to find another way for the *Post* owner to get his money. At last McLean agreed to sell not the newspaper but his 1,200-acre Ashburn, Virginia, estate, Belmont, to Patrick Hurley for $100,000. (Later, Hoover's colleague Eugene Meyer would purchased the *Post* at auction.)

Ned McLean set off by ocean liner with Rose Davies and his Dusenberg for Paris in the fall of 1931 and Patrick Hurley took possession of Belmont. Within a few years Evalyn Walsh McLean had her husband declared insane and the *Post* remained a Republican newspaper.

* * *

Donations of food and money from private citizens and veterans groups continued to pour in to the small BEF headquarters on 11th Street, SE. The gifts, which came from all across the country, were often accompanied by notes such as "Stick it out 'til 1945," and "Stand up for your countrymen."

Clark Griffith, owner of the Washington Baseball Club, made the stadium available for a benefit on June 7 that raised $1,500. Another gift of $206.84 came from a collection taken by a black evangelist, Elder Lightfoot Michaux, in thanks for the BEF's support of all veterans regardless of their race.

One elderly woman wrote, "I have nothing but a sewing machine and my eyesight, but I will gladly come to Washington to make shirts for you." Fifty cents in dimes and nickels was enclosed.

By mid-June the BEF had received $12,895.56. Each contribution was recorded by Waters and passed on to Glassford to buy supplies. While this required the commander-in-chief to spend several hours each day processing mail, Waters did not trust the handling of money to others.

Some letters included suggestions of ways for the BEF to help to end the Depression. One man thought the veterans should be sent to Alaska to mine for gold. Another letter-writer from New York offered a fleet of boats for the veterans to use for fishing along the coast.

A few of the ideas had far-sighted merit, although they were laughed off at the time. One man suggested using the vets to drain Florida swamps for real estate. Another advocated creating state lotteries to generate extra revenues. Yet another suggested that they build an interstate highway.

Of the thousands of letters that the BEF received, not one advocated violence.

Many con artists were eager to take advantage of the veterans and tried to use the BEF to sell raffle tickets, foot powder, badges, and pamphlets on the streets of Washington. Before he became wise to these schemes, Waters was lured to Camden, New Jersey, where some men put on a wrestling match to benefit the BEF then disappeared with the proceeds, leaving Waters with the bill for his hotel room.

There were so many requests to visit and speak to the veterans from evangelists, salesmen, aspiring performers, and politicians that Waters and Glassford instituted a policy: no speakers on any subject other than the bonus legislation.

* * *

President Hoover still refused to meet with the veterans even though his schedule included visits from Boy Scouts, beauty queens, and wrestling champions. Walter Waters went to the White House several times only to be firmly turned away by Hoover's secretary, Walter Newton.

But when Hoover heard that 350 veterans a day were visiting the small infirmary made available to them at the Sixth Marine Brigade, the president's humanitarian instincts surfaced. Quietly, Hoover ordered Veterans Affairs chief Frank Hines to establish a larger 300-bed hospital facility at nearby Fort Hunt in Virginia.

Herbert Hoover received no credit for this anonymous act of charity.

* * *

Once the provision of basic food and shelter for the veterans was under control, Waters turned his attention to the BEF's primary objective of lobbying.

Activity surrounding HR 1 had been dormant since the House Ways & Means Committee failed to forward the bill for consideration. Only execution of a "discharge petition" that required the signatures of 145 Representatives could cause the bill to be reconsidered. Waters appointed Harold Foulkrod, a former Burns Agency detective from Philadelphia, as "legislative representative" for the BEF.

Within a week Foulkrod recruited 150 of the more articulate and aggressive veterans from Camp Marks to begin lobbying the congressmen and turned them loose.

To the anger of many Representatives, Foulkrod's troops marched to Capitol Hill where they confronted their elected officials face-to-face. Their approach was blunt: support HR 1 and you will be re-elected; oppose it and the veterans' vote will mean certain defeat in the fall.

There was no escaping Foulkrod's men. They cornered Representatives and their staff members in restrooms, elevators, parking lots, and even in the private dining room where a few sympathetic congressmen invited them. If a Representative refused to see them, a half-dozen veterans would crowd into his small waiting room until he changed his mind.

The second morning Foulkrod announced that he would add 100 men per day to the lobbying effort. He certainly had the manpower at his disposal to make good his threat. The House leaders reluctantly agreed to put forth a recall petition to re-activate Patman's bill.

The famed populist Will Rogers said at the time, "These World War veterans have the same right to be lobbyists that other people have and their standing is better than corporate lobbyists because they are not paid for it."

The discharge paper for HR 1 was placed in the well of the House where the opposing Republican party leaders kept an eye on any who might dare to sign it. Scores of veterans also watched hawk-like from the House gallery. When a member capitulated and walked to the well to sign the petition, the veterans reacted with cheers and shouts of encouragement. Just three days after the BEF began its lobbying effort, the recall petition secured the necessary votes and Wright Patman's Bonus Bill became live again. The petition to have the Bill considered by the full House was filed on June 4.

Six of the thirty-four Republicans who reluctantly supported the recall went as a group to District Commissioner Crosby and complained bitterly about having been intimidated. Crosby, a slender man with a high forehead and enormous eyes, sympathized with them. He shared Patrick Hurley's desire to drive the veterans from the capital by force and he was furious at the BEF's tactics. Crosby blamed his own police superintendent, Pelham Glassford, for making all of this possible.

* * *

If the steady influx of veterans was out of his control, one group that Glassford did have under his thumb was the Communists.

Emanuel Levin's office on Eye Street had just one entrance in the front, making it convenient for Ogden Mills' Treasury agents, Hurley's Army Intelligence, and J. Edgar Hoover's Bureau of Intelligence men to trail virtually every "commie infiltrator" on a daily basis.

The presence of Communists was abhorrent to the intensely patriotic veterans. Glassford did not have a hard sell when he spoke to the men of Camp Marks about the need to avoid "Red" influence. Waters ensured Glassford that his men would take care of any radicals who came around.

The first complaint from Emanuel Levin about the murder of one of his men reached Glassford in early June, but nothing could be verified.

* * *

June in the nation's capital usually marked the start of a long, hot, summer siesta.

This year Washington had a Mardi Gras-like atmosphere of activity.

The veterans continued to come. Every day hundreds of exhausted, road-dirty men, women, and children arrived in the District by car, truck, train or on foot. One afternoon a one-legged man fell into Camp Marks after making his way by foot and crutch from New York. Some mornings the registration line was so long that it took the entire day to sign up new recruits.

Taken from *Veterans on the March*, Jack Douglas, Workers Library Publishers, 1934

Veterans and their families make their homes in tents at Camp Marks.

In addition to Camp Marks, Glassford established shelters at twelve other sites including "Camp Glassford" on Third Street and Pennsylvania Avenue near the Capitol in the area today known as the Federal Triangle. In time there were twenty-seven encampments. Over the eight weeks of the siege, approximately 30,000 people came through the camps (Glassford estimated 38,000) but at the peak no more than 22,000 were estimated to be in Washington at any one time.

Veterans and their families went into the city each day to seek discarded items that they could use. They crowded the sidewalks and acted just like tourists. Everything was peaceful. During the Bonus March episode there were only 350 arrests of veterans, and just twelve of those were for offenses more serious than panhandling or loitering. In fact, overall crime in the nation's capital actually decreased during that time, perhaps because of the veterans' presence.

Although most veterans at Camp Marks were in dire straits, their mood was positive, even uplifting. First, they were there for a purpose. Secondly, they were there together. As reporter Tom Henry wrote in the *Washington Star*:

> "This bonus march might well be described as a flight from reality—a flight from hunger, from the cries of starving children, from the humiliation of accepting money from worn, querulous women, from the harsh rebuffs of prospective employers. It is very like the peace of infancy there in the warm June sunshine of the Anacostia field."

Perhaps this explained the orderliness of such a diverse group of people, "orderliness (to which) they have fled from the mysterious, heartless forces that are crushing them in the outside world."

* * *

Pelham Glassford was in a no-win situation. He described it as "being in a cross-fire between political pressure and humanitarianism. Hectic days, sleepless nights as I did all in my power to care for the veterans and their families who were already in Washington while carrying out an active campaign to discourage any more from joining them."

The lukewarm support given to him by the commissioners became clear at an early confrontation with Herbert Crosby following a meeting with local welfare agencies.

"If you continue to feed and house them," Crosby warned, "the veterans will come by the thousands."

"It is far better to have 10,000 orderly veterans under control than 5,000 hungry, desperate men breaking into stores," Glassford replied.

"What is your police force for?" Crosby demanded.

"Are you making a suggestion or issuing an order?" Glassford shot back.

Falling back on their prior military relationship, Crosby replied, "In the Army it has been my experience that a suggestion is obeyed just the same as an order."

"We're not in the Army now," Glassford shot back. "I cannot follow suggestions. If you want to take the responsibility yourself for such a policy, all you have to do is issue written orders and they will be carried out. In the absence of such orders I shall take what I consider to be the correct course."

Dr. Luther Reichelderfer, chairman of the District's Board of Commissioners, reported directly to Herbert Hoover. Thus it was actually the President of the United States who had the final say regarding the BEF.

However, in the spring of 1932, Herbert Hoover was busy with a host of other critical issues. In Asia, Japan had just declared war on China. Closer to home, Congress had finally approved Hoover's Reconstruction Finance Committee bill that would pump $3 billion into the nation's economy from the top down. Appointments to staff the RFC had to be made.

Also, the Republican Convention was to take place in just three weeks, followed by a difficult campaign. While party leaders had whispered about replacing Hoover on the ticket, they were now committed to sail into the electoral storm with their embattled leader.

The greatest difficulty that the president faced with the veterans was that, while many influential people in Washington, D.C. wanted them gone, the rest of the country saw the veterans as heroes. With the election just six months away, Hoover could not afford to further alienate the electorate.

Hoover reacted to the BEF the same way that he responded to many difficult problems during his presidency—from a distance, through intermediaries, and by refusing to take a specific position. This left a vacuum into which Douglas MacArthur soon moved.

* * *

The BEF drama was followed closely by Patrick Hurley. On June 8, he received a confidential assessment from George Paddock, a War Department intelligence agent, that described the camps as "orderly" and the men as "disciplined." Paddock recommended benign treatment and said the danger of radical influence was "not great" unless the veterans believed "their requests have been unjustly disregarded."

Photograph taken by Acme. Taken from *BEF*, by W. W. Waters and William C. White, John Day Company, New York, 1933.

Superintendent Pelham Glassford was a friend
to the veterans during their time in Washington.

At the same time, from private conversations with Herbert Hoover, the Secretary of War knew that the president was unhappy with Glassford for his "friendly" attitude toward the veterans. In early June a piece of information reached Hurley that ran counter to Paddock's studied report and seemed to confirm his deepest fears.

Two of Hurley's children, Wilson and Mary, were playing on a Persian rug in the living room at Belmont when the secretary slammed into the large front hallway in a fury. Ruth Hurley rushed in from a sun room where she had been working with her social secretary.

"Do you know what those damned Communists are doing?" Hurley roared. "My God, the impertinence of it!"

"What is it, Pat?" Ruth asked.

"They've named their main camp after Karl Marx!" Hurley declared. "They're calling it Camp Marx!"

Someone had convinced the Secretary of War that the BEF was honoring the memory of the man who in 1866 had written *Das Kapital*, the 882-page intellectual underpinning for the Communist Party. In reality the camp at Anacostia Flats was named for J.P. Marks, the Anacostia police captain.

More fuel was added to Hurley's fire a few days later when Emanuel Levin, head of the Communist WESL organization, held a press conference to falsely claim that the Communist Party was behind the bonus march.

Soon afterwards Allen Straight, a Secret Service agent from New York, told Glassford that the Party had called for thousands of Communists to mass in the District of Columbia on June 8. Some 750 were reported to be on their way from Baltimore. Another 300 from Detroit, led by Communist agitator John Pace, were penned up by police in a B&O rail yard in Cleveland.

Their plan was to provoke a violent confrontation with Waters' men, during which the Communists would force their way into the White House, thereby sparking a revolution. A similar report came from a New York police lieutenant, B.H. Lacherman.

This warning threw Douglas MacArthur's chief of staff, Brigadier General George Van Horn Moseley, into a panic. Moseley was a closet fascist whose fear and hatred of Communists was almost as great as his antipathy toward Jews and Negroes. If communist cells all across America were to launch thousands of red agents toward Washington, it could mean the end of democracy.

Moseley pleaded with MacArthur to react forcibly to this latest news. After he took an evening to think about it and discussed the situation with Secretary Hurley, the Army chief instructed Moseley to accelerate his military plans to deal with a possible civil emergency.

Pelham Glassford had already been told by MacArthur that Army troops were at his disposal. But Glassford knew that if he called for troops to head off the Communists he would give the War Department its chance to drive the veterans out as well.

Once serious fighting started, there would be no differentiating between friend and foe. The inevitable slaughter of innocent veterans would play right into the Communists' hands and could start the very revolution that Moseley and others feared.

Complicating things further was the fact that Congress remained in session and the recent vote to reconsider the bonus legislation had temporarily legitimized the veterans' presence in Washington. No one, not even Patrick Hurley, wanted to move against the veterans while their elected representatives were in town.

With the Communists reportedly on their way and nowhere else to turn, Glassford called for an emergency meeting with Walter Waters.

* * *

Overnight, the charismatic commander-in-chief of the BEF had become a nationally known figure with all of the requisite trappings and authority. Waters now had a personal adjutant, Owen Lucas from the Bronx, to handle his massive amount of correspondence and to make appointments with the many people who wanted to see him.

The numerous BEF camps were run with strict military precision by layers of officers that Waters appointed. There was reveille at 7:30 in the morning and taps at 9:30 each night. In between, every veteran had an assigned work detail.

To further maintain control, Waters had formed his own "intelligence service" run by Eddie Atwell, a former bookie from the Bowery. Within six weeks this group grew to more than 300 men, their names known only to Waters and to a few others on his executive committee.

Although the stated purpose of these agents was to inform Waters of any radical movements among the veterans, the secret BEF security force soon took on broader responsibilities, including policing of the veterans themselves. They also fraternized with Glassford's police and Hurley's War Department agents, many of whom were more sympathetic to the BEF than to the Hoover Administration.

The relationship between Waters and Glassford was unusual. The superintendent was glad to have a commander who would operate under his direction. So long as he could trust and prop up Waters, Glassford knew that he could keep the veterans in line.

Waters understood that Glassford had two agendas: to keep the veterans under control and to rid the city of them as soon as the bonus matter was resolved. Waters also knew that only Glassford stood between the BEF and a hostile War Department. To keep his men under control, Waters relied upon the veterans' deeply imbued patriotism and their respect of military discipline.

These complex dynamics were not understood by the veterans, many of whom disapproved when they saw their commander ride with the superintendent in his fancy yellow car. The men did not fully appreciate the fact that Glassford alone kept them from starving and from the wrath of Patrick Hurley.

At their meeting to discuss the communist threat, Waters and Glassford decided on a daring plan. The BEF would stage a massive parade on the evening of June 7 in order to trump the communist rally. The next day the veterans would be kept out of the city to avoid any possible confrontations with the Communists, who would be closely monitored by Glassford's police.

When they were told of this plan, Hurley, MacArthur, and Moseley held an urgent meeting with the president at which they implored him to authorize the use of Army troops to protect against the expected violence.

Hoover, who was reassured by his own intelligence reports, refused to do so.

Each new group of veterans that came to Washington had been infiltrated by Treasury agents. So far there was no evidence that the BEF was controlled by Communists. The War Department did not have the right to interfere with a private event.

With great trepidation, the officials of the federal government and the city of Washington looked toward June 8.

* * *

When he visited Camp Marks two days before the planned march, Glassford was dismayed to find that the physically frail Waters had suffered a collapse.

From his sickbed Waters relinquished leadership of the BEF to George Alman, who had been waiting in the wings for this opportunity.

Glassford arranged for medical care for Waters and continued to reassure Patrick Hurley that things were under control. To his relief, by late afternoon on June 7, Walter Waters was well enough to take his place at the head of the BEF parade beside the glowering lumberjack Alman.

The 8,000 marchers assembled on the ellipse in the shadow of the Washington Monument. From there they were to walk up Pennsylvania Avenue and end the parade short of the Capitol building. More than 100,000 Washingtonians crowded the sidewalks along the parade route, behind a cordon of police stationed every 50 feet.

It was dusk when the parade started. The crowd saw at once that this was a grim and somber affair, very different from the parades that the soldiers had walked in twelve years before on their return from France. Then the streets of Washington had been lined with wildly cheering friends and families. There had been bands with loud trumpets and at the end of the parade there was cavorting with kegs of beer, fireworks, and pretty girls. They men had been young and strong, their uniforms clean and crisp.

Now, although the oldest marchers were only in their early 40s, the men appeared old and stooped. There was no patriotic music, just the slap of their feet hitting the pavement and the cadence of drums like a slow heartbeat.

In the front ranks of the funereal procession were disabled soldiers, many wearing their purple hearts. Some were on crutches, others in carts and wheelchairs. Next came camp regiments in the order in which they had arrived in Washington, Oregon and Pennsylvania being first.

Many veterans had brought remnants of their old uniforms to Washington. Some wore olive-green wool short coats or breeches, others boots and soft service hats. Large American flags were carried at the front of each regiment and two or three former soldiers in each group held rifles at arms over their shoulders.

The signs that the marchers carried reflected bitterness and fear. "Won in '20, Done in '32" read one. "Here We Stay 'Til the Bonus They Pay" declared another.

The spectators watched the parade in silence. Hurley's War Department had issued a release that warned the women of Washington to stay off the streets and so there were few female spectators.

This silent, determined procession on a balmy summer evening was captured on newsreels and relayed to sympathetic audiences in movie theaters across the nation.

Hearst reporter Floyd Gibbons, himself a one-eyed hero of the Great War, felt special compassion for the men. In Gibbons' words the next morning:

> "I saw them march last night, thousands of hungry ghosts
> of the heroes of 1917. Not so young now, carrying the flags
> they fought for...ragged remnants of Pershing's own...They

were not allowed past the Capitol as they would bring distress to the congressmen. And not past the White House, which would bring distress to the president of the richest nation in the world."

Although they had traveled to the nation's capital on a selfish mission, the veterans' march was being transformed into a force demanding justice for all.

The next morning only 160 "Red" agitators showed up for their scheduled parade and it was quickly abandoned. Later that day Walter Waters reclaimed his role as BEF commander.

CHAPTER SEVEN

Learning to Salute

The BEF army reached Walter Waters' predicted size of 20,000 by June 14 and their twenty-two camps had created a city within the city of Washington. One of these sites was a half-demolished former car dealership on lower Pennsylvania Avenue. There, 200 people lived on the second and third floors in rooms without front walls and in shacks and tents surrounding the base of the building.

Camp Bartlett was the largest secondary camp. It was located three miles north along the Anacostia River on thirty acres of land owned by John Bartlett, the assistant postmaster general and a former governor of New Hampshire. While the camp was dry and had electricity, it was not a popular site due to the time it took to walk from there to the Capitol building.

John Bartlett was a kindly bespectacled man who felt sympathy for the veterans. With his white hair parted in the middle and his rumpled herringbone suits, Bartlett cut a grandfatherly figure as he moved among the 1,200 campers who stayed at his farm.

Bartlett several times told Waters that the BEF could use his land to create a permanent camp for the men whenever they wished to do so. In weeks to come Bartlett would regret that promise.

* * *

Cissy Patterson, the colorful publisher of the *Washington Herald*, had a complicated relationship with the Hurleys and with Douglas MacArthur.

Of the six Washington newspapers, Cissy's was the most critical of President Hoover and his administration. She was the first to subscribe to her former son-in-law Drew Pearson's vitriolic "Washington Merry-Go-Round" column and she ran regular features about the condition of poor people in the District.

The *Washington Herald* also published the city's most popular and influential society section that frequently flattered the Hurleys and MacArthur with its coverage.

Further complicating things was the fact that Cissy's brother, Joe Patterson, publisher of the successful *New York Daily News*, had served under MacArthur in his famed Rainbow Division. When in town Patterson often joined his old commanding officer for lunch at the Chevy Chase Club. Patrick Hurley sometimes accompanied them, MacArthur having sponsored his membership there.

MacArthur called Joe Patterson "the most brilliant natural-born soldier who ever served under me." Patterson accompanied MacArthur in five major engagements until Joe was gassed and discharged. Even though his combat experience caused him to become virulently anti-war, Joe Patterson continued to worship the ground on which MacArthur walked.

* * *

The treasury of the BEF got an unexpected infusion of $5,000 from Father Charles Coughlin. This was followed by a flood of smaller donations that resulted from the radical Detroit priest's radio exhortations on behalf of the veterans. A terrible anti-Semite and a secret fascist like Van Horn Moseley, Coughlin hoped that the BEF would stir revolt in Washington.

For a few days in early June things looked promising for the BEF mission. Its primitive lobbying efforts had been highly successful and there was good reason to expect passage of HR 1 by the House. The BEF revenues were robust and the support of the nation was clearly with them. Most of the men were comfortable if generally bored in their temporary shacks. Importantly, there was almost always food even though the chow line sometimes stretched for a half-mile.

Then in mid-June it began to rain and for a full week it did not stop. The bowl-shaped Anacostia flatlands quickly turned to mud and the primary goal of the 10,000 people living there became finding some way to stay dry.

Glassford decided that this was an ideal time to persuade the veterans to head home. First he announced free transportation for any group of forty or more. Then he arranged for the Navy and Marine bands to perform under large tents with sentimental songs like "My Old Kentucky Home" and "Carry Me Back to Old Virginny."

Some veterans did leave, mostly due to illness or family emergency. One day fifteen men from Canton, Ohio, accepted Glassford's offer; another day fourteen from Alabama left. Some simply took the train fare and remained. But for every man who left, 100 more arrived.

Many newcomers brought "proof" of who they had been in their former lives—a cancelled bankbook, an old country club membership, a wrinkled pay envelope. A man named Garrison passed around a newspaper clipping. The other veterans read it and nodded at the photo of Garrison and the story of a judge who ordered him to pay $300 per month in alimony.

"You wouldn't think it now," Garrison said, "but by God, I had it once."

Another new arrival was the former congressional witness Joe Angelo. The thin little man with large brown eyes built his shack out of old crates and entertained his new comrades with his tale of saving George Patton's life.

It was Angelo, Patton, and 15 men. They were the vanguard of a force of 300. Two German machine gunners opened fire from behind a bush. Angelo returned their fire and killed one. Patton yelled to him, "Come on, we'll clean out those nests." But when they attacked the other advance, men were killed, leaving only Patton and Angelo.

"Boom! Just like that, the colonel goes down, and I asks him, 'Are you hit?' and he says 'Yes I am.' A slug went right through his left thigh and out the back of his leg, making a hole the size of a silver dollar."

Angelo pulled Patton into a shell crater where the colonel passed out. Angelo left him only once, to warn away two American tanks. "I'm his batman, see, so I stayed with him the whole time, even in the hospital."

The first company that reached Angelo and Patton was shocked at the carnage.

Among the replacements in Battery D was a reserve captain who kept losing his glasses named Harry Truman.

Angelo reached into his hip pocket and pulled out a tie-pin with a sliver of white glued to it. "See this?" he said. "That's what they took outta Patton's leg, his own bone. We're great friends," Angelo said proudly, "to this very day."

* * *

As he walked to his father's office, Wilson Hurley gazed solemnly up at the oil portraits of previous secretaries of war hanging along the corridor. Each secretary was allowed to select his own artist and the painting of his father by Frank Townsend Hutchens had not yet been completed.

A military aide, probably Eisenhower, held the seven-year-old boy by the hand. When the office door opened, Wilson saw his smiling father perched on the edge of a big wooden desk. Wilson noticed green leather chairs, flags on brass stands, and dark wood paneling.

The room would have been gloomy except for sunlight streaming in through the side windows. Sitting on the edge of a window ledge was another man, also smiling. He was balding, Wilson noticed, and had a thin nose and a strong, square chin. The man was dressed in shiny brown riding boots, jodhpurs, and a green shirt with black tie. A wide Sam Browne belt crossed his chest. His face and shiny dark eyes reminded Wilson of an eagle.

"Willie," his father said, "meet the general who commands the entire United States Army." Wilson, who was a serious little boy, stared at the man.

"Aren't you going to salute him?" his father asked. After a few seconds Wilson, a lefty, raised a tentative hand toward his forehead.

"Not with your left hand!" the Secretary of War exploded and Wilson stiffened.

The man in the uniform walked over to the little boy and bent down.

"Here, let me show you," MacArthur said. "You have to stand like this. Put your left hand straight down to your side. That's good. Now bring your right hand up—here's the secret, you need to straighten your wrist…touch your eyebrow then bring your right hand straight down to position. Now let's try it."

The general stepped back and received a sharp, right-handed salute from Wilson, which he returned.

"Good boy," he said.

* * *

Charles Frederick Lincoln, the sixth cousin of the former president, made his way to Camp Marks from California in mid-June. Slight of frame and deeply tanned, Lincoln was a painter and composer who was desperate for funds to support his wife and five children.

The camp attracted hundreds of visitors every day. Women came seeking lost sons and husbands—so many that a "Bureau of Lost Husbands" was set up in a designated tent.

Washington residents usually came on weekends. One Sunday over 25,000 people visited Anacostia Flats. Couples and families parked along the shoulder of 11th Street, changed into old shoes in their cars, and strolled through Camp Marks as though they were at the National Zoo. They pointed out the clever ways in which the veterans had built and decorated their small shacks. Some visitors handed out candy and coins to the children, others brought used clothing to donate.

Most of the veterans enjoyed the attention, especially from reporters. When they saw someone carrying a camera campers flocked to be in the photo. To Walter Waters, who was now quoted in the press every day, this showed a pathetic need of the veterans to have the value of their lives affirmed.

Various ways to take money from the tourists were conceived, ranging from the sale of soft drinks to having their photos taken by Eddie Gosnell, the "official" BEF photographer whose mysterious death a few months later would never be solved.

Joe Angelo was "buried alive." He breathed through a stove pipe and charged a dime to allow people to look at him through a tube.

A group of camp urchins hovered near a disabled veteran who sold hard candy in front of his tent. When visitors approached, the ragged youngsters rubbed their eyes to make them red and watery. This trick often earned them pennies for candy. When there were no visitors the disabled man chased the children away.

Tourists were amused by the camp barbershop run by a man named McCurdy.

Customers sat on an overturned nail keg and McCurdy put a newspaper with a hole cut in it over their heads as a bib. A cut cost ten cents, for which he apologized. Each time McCurdy placed the newspaper over a customer, he said that they could read while he trimmed.

Many congressmen came to visit the veterans who were there from their states and have their photos taken with them. One day Huey Long, the flamboyant "Kingfish" from Louisiana, showed up to organize an impromptu protest parade against Herbert Hoover for his promise to veto the bonus bill. Long was dressed in a fawn-colored suit and a purple shirt. He departed right after the photos were taken.

Reporters seeking quotes were there every day, including Drew Pearson, John dos Passos and Ernie Pyle. Mark Sullivan, a reporter for the *New York Herald Tribune* and one of Herbert Hoover's few friends in the media, visited Camp Marks often and he wrote of the men:

> "To go among them was to recognize instantly their complete harmlessness. A child or a lost pocketbook would be safer among them than among any average cross-section of a city's population."

* * *

Heavy rain continued to drum on the roof of the Capitol dome as the congressional debate over the bonus bill droned on. Each day hundreds of wet veterans filled the gallery to watch the show below.

The House chambers were banked like a theater and sloped down to the speaker's rostrum in the well. Unlike the Senate, House members had no assigned desks but sat on hard benches covered with black leather, reading, sprawling, laughing, and talking with one another. Occasionally one would walk to the well to make a speech about the bonus.

The debate was all for show. Once the bill was reported out there was never any doubt that the more liberal House would pass it—just as there was no question that the legislation would go down to defeat in the Republican Senate.

Even should a bonus bill pass the Senate, it faced a certain veto by President Hoover with no chance of a congressional override. All of this was made clear to Walter Waters early on, but by now the BEF commander was playing for higher stakes. The veterans were kept in the dark.

The most dramatic thing to occur during the debate was the death of Representative Edward Eslick, an obscure Democrat from Tennessee. The sixty-year-old Eslick was comparing the conditions faced by the veterans at Camp Marks with those they experienced overseas when his heart gave out and he slumped to the floor dead. His wife was in the audience.

Speaker John Nance Gardner immediately adjourned the proceedings, which resumed the next morning. On June 15 the House approved a $2.4 billion bonus bill by a vote of 211 to 176.

Following the vote 15,000 veterans filled the streets of Washington, shouting and cavorting with glee. This caused the Senate to schedule consideration of the bill the very next day. The veterans returned to Camp Marks that night for a joyous, dancing celebration.

* * *

Although Washington in 1932 was not yet the imperial city that it is today, it was fast becoming magisterial and its white granite buildings and monuments had a profound effect on the intensely patriotic veterans. Just the view of the monuments from Camp Marks inspired many with pride and awe.

As they made their way to the Senate galleries, the homeless, shabby vets walked past intricately carved marble statues and busts of Washington, Lafayette, and Jefferson. Abraham Lincoln was also there, holding his law book. The veterans paused before huge paintings including Trumbull's *Signing of the Declaration at Independence Hall.* What a contrast these threadbare former soldiers made, mingling open-mouthed among the well-dressed senators and their staff members under a vaulted ceiling graced with the American history murals of Constantino Brumaldi, enhanced with fresco laureates and decorative inlays.

All that the Senate artwork represented—the constant forward movement of society toward an ever-better national well-being— seemed refuted by the destitute men who passed by it every day. On the country's path from barbarism to universal enlightenment, evolution had suddenly gone into reverse.

Yet the men of the BEF still believed in their country's future.

* * *

Other than the kidnapping of the Lindbergh baby, the sudden arrival of 20,000 destitute former soldiers in their privileged city was the primary topic of conversation among Washington's elite. For many the topic was passing from curiosity to irritation.

The social lions spoke of the impoverished men and women with a feigned bravado during their nightly gatherings, their scorn coupled with nervousness. It had been only fifteen years since another ragged army seized control of Petrograd, grabbing all of the property and wealth of those wealthy people in the process. Whenever asked, Patrick Hurley assured his rich friends that everything was under control. He had special plans for the BEF, Hurley said, smiling.

Cabinet positions in 1932 were mostly social in nature and Pat and Ruth Hurley were the most attractive members of Herbert Hoover's mostly dull cabinet. In the evenings the couple was always in demand, if not at a White House function then at a host of embassy parties, lobbyist functions, small affairs with businessmen and publishers, private dinners with the wealthy and powerful, and late desserts with prominent Washington hostesses. They were especially busy during "the season," October through early June, that roughly conformed to when Congress was in session and when the weather was bearable.

It was said that in Washington there were three parties: the Republican, the Democrat, and the cocktail. For the extroverted and ambitious Patrick Hurley, Washington, D.C. was a stage on which to perform. He seldom turned down an invitation and was a regular at Cissy Patterson's Sunday evening parties for 300 or more.

Occasionally Alfred and Jessie Ball duPont drove over from Nemours to stay for the weekend; in summers they took the Hurley family out on the Chesapeake Bay on their yacht and let Wilson fire the mounted machine gun. The DuPont Company was the nation's largest manufacturer of munitions. Wilson knew duPont as "Uncle Al."

In such company Hurley felt like royalty. The ability to make someone like Patrick Hurley feel fully accepted was old Washington magic that he would not fully appreciate until it ended.

The Hurleys' former neighbors from Belmont Avenue, Eugene and Agnes Meyer, were often at the same parties. Agnes was considered by many to be the most beautiful woman in Washington and she had been instrumental in introducing the Hurleys to her close friend, Cissy Patterson. Much talk also centered around Eugene Meyer's plans for the Reconstruction Finance Committee and his disagreements with Herbert Hoover, and whether he intended to buy the *Washington Post*.

While Patrick Hurley loved these engagements, for Ruth they became an enormous burden. Just keeping track of their social responsibilities was a full-time job. What's more, Ruth did not like many of the people with whom they had to associate, including Lou Henry Hoover and especially Douglas MacArthur, whom she considered vain and pompous.

Ruth Hurley was also appalled at her husband's naked ambition and embarrassed when he sought the approbation of the wealthy and powerful. As a third-generation Chapman, Ruth had experienced wealth and social power all her life. Unlike her husband, she understood that their popularity was temporary—that nothing about Washington was real. It was the position that was invited to dinner, not the person.

Ruth Hurley preferred down-to-earth, forthright people regardless of their status. She did not share her husband's ribald sense of humor, nor was she intimidated by his explosive temper.

And so after four years of immersion in Washington society, Patrick Hurley found himself attending more and more social functions alone while Ruth remained perfectly content at Belmont, an hour's drive away.

* * *

On June 16 the rains finally stopped and Washington descended into the stifling summer humidity for which it was famous. Daytime temperatures at Anacostia Flats usually exceeded 100 degrees while at night in June they could drop below 50.

Inside the Senate chambers one day after the House approval, the Senate Finance Committee voted against the bonus bill without discussion, essentially killing it.

Elmer Thomas of Oklahoma, the leading advocate for the bonus in the Senate, argued that this action was too quick and harsh and so the bill, already defeated, was brought to the floor for a faux debate and vote on Friday, June 17.

On this same day Herbert Hoover and Charles Curtis were re-nominated by the Republican Party in Chicago. According to tradition, neither man attended the convention.

Prior to the Senate debate, Alice Longworth's lover, Senate leader William Borah, announced that he would vote against the bonus, thereby giving permission for everyone else to follow. He thundered:

> "Even had I been for it I would be against it now with these veterans in Washington, seeking by their bodily presence and numbers, amounting to force, to compel Congress to pass this legislation."

Although he knew that the legislation would not pass, on the morning of the vote, Walter Waters took the stage at Camp Marks. He was dressed in his new trademark uniform: a tight-fitting brown leather jacket partially opened over a white shirt and bow tie; tan whipcord riding breeches; and polished black leather boots, free of dust from the camp. The latter were a gift from Evalyn Walsh McLean. He had also started to carry a riding crop as an accessory.

The BEF commander's curly blonde hair was carefully combed and his blue eyes sparkled as he faced the eager assembled crowd.

Waters said that when they first came here to Washington there didn't seem a chance that the House would consider the bonus bill. "They thought we were a bunch of weaklings," he said, "that we couldn't stand together. But now they know that the BEF means business and our next move will be to convince the Senate." The shouts and applause were thunderous.

Waters then said something new: that they had to stand not only for themselves but for the rank and file of unemployed Americans, veterans or otherwise, who they represented.

Waters paused then pointed his outstretched hand rigidly above the heads of the crowd below him. This was another new gesture that he had borrowed from the fascist leaders of the time.

"I understand that if the measure passes the Senate today, Hoover…"

"Who?" the crowd yelled, and Waters smiled.

"Hoover will veto it!" There was hearty booing. "If he does, I want you men to pledge to do your stuff in November!"

After Waters climbed down from the stage to leave in his car for the Capitol, the veterans were given their orders. Eight thousand men were to depart for the city on foot at once. Another 5,000 would join them in the late afternoon to make a final show of strength on the Capitol grounds.

* * *

Pelham Glassford had carefully prepared for this day. Just before noon, after the first contingent of veterans crossed the river, the police superintendent ordered the Anacostia drawbridge raised, isolating more than 12,000 people on the Flats. The bridge sections extended skyward like Water's rigid hand as curious veterans and their families gathered in a mass along the banks of the river.

Two police boats took position near the raised bridge to discourage anyone from trying to swim across the tainted water. Overhead a war plane from nearby Bolling Field flew in a low threatening pattern above the camp.

Photograph taken by Acme. Taken from *BEF*, by W. W. Waters and William C. White, John Day Company, New York, 1933.

8,000 men mass at the Capitol, unaware that Pelham Glassford has raised the drawbridge at Anacostia Flats.

The drawbridge controls were on the Anacostia side of the bridge. A line of policemen stood there shoulder-to-shoulder, flanked by police cars. Other officers were positioned nearby armed with Tommy-guns.

The usual friendliness of the police was nowhere to be found; instead they stared dispassionately over the heads of the growing crowd of taunting men in front of them.

Unaware of this, the 8,000 men who had joined Waters at the Capitol grounds took their positions in the shade of the trees and on the cool marble steps of the building.

Within the Capitol seventy heavily armed Metropolitan Police hid in the wings. At the Marine Barracks in the Navy Yard, Commandant Charles Taylor placed three companies of 180 Marines on alert, awaiting a possible summons from Vice President Charles Curtis who was reluctantly serving in his capacity as President of the Senate.

* * *

While the Senate debate was underway, former Vice President Charles Dawe visited Herbert Hoover to make his farewells. Dawe had served as the temporary chairman of Hoover's new RFC until Eugene Meyer could take charge, after which Dawe secretly applied for an $80 million loan for his bank in Chicago.

Hoover assured him that the loan would be made, even while thirty-nine of Dawe's competitors were forced to close their doors.

* * *

Walter Waters stood on the Capitol steps and gave interviews. "The bonus was just a break," Waters said. "A little bit of capital that they can use for a fresh start. That is all every man wants and they think they've earned it."

Asked whether the men of the BEF considered themselves radicals, Waters said that they were hungry and desperate but not radicals—although radicalism was always possible if men believed they didn't have a chance.

* * *

At his estate on Broad Branch Road, Senator Thomas Gore began his transformation from a frowzy-haired old man in a bathrobe to a distinguished U.S. Senator.

His seven-year-old grandson Gene always enjoyed this daily activity. Gene stood in the bathroom door watching as "Dah" inserted first his upper, then his lower, sets of false teeth. Then Gene watched Tot gently wet down and comb the old man's unruly white hair.

Finally it came time for the boy to open the small black leather case and remove the single bright blue glass eye. Dah carefully wet and inserted the eye into his empty socket. After Gore put on his starched white shirt and black suit with tails, the old man stood military-straight, chin raised, his blind eyes fixed on a distant horizon—the very picture of a distinguished senator.

The senator had promised to take young Gene with him that afternoon to watch the U.S. Senate vote on the bonus. As always they rode to the Capitol in the senator's chauffeured car. When the car approached the reserved parking area, the driver had to slow and negotiate his way through a throng of men in ragged clothing. The senator and Gene sat together in the back seat.

Suddenly someone threw a large rock through the open side window of the limousine. It bounced off the back of the front seat and landed between them. Gene fell back into the corner of the car, his eyes wide. The senator reached out and felt the jagged edges of the rock.

"Roll up the window," he instructed his grandson.

There was, after all, something to fear from the "boners."

* * *

The Senate debate lasted all afternoon and into the night. Purely for show, the senators re-hashed the arguments and speeches that they had been making for years.

Elmer Thomas of Oklahoma characterized the legislation as a titanic battle between the rich and the poor. Others spoke of the nation's great unpaid debt to its veterans.

Within the adjoining Senate offices, tensions ran high. From outside in the park the veterans frequently saw the white faces of staff members peeking from their windows down onto the Capitol grounds.

The hot day ebbed into evening and a vaudeville entertainer named Jack Frost from Camp Bartlett began to lead them in song—the BEF's own version of "Over There" that went:

"All you there. All you there.
Pay the Bonus. Pay the Bonus. Pay the Bonus.
For the Yanks are Starving. The Yanks are Starving.
The Yanks are Starving Everywhere."

Senator Brookhard emerged and asked Waters to quiet the men whose loud singing could be heard inside the Senate chambers. Waters, who had been going in and out of the Capitol all day to confer with Foulkrod, moved to the top of the steps and said: "Men, this noise is going to hurt us. Please keep silent. We can do our cheering later on."

A military kitchen was set up and then dismantled at the insistence of the Capitol Police. It was assembled again off the grounds and the men were served a dinner of hot dogs and beans.

By eight-thirty it was dark and the veterans watched anxiously for the second contingent of men who were supposed to be on their way. Waters, who had been told of the drawbridge being raised, remained quiet. Dozens of Capitol and Metropolitan Police moved constantly among the veterans as they lay about on the Capitol lawn.

From time to time a reporter or policeman approached Walter Waters. "What's gonna happen?" they asked. "What will the men do if the bonus is voted down?"

Waters simply shrugged. "Nothing," he said. "Nothing will happen."

The vets talked quietly among themselves about what they would do with the bonus money. Many intended to buy new clothes for their wives and children, then use the balance to start a business. For $470 a man could buy a truck and do a little hauling.

"I'm going to Florida to buy a little fishing shack," one man said.

"I'm getting a hotel room and a hot bath. I'll stay there 'til the money runs out."

"I'm paying back taxes."

"I'm buying new teeth."

The men's eyes shone with hope as they discussed their plans.

Inside the Senate chamber the debate droned on. Conservative Democrat Burton Wheeler from Montana rose and said in carefully phrased support:

> "If I could see a ray of hope that some means would be found to put more money into circulation than by the method here proposed, I would not vote for the pending bill…but I have sat here waiting month after month…in vain for the Great Engineer at the other end of Pennsylvania Avenue to come forward with some proposal to take care of these veterans and the other millions of men and women…but nothing has been done, and nothing will be done."

An occasional current of anger would build up among the veterans outside and their raised voices could be heard inside the chambers. When this happened a senator would emerge, walk to the top of the steps, and make a brief speech to the assembled men to explain his position.

As the night wore on, more and more senators came out to weakly explain that if the legislation seemed headed for defeat, they would vote "No" themselves in order to be able to move to reconsider it in the fall when Congress reconvened. They asked the veterans not to hold these "no" votes against them.

The Army band arrived, summoned by Pelham Glassford, and began to softly serenade the veterans. Glassford knew that music was an effective way to control their tempers. (Camp Marks even had an official "camp clown" who broke into song whenever tensions arose at Anacostia Flats.)

Walter Waters was summoned inside the Capitol by Senator Elmer Thomas at 11:00 p.m. After several minutes, he returned to the top of the marble stairs to address the men. The silence below him seemed to resonate with tension.

"Prepare yourselves for a disappointment, men," the BEF commander-in-chief said. "The bonus has been defeated 62 to 18."

The 8,000 men standing at the foot of the Capitol steps seemed stunned. Then an angry muttering began to build.

"This is only a temporary setback," Waters said. "We are going to get more and more men and we are going to stay here until we change the minds of these people. You are ten times better Americans than these senators who voted against the bill."

Now the mass of ragged veterans started to advance toward the Capitol, their voices raised in angry shouts, their fists clenched.

A dozen reporters who had gathered around Waters bolted away for safety. Inside their chambers the senators sat motionless, waiting. Hiram Johnson of Connecticut turned to his colleagues and said, "The time may come when these trappings of government will disappear and fat old men like you and me will be lined up against a stone wall."

Elsie Robinson, a Hearst reporter, stood behind Waters at the top of the steps. She leaned forward and said, "Tell them to sing 'America.'"

And so he did. After several tense moments, the angry shouting began to subside. A few voices lifted from the crowd below, softly at first then with growing intensity as the Army band began to play:

> My country 'tis of thee
> Sweet land of liberty
> Let freedom sing

The men sang fervently, their emotion and anger channeled into this song that reflected their love for America.

> From every mountainside
> Let freedom ring.

Pelham Glassford watched with pride as the men then placed their hands over their hearts and recited the pledge of allegiance. Then, in small groups, the veterans turned away from the Capitol and began their long walk back to Anacostia Flats. The drawbridge had been lowered for their return.

CHAPTER EIGHT

The White Plan

The morning after the Senate vote an angry Walter Waters summoned Pelham Glassford to the new BEF headquarters at 1841 N. Capitol Street. He told the superintendent that the veterans were furious over his "drawbridge stunt" and demanded an explanation.

Glassford said they were right to be angry. He claimed the police had received false information about a plot. "What sort of plot?" Waters demanded. Hadn't they been working together? Weren't his men keeping the Communists under control?

At Waters' insistence, Glassford dictated a written apology to the BEF.

Soon after this episode, Glassford installed Waters and his wife in the home of Don Alphonso Zelaya, a well-known concert pianist. Don Zelaya and Glassford had been plebes together at West Point in 1898. Glassford used Zelaya to reward Waters with more comfortable surroundings and helped pay for the related costs. Given Zelaya's hidden radical politics, this may have been a mistake.

* * *

Taken from *The Bonus March and the New Deal*, John Henry Bartlett;
M.A. Donohue and Company, Chicago, 1937.

*Walter W. Waters (left) and chief of staff Doak Carter
leave the Senate Office Building.*

The mood of the veterans at Camp Marks the day after the devastating Senate defeat was grim. For the first time men would not respond to roll call. Those who did fall out were sullen and refused to come to attention. Visitors to the camp overheard many muted conversations punctuated with angry outbursts.

Assembly was called later in the morning and a camp officer took the stage and read aloud Glassford's letter of apology:

"Dear Waters—I wish to express to you and to the Bonus Expeditionary Forces my regret over the incident which occurred last night when the drawbridge at Eleventh Street was raised under instructions from the Police Department."

Glassford described the state of official concern over "so many visiting veterans" and the fear by residents of "mob psychology should the bonus bill receive unfavorable action by the National Legislature." This required plans to raise the bridge should the veterans at the Capitol become disorderly, although Glassford was sure they would not. He placed the blame for raising the bridge on an officer at the scene.

"The exemplary conduct, discipline, and loyal attitude of your officers and men has been remarkable." Glassford concluded his apology with hopes that the incident would not cause the BEF to believe the policy of the police toward them had changed.

There was only silence after the letter was read. Then one veteran shouted, "Just get us our damn bonus!" to which a chorus of cheers responded.

* * *

After the Senate rejected the bonus bill, the District commissioners increased their pressure on Glassford to hasten the exit of the BEF. In response, the police superintendent sent telegrams to the governors of all 48 states in which he urged them to make arrangements to bring their citizens home.

Only three governors responded. The most aggressive was Franklin Delano Roosevelt, who offered the large New York contingent free passage as well as jobs on their return.

Glassford placed another call to Daniel Willard at the B&O to arrange for discounted passage out of Washington at the cost of a penny per mile. He proposed using the veterans' own treasury to pay for it but the BEF executive committee objected so loudly that Glassford said he would raise the money from "wealthy Washingtonians."

President Hoover finally acknowledged the BEF's presence when he asked Congress to pass an emergency measure authorizing $100,000 toward the advance of travel costs, which would be deducted from each veteran's eventual bonus.

Patrick Hurley sent word to Walter Waters that the War Department would transport people to nearby states after which Waters could coordinate further transport with the state National Guards.

Glassford printed flyers to promote these various options. When Camp Marks officials refused to hand them out, the resourceful superintendent had an Army plane drop 3,000 flyers over Anacostia Flats.

These offers led about 5,000 veterans to leave Washington. Another 17,000 or so remained. The rains had stopped (as one vet said, "They were never as bad as France anyway") and Camp Marks still provided two meals a day. There was a racetrack nearby and many men had their families with them. Besides, Congress was still in session and their job wasn't done.

The bottom line was that for many in the BEF, life on Anacostia Flats was better than the life they had left behind.

* * *

Cissy Patterson and her best friend Evalyn Walsh McLean paid a visit to Anacostia Flats one afternoon in late June.

Evalyn had been a patron of the BEF almost since their arrival in Washington. She called on their behalf to local service agencies; purchased food for them; donated her own family's clothing; funded a large tent for the BEF registration area; sent the veterans books for their library; and she met often with Walter Waters. When Waters' slender young wife arrived by bus in Washington dressed in men's clothing, Evalyn even brought Wilma into her home for several days.

This charitable activity helped keep the heiress's mind off her personal troubles. Evalyn had been in despair ever since her husband Ned ran off to Paris with Rose Davies, an excursion made possible by Patrick Hurley's money.

Then in April, desperate for a way to save the *Washington Post* from bankruptcy, Evalyn had foolishly paid $104,000 to a swindler named Gaston Means who told her that he could recover the Lindbergh baby. A scoop of this magnitude, she reasoned, would revitalize the newspaper's flagging reputation and circulation.

Evalyn sent *Post* reporters with Means on a wild goose chase through swamps in South Carolina and Texas. The charade lasted until the baby's body was discovered on May 12 not far from the Lindbergh home in New Jersey.

The baby had actually been killed on March 2 when a homemade ladder broke under the kidnapper's weight and the child's skull was fractured in the fall. The *Post* was scooped itself when rival newspapers ran the story of Means' arrest. Evalyn was subjected to enormous ridicule as a result.

Even Evalyn's fabulous 75-acre estate Friendship—site of a former monastery called Old Friendship—was going to seed and she was thinking of selling her family home and moving to Georgetown. (Her estate would eventually become an unsightly post WW-II community of brick apartment buildings in Bethesda, Maryland, morphed today into upper-income condominiums at "Friendship Heights.")

This was not the first time that Cissy, either, had descended among the poor. A few months before the veterans arrived, she had dressed in an old brown corduroy skirt and a floppy hat and spent seven days and nights posing as a destitute woman, standing in food lines and sleeping on narrow Salvation Army cots. Cissy wrote a compelling eight-part series about her experiences for the *Herald*.

The two friends drove to Anacostia Flats in Evalyn's chauffeured limousine, accompanied by Cissy's team of six leashed poodles, five black and one white. Evalyn wore the Hope Diamond, which she only removed when she slept.

The women were welcomed by Waters and escorted to the large green Salvation Army tent dubbed "The Hut" where Cissy and Evalyn were given refreshments before being taken on a walking tour of the camp. The veterans, used by now to all sorts of visitors, were especially accommodating when tourists arrived in limousines and strolled about under parasols.

After their tour the women returned to Patterson's DuPont Circle mansion for afternoon cocktails where Cissy wrote out a check for $500 and sent it to Pelham Glassford with her best wishes.

* * *

Herbert Hoover's one salvation in these difficult times was his devoted wife Lou Henry, who affectionately called her husband "Bert."

The two had met as geology majors at Sanford University and married in 1899.

Lou Henry followed Bert around the world as he made his fortune as a mining engineer, and they were married in Australia.

The couple was living in London when the first World War broke out and they dedicated themselves to helping 12,000 Americans escape Europe. Of the $1.5 million that Hoover loaned to his countrymen for passage home, all but $300 was repaid. Later Hoover oversaw a massive food rescue effort to save the people of Belgium from starvation.

These humanitarian projects led the *New York Times* to proclaim Herbert Hoover among the ten greatest living Americans in 1920. President Coolidge, on whose cabinet Hoover then served, was fond of calling him "wundah boy."

The Hoovers were both intellectuals who loved the outdoors. They were tender-hearted people who gave of their wealth generously and, as Quakers, anonymously. (Few knew that Lou Henry often sent her servants to Camp Marks with sandwiches and coffee.)

But Herbert Hoover also had an imperious side, and after being elected president, his aloof manner grew. Because he did not wish to see servants other than at meal times, a bell was sounded when the president walked the halls of the White House, giving the servants time to scurry behind doors and curtains.

At dinner the Hoovers were trumpeted in and a Marine color guard stood at attention throughout their meals. The table servants had been carefully chosen so that they all were the same height. The president and Lou Henry sometimes spoke in Chinese so that the servants would not overhear their private conversations.

* * *

Dissatisfaction with Walter Waters' leadership grew following the Senate defeat. Some BEF officials wanted to affiliate with the Democratic Party, but Waters refused to "politicize" their cause.

Waters learned of a secret meeting convened by George Alman, Mike Thomas, and other camp commanders to identify another leader.

The commander-in-chief was subjected to heckling when he visited the Camp Marks billets and on several occasions his orders were not carried out. There were rumors of plans to harm or kidnap Waters.

Waters stepped down on June 25 and named his friend George Kleinholz as his successor. Kleinholz lasted one day before he was replaced by Alman. Neither man was recognized as BEF commander by Pelham Glassford, who immediately cut off all food and water to Camp Marks. After two days of hunger, the veterans re-elected Waters as their leader.

Waters moved quickly to secure his position. He fired the six camp commanders who had opposed him and doubled the size of his military police, who were given new powers to act with force against anyone who dared to speak out against the BEF commander.

"Any man who disobeys my orders will be dragged out of Washington by the (BEF) military police," Waters told the veterans at assembly the day after his return.

"General Glassford says that is illegal!" a veteran shouted.

"To hell with civil law and General Glassford!" Waters yelled back. "I'm going to have my orders carried out!"

To help re-establish discipline, rifle-sized wooden sticks were issued to the men at Camp Marks and they were required to undertake three hours of drill each morning. Waters' top officers now dressed in the same khaki shirts that Waters wore and his bodyguards were placed on round-the-clock duty.

* * *

Life on Anacostia Flats fell back into its old patterns. Some veterans attended Bible readings and services at a religious tent. Others spent time at the canteen provided by the Salvation Army and borrowed Evalyn McLean's donated books and magazines. At the small BEF post office there was a table where the men sat to write letters and postcards home.

Baseball games resumed on a rough field between teams of veterans and P.J. Marks' local police or Marines from the Navy Yard. Meals continued to be served twice a day. Camp Marks missed just one thing—its commander-in-chief.

As the summer slipped into July, Waters and his wife spent most nights at the cool, comfortable downtown mansion of Don Zelaya. Waters later wrote in his memoirs, "We made no finer friend in Washington."

During those evenings, sipping a glass of wine under slowly rotating ceiling fans, the BEF commander was enthralled by stories from his cultured host, for Don Zelaya was the son of Jose Santos Zelaya, the ruthless deposed dictator of Nicaragua.

The elder Zelaya had dominated his country for sixteen years until his rule was overthrown by the United States in 1910. By 1932 Nicaragua represented the very worst example of American meddling in Latin America. Don Zelaya had no fondness for the Hoover Administration and he was quite happy to assist Waters and the BEF.

* * *

Thanks to his family's wealth from California vineyards and his wife Bea's personal fortune, Colonel George Patton could do whatever he wanted. What he wanted most was to be at war. Thus, despite severe dyslexia, Patton worked his way through the Army War College with enthusiasm and earned outstanding reviews.

Patton recalled fondly his first action in Mexico. He and two other National Guardsmen went on a raid across the border to capture Cardenas, one of Pancho Villa's lieutenants. In a small, dusty village they engaged four banditos in a shootout. Patton drove back to Texas with Cardenas strung like a deer across the hood of his car and presented him to General Pershing. In a letter to Bea Patton he described his feelings at killing two men as being much like when he landed his first swordfish.

Patton met Douglas MacArthur in France prior to the battle of Saint-Michiel. MacArthur stood alone on a knoll staring toward the German front. Major George Patton joined him. Soon a wave of German shells began to fall across the battlefield. The explosions came closer and closer until they were blasting craters all around the two men.

When Patton flinched at one near miss, MacArthur said, "You never hear the one that gets you." The shelling passed on, leaving them miraculously unscathed, and the men remained close friends from that day forward.

Although the War College at Ft. McNair was near Anacostia Flats, Patton had been consumed with his final papers and not concerned with the bonus march. When he graduated in early July, Patton moved his family into a large rented home in Rosslyn, Virginia, directly across from Douglas MacArthur's quarters at Ft. Myer.

Patton was appointed executive officer at Ft. Meyer, a ceremonial post that allowed him to take part in the fox hunting and the equestrian events that he enjoyed. Now that he had time to size up the BEF situation, Patton criticized the "weak handling" of the veterans by Glassford. He pressed MacArthur for a decisive military solution.

It was Patton who provided the final ingredient to the simmering bonus situation.

* * *

Nicaragua was actually two countries divided by a thick jungle. On the Pacific side was the cool lake district. On the east was the hot Mosquito Coast. In the middle was huge Lake Nicaragua, offering a possible canal route to the Pacific.

In 1901 Zelaya's father and President McKinley agreed to build an ocean-to-ocean canal. However, Momotombo, a dormant volcano on the edge of Lake Nicaragua, erupted. President Zelaya downplayed the event, but a local artist painted it and stamps were made from the painting.

The chief engineer for the competing French project in Panama obtained sheets of the stamps and sent one to every U.S. congressman with a note: "Do you want your canal built here?" The next year the U.S. bought the French interest in the Panama Canal and the Nicaraguan canal was never built. Nicaragua was left in great debt and Zelaya's father negotiated loans with other countries. Fearing that foreign interests would take over Nicaragua, U.S. officials deposed the dictator.

In the 20 years since, Nicaragua had been ruled by one military regime after another. Now Sandino, a peasant Robin Hood, was fighting the American Marines in order to put a new leader, Juan Sacasa, in control. Sacasa had recently spent two years working with Don Zelaya in Washington.

Zelaya smiled and raised his drink. He was secretly providing financial support to the bandits.

By July the flames of ambition were burning white hot in Walter Waters. He had spent a month walking among men of power as their equal. It was a role he did not wish to abdicate.

The lesson that Walter Waters learned from Don Zelaya was clear. When the revolution occurred, anyone could end up in control, whether he was a printer in Italy, a paper hanger in Germany, or a fruit picker from Oregon.

* * *

The greatest threat to Democracy in 1932 was not Communism whose arcane proposals often seemed laughable but violent, intolerant

Fascism. Some prominent American business leaders had begun to advocate for a form of Fascism that they believed could be an alternative to democracy, which was clearly failing.

Walter Waters and the BEF were not invisible to these people. Waters was a compelling speaker, physically attractive, and well organized. He had also demonstrated an uncanny skill for maneuvering and manipulation.

By July, Waters and Wilma enjoyed a suite of rooms at the Ebbitt Hotel that he said were paid for by Evalyn McLean. However, he also had a chauffeured limousine and a private airplane that was kept at Bolling Field for his use in attending secret meetings and distant speaking engagements. These extraordinary luxuries caused Pelham Glassford to question who was supporting the BEF commander.

A rumor was circulating among the veterans that a secret right-wing military group called the "Key Men," led by radical Marine General Smedley Butler, had gained control of Waters and his commanders. The top leadership of the 4,000 Key Men was said to be so secret that one member did not know another. Waters denied this but never accounted for the source of his unusual financial support.

(The Key Men actually existed. Their headquarters, under executive director Thomas N. Jarrell, was at 1116 Vermont Avenue in Washington. Their slogan was "For the improvement of Economic and Social Order." On June 25, 1932, Jarrell wrote to Pelham Glassford telling him that they had secured 100,000 acres of land in southern states where the veterans could engage in farming, paid for by funds from the new RFC. If needed, Jarrell felt they could "furnish a million more acres.")

Butler confirmed in 1935 that he had led a fascist-inspired movement during this time. He said that the Key Men had approached Major General Douglas MacArthur to serve as a possible dictator but abandoned that idea because of the highly negative public response to the Bonus Army episode. MacArthur, a staunch supporter of democracy, would probably have rejected fascism, but perhaps not the opportunity to run the country.

* * *

Frustrated by the BEF's refusal to allow Red agitators inside Camp Marks, Emanuel Levin summoned help from the large communist cell in Detroit. Within a few days more than 200 thugs arrived and mounted an evening attack on the camp with baseball bats. As reported the next day by Cissy Patterson's *Herald*:

> "Husky buddies from the Texas plains vied with lanky New Englanders for the privilege of going to work on the Communists."

Pelham Glassford was summoned to escort the agitators out of Camp Marks. He found them beaten and cowering under guard in a dark corner of the Flats.

In July, a new leader was brought in to stir up the ineffectual communist organization in Washington. John Pace was an unemployed small businessman from Cleveland who had recently made headlines by leading a standoff between communist agitators and railroad authorities. Although averse to violence, Pace was the best organizer that the Communists had in America.

Soon after Pace's arrival, the Communists turned to propaganda. They created a counterfeit "BEF News" that they paid children to carry into Camp Marks. One story referred to Walter Waters as "Puss in Boots" and ridiculed his new way of addressing the veterans in the fascist manner, in which he extended one arm palm out and spoke with his eyes focused on the ground.

* * *

In ten weeks' time Walter Waters underwent an astonishing metamorphosis, from a desperate unemployed worker to a national leader. By July the bonus issue looked like small change compared to the opportunity of a national organization, perhaps a third political party that some were dangling in front of him. As Waters later wrote:

> "Letters received by hundreds assured me that such an organization would find plenty of support at home; and if its purposes were broadened from the special interests of the veterans to include a demand for general political reform, we should have in our hands the nucleus of a new party…seemingly, the BEF was the nucleus for a powerful movement."

Waters portrayed himself in heroic terms in a July article in the official *BEF News* headlined: "W. W. Waters Imagines One Million—Waters Outlines Road Ahead for New Organization." He wrote:

> "What matters…if I go down fighting! The cause is the greatest thing in America today. My own health means nothing if I can help the millions in need. I might have to die with my boots on. All that I have, all that I am, I shall give to the people of my country."

In the same article Waters compared himself favorably to Hitler and Mussolini.

* * *

A swarm of activity occurred around the Bonus Marchers involving Pelham Glassford's police, Ogden Mills' Treasury and Secret Service agents, the Communists under John Pace, the fascists under Smedley Butler, J. Edgar Hoover's Bureau of Intelligence operatives, and Frank Hine's Veterans' Affairs officers. Everyone fell over each other with different agendas and orders.

Pelham Glassford again offered free train tickets to little avail. Some 1,769 veterans came to Washington in one July week compared to 258 who left. Each new group was infiltrated with government agents.

Glassford arranged for a photograph to be taken of a dozen derelicts in the back of an Army truck under a banner reading "We're Going Home." The Republican-friendly *Post* dutifully ran it on the front page with a story predicting an exodus by the veterans.

In nearby Anacostia rooms were leased by covert groups with fascist leanings and veterans were lured there with poker games and free liquor. More and more infiltrators entered the camp to plant rumors and instigate quarrels.

Eddie Atwell's Khaki Shirts created an undercurrent of fear and tension at Camp Marks. They regularly beat agitators and suspect campers alike and tossed them into the polluted Anacostia River.

Another activity during this time was shrouded in secrecy. The Army, under Patrick Hurley and Douglas MacArthur, was putting in place its White Plan.

* * *

As early as June 3, before the veterans proved themselves to be docile and easily controlled, Pelham Glassford had suggested to the commissioners that they create a "White Plan," the military term for a strategy of force to deal with serious civil disorder. His concern was that the veterans might riot if food supplies dwindled. Even earlier, on May 25, MacArthur had authorized Van Horn Moseley to begin similar preparations.

By mid-June at the continued urging of Van Horn Moseley and MacArthur, Patrick Hurley authorized funds to accelerate the assembly of military personnel and weaponry that could be deployed against the veterans' army.

The primary staging point for cavalry troops was Ft. Myer, the Arlington, Virginia, Army base across the Potomac from Washington. The newly involved Patton placed an order for 100 brown cavalry horses, trained to support crowd control.

The infantry troops were barracked further down the Potomac at Ft. Washington in Maryland, across the Potomac River from Alexandria, Virginia. Because older enlisted men might not take up arms against their former comrades, MacArthur amassed younger soldiers from Army bases around the country.

By mid-July, about 600 soldiers had been deployed to these two locations, their summer leaves cancelled. During the day the soldiers were rigorously trained in crowd control and the use of tear gas. Most evenings all but the officers were restricted to their hot barracks so that they would not fraternize with older soldiers or veterans.

A new officer, Perry L. Miles, was assigned as Commanding General of the Washington Provisional Brigade. Hurley approved Miles' request for more than 2,500 canisters of tear gas from the Army Weapons Division at a cost of $2 apiece. This was the same caustic gas once used against German soldiers to drive them out of trenches and underground bunkers.

Measures were quietly taken to secure Camp Marks. At nearby Bolling Field, 120 soldiers were drilled in armed crowd control. Across the greasy Anacostia River several hundred Marines were kept on alert in their Navy Yard barracks.

Even the battleship *Constitution*, anchored at the Navy Yard for exhibition, was armed. Sixty loaded rifles were kept under canvas on the deck for a team Marine sharpshooters. Mothers and children from Camp Marks played by the river and enjoyed the view of the tall-masted ship, never suspecting that it might be used to fire upon them.

Six small M1917 tanks were shipped in late June to the Aberdeen Training Grounds in Maryland where the number of soldiers had been tripled to guard the base's large weapons supply. The tanks were sent on to Ft. Myer on July 22 as the White Plan neared its execution.

There was much to be done. Farriers had to tap special shoes onto the horses' feet to protect them from the rough asphalt of the city's streets and ensure sure footing.

Rooftop sirens were installed across the District, and codes for siren blasts communicated to the police and Army units to summon them into immediate action. The White House, Treasury building, Bureau of Engraving and Printing, and the Capitol were designated as critical points whose protection was primary.

Several older soldiers came in secret to Walter Waters to advise him of the build-up of troops and weapons. They told him of armories in the region where friendly guards would provide the BEF with weapons so that the veterans could defend themselves.

* * *

A new worry whispered about in Washington social circles concerned disease coming out of the encampments. Vaccines for viral killers like scarlet fever and smallpox had not yet been discovered and Camp Marks in particular was becoming more unsanitary every day. The newspapers began to warn of an epidemic.

The veterans, trained in waste disposal from their Army days, had created a serviceable latrine system, and periodic inspections from the

District health department pronounced Camp Marks fit for habitation (although health officials later denied this). The supply of fresh water, however, was inadequate—only 700 of the 10,000 residents could shower on any given day and the camp bottomland created a haven for mosquitos and diseases like trench mouth. Despite its polluted condition, many bathed in the Anacostia River.

The growing mountain of garbage near the entrance to Camp Marks had also become a smelly nuisance for every visitor to the camp. A low fire burned there around the clock.

That summer, a thin man, aged 34, strolled by Camp Marks. Against his wishes, Ernie Pyle had just been named managing editor of the *Washington Daily News*, the Scripps-Howard tabloid newspaper on 13th Street.

Pyle, who would become the country's most revered war correspondent, had worked for the past four years as the Scripps-Howard aviation editor. During that time he spent enjoyable days at nearby Bolling Field with pioneer aviators like Wiley Post, Charles Lindbergh, Amelia Earhart, and Gene Vidal.

Ernie Pyle and his wife Jerry lived in a cramped apartment in the city and spent their money on rent, a modest amount of food, cigarettes, and booze. The couple, who were originally from the Midwest, planned to leave Washington. Their odyssey would lead Pyle to seven years of reporting for Scripps-Howard from the road and then to the battlefields of World War II.

As he stood at the edge of Camp Marks and watched the burning fires and the thousands of lost souls who had journeyed there, Pyle no doubt shook his balding head. This was tragedy, pure and simple, and there would be no happy ending.

CHAPTER NINE

The Death March

Few top Republicans gave the sitting president a chance for re-election in the 1932 contest. Their reluctant re-nomination of Herbert Hoover was largely done out of fear that switching to a new candidate might lead to the loss of more seats in Congress. Republican leaders never considered that they could lose not only the presidency but both the Senate and House in the greatest single-party defeat in election history.

For a while it appeared that the Democratic nomination would go to John Nance Garner, the grizzled secretary of the House of Representatives. A short man with a gray crew-cut, Garner was the early favorite of publisher William Randolph Hearst who had come to believe that Hoover represented a threat to continued U.S. democracy.

The millionaire Garner was known as the cheapest man in Congress. He lived in a one-room boarding house apartment with his wife Etti who served as his cook, laundress, secretary, and errand person. He insisted that she call him "Mr. Garner."

(After he lost a $5 bet at a baseball game, Garner asked the winner what he would do with the bill. The man said that he would frame it. "Then I will write you a check," the congressman replied, snatching back the bill.)

When the Democrats nominated Franklin Delano Roosevelt on July 2, Herbert Hoover was relieved. He had not wanted to run against Garner, who was a master legislator. Because Hoover considered Franklin Roosevelt to be a weak candidate, he did little campaigning early on. Instead, Hoover stayed sequestered in Washington where the public saw him as being surrounded by the veterans' army.

To counter rumors about his health, Roosevelt threw himself into a coast-to-coast election campaign, promising the country a "new deal." Roosevelt specifically mentioned the veterans and pledged that he would dedicate his campaign to the "forgotten man at the base of the pyramid."

* * *

Harold Foulkrod, the BEF's effective chief lobbyist, returned to Washington from the Democratic convention in Chicago where he had been heavily lobbied and converted to their cause. Foulkrod, who was also a member of the BEF Executive Committee, broke ranks with Walter Waters on July 12 after several weeks of deteriorating relations.

Alarmed by Waters' growing militancy, Foulkrod called the new BEF slogan, "We Stay Here Until 1945," "stupid" and told the veterans at Camp Marks that there was "no room for a dictatorship."

Foulkrod's desertion gave voice to what many veterans had been feeling for weeks—that Walter Waters no longer cared about the bonus issue. There appeared to be other plans and priorities at work.

* * *

With just four months remaining before the election, Herbert Hoover had yet to begin campaigning. Although many in the administration began to distance themselves from the president, Patrick Hurley still defended Hoover at every opportunity. It was only when the gubernatorial election in stalwart Maine unexpectedly went to a Democrat that the president finally agreed to go on the road.

On his first night of travel, Hoover saw the glowing lights from hundreds of campfires from the window of his train. He asked his secretary Lawrence Richey about them and was surprised to learn that they were the fires of thousands of homeless people who were camped along the railroad tracks.

The thin-skinned president was shocked when he stepped onto the platform at a Kansas whistle-stop and was heartily booed by the crowd, many of whom then pelted his train with eggs and tomatoes. Hoover retreated into his railroad car ashen-faced.

Never having visited a bread line or a soup kitchen, having blissfully believed the self-serving reports from his underlings that "no one in America was starving," the president had lost all touch with the people he was elected to serve.

* * *

The growing divide between Patrick Hurley and his wife did not improve the mood of the Secretary of War.

Traditionally, Washington wives were submissive to their powerful husbands. Mamie Eisenhower considered herself "thankful for the privilege of tagging along at Ike's side." After leaving the White House, Lou Henry Hoover admitted having yearned for the "loss of all kinds of projects...I should have liked to follow." Bea Patton was fiercely protective—once at a party she physically attacked a man whom she thought had berated her husband.

Ruth Hurley was the exception. Although initially impressed and even overwhelmed by her husband's strong personality, in time Ruth began to question her life with him. Her son Wilson came across a packet of undelivered letters that Ruth had written to her father about Patrick. The words leaped out at Wilson: "Ambitious…insensitive… driving only for what he wants…divorce unthinkable, but…" A life-long battle of wills between his parents had begun.

When Ruth retreated to their Belmont estate and left her husband to negotiate Washington society alone, Patrick Hurley did not react with affairs and deceits as other power figures so commonly did. The Secretary of War was at his core a strongly principled man. He remained married to Ruth but from 1932 on he made his own way in life.

* * *

An apparent new threat arrived in Washington in mid-July that gave Hurley and MacArthur the excuse they needed to step up military preparations.

For weeks, military intelligence reports warned of a large build-up of activist veterans in the state of California. Their leader was Royal Robertson, a disabled former naval enlistee.

Before the war, Robertson had been an actor whose biggest role was as a disabled French soldier in Rudolph Valentino's silent film *The Four Horsemen*. Ironically, soon after he joined the Navy, Robertson broke his neck in a freak accident. Other sailors had tied a "fool's knot" in his hammock that came loose in the middle of the night.

Surgeons kept Robertson alive by stabilizing his head over his spinal cord. This required a steel back brace that extended above his head from which hung a leather strap that fit under Robertson's chin. This apparatus made Robinson look as though his head was in a permanent noose.

Inspired by the bonus marchers from Oregon, Robertson assembled more than 1,000 California veterans whom he led on a June 9 parade through downtown Los Angeles. A huge blanket was carried by twenty veterans into which bystanders threw donations.

The event's carnival-like atmosphere was enhanced by Robertson and his chief aide, a puffy red-faced little man named Urban LeDoux who had used the stage name of "Mr. Zero" during his vaudeville days.

By the time he left Los Angeles, Robertson had collected more than $4,000 in donations and assembled a fleet of 350 old cars and trucks to carry more than 2,000 veterans across the country. Free gasoline donations had been lined up along the way.

Because of rumors that the men were heavily armed and dangerous, "Robertson's Army" was infiltrated by Treasury agents who began to plant rumors and cause dissension. By the time his marchers reached Phoenix, Robertson had been accused of stealing funds. As a result, he split off on his own with a smaller group of primarily disabled veterans.

When Robertson finally marched into the nation's capital on July 12 after 30 days on the road, he was accompanied by only 450 men, but his reputation had arrived far ahead of him.

Waters had heard stories about Robertson and his boast, "Just wait until I get to Washington" for several weeks. The wise-cracking Navy vet also said, "All (the BEF is) doing is sitting in a puddle and whittling a stick."

What was needed, Robertson said, echoing Father Coughlin, was direct action.

* * *

The Hurley family enjoyed a visit of several days from Patrick Hurley's boyhood friend Will Rogers when he came to see Anacostia Flats.

Since their early cowboy days together, Will Rogers had become one of America's most beloved movie stars and a highly regarded sage and wit. Accompanied by his son, Rogers was flying coast-to-coast to give away much of the money he had earned that year to poor families.

While at Belmont, Will Rogers spoke frankly to his old friend about his dissatisfaction with the ineptitude of Herbert Hoover and how impressed he was by the charismatic Democratic nominee, Franklin Roosevelt.

Despite his compassion for the unemployed, Will Rogers did not support the bonus marchers, feeling that their cause was too narrow. Still he spoke well of their composure, saying, "These soldiers...were the best behaved 5,000 hungry men that ever lived in the world"—better, Rogers said, than 15,000 hungry bankers or club women would have acted under similar situations.

When Patrick Hurley tried to make a clever comment of his own at dinner one night, it came across as cruel. Rogers squinted at him and said, "Listen, Pat, don't you try to be funny. That's my job. You have more important things to do."

* * *

Royal Robertson's primary concern was to achieve benefits for physically disabled veterans like himself. Therefore, his petition to Congress was to pay the bonus first to those with disabilities.

When he was met by BEF men at the District line, Robertson refused to accompany them to Camp Marks for registration. "I wish I had been here seven weeks ago when this thing started," he said. "It would never have dragged this long."

Walter Waters went to see Robertson personally to invite him to join the BEF.

But again the crippled sailor curtly dismissed him. "We ain't here to go on no picnic," he said. Robertson instead led his 450 men to the U.S. Capitol grounds where they spent their first night sleeping on newspapers on the ground.

The next morning Robertson and a half-dozen men barreled down the Senate hallways and burst into the massive office of Vice President Charles Curtis, where Robertson handed the startled and thoroughly frightened Senate president his petition.

"You'd better get busy on this," Robertson said. "I might be dead in a year." He then led his team across Capitol Hill to give the same treatment to Jack Garner.

When they left Garner's office, Robertson and his men were intercepted by an angry Captain J. Gnash, Chief of the Capitol Police, who threatened to arrest them for loitering on the Capitol grounds. Robertson asked if there were any laws against walking on the sidewalks, and Gnash reluctantly said that walking was permitted. Thus began the infamous veterans' "Death March."

* * *

In his role as secretary and treasurer for the BEF, Pelham Glassford was glad to report that it cost just thirty-eight cents per person to feed the men and their families two meals a day at Camp Marks. (By comparison, a full meal at a Washington, D.C. diner in 1932 cost a quarter.) The two daily meals were not fancy. They often consisted of mulligan stew ladeled into folded newspapers or turtle soup with grits. Salted kippers were a frequent if unpopular menu item. Only twice did the kitchen at Anacostia Flats fail to deliver a meal.

For many at Camp Marks, the two meals were more than they had been getting before they arrived. To Glassford's dismay, increasing numbers of wives and children arrived every day. Although he hated to do it, the superintendent realized that, apart from force, cutting back the food supply would be the only way to force the veterans and their families to leave.

* * *

Although he had been re-elected as commander just three weeks before, dissatisfaction with Walter Waters reached a fevered pitch again by mid-July.

To many of the men, Waters had become star-struck. Immediately after Roosevelt's nomination, the BEF commander announced that he would fly up the Hudson River to Hyde Park to personally meet with the presidential hopeful. (Apparently, this did not happen.)

Despite the efforts of Eddie Atwell and his intelligence unit to hold the BEF together, communist and fascist elements were luring away some of the organization's leaders. Both George Alman and Mike Thomas, the former chief of Camp Marks, had already departed.

The counterfeit *BEF News* being published by Pace and the Communists had achieved wide readership both inside the camp and on the streets of Washington. (It was put out by Scott McCaffrey, the original publisher whom Waters had accused of embezzlement.) The newspaper claimed that Waters received daily expense money from Pelham Glassford and it quoted Royal Robertson as saying that the BEF deserved a leader, "not a weakling who is always pulling fainting tricks (and) who finds a swell apartment far from the scene of the action."

In truth, Waters had come to agree with Glassford that it was time for most of the veterans to withdraw from Washington, perhaps keeping a core group to maintain a national BEF headquarters.

Now that he had become a national figure, the cumbersome army of veterans was becoming an inconvenience to Walter Waters.

* * *

On the winding paths of the Capitol grounds, Royal Robertson's "Death March" was underway. A single line of 250 gray and weary men shuffled silently up Capitol Hill, around the parking lot and down again, winding under the hundreds of ornamental trees planted there by the various states of the union. Another 200 men sat in a nearby vacant lot awaiting their turns as substitutes. Many of the marchers sported fake slings and head bandages to dramatize their plight.

Although Pelham Glassford's jurisdiction did not include Capitol Hill—he and Captain Gnash were enemies and did not speak—the District police were pressed into service to help. Upon meeting Glassford the deformed Robertson told him: "You'd better have ambulances standing by as my men are mostly disabled and will soon begin to keel over."

As Robertson predicted, his men began to topple and ambulances were summoned to take them to local hospitals. Robertson himself "collapsed" three times in front of the press and was dramatically revived and pressed into action again after each episode.

By the second day 1,500 men took part in the march, and by the third 3,000, most of them joining Robertson from various BEF camps. The Capitol Police turned on the lawn sprinklers around the clock to keep the exhausted men from lying on the grass.

All of this was great theater and thousands of spectators came each day to watch. The "Death Marchers" put the bonus issue once again onto the front page of the nation's papers—but this time the leader was Royal Robertson, not Walter Waters.

Charles Curtis, the 72-year-old vice president, continued to be terrified of Royal Robertson. He had not recovered from the deformed veteran's sudden appearance in his office. By the third day of the Death March, with the temperature well into the 90s, the vice president snapped.

Using his authority as president of the Senate, Curtis called Admiral Henry Butler, commandant of the Navy Yard. He ordered Butler to send the Marines to defend the Capitol and drive off the Death Marchers.

Pelham Glassford was summoned to the War Department by Commissioner Crosby. There, he found Crosby, MacArthur, Van Horn Moseley, and Pery Miles, all in confusion. Someone had called out the troops without going through legal channels, but no one knew who. When Admiral Butler arrived to clear things up, a call was made to stop the Marines, but it was too late.

Glassford rushed to the vice president's office where the two men engaged in a brief but furious argument. Glassford then found Senator Hiram Bingham and urged him to intervene with Herbert Hoover. Bingham called the president at once.

"Do you want to take personal responsibility for calling out the Marines on these men?" the Alabama senator boomed. No, Hoover replied, he did not.

A second call was made from the White House, but the president was told that the Marines would arrive at any minute. Only 60 members of the 95-man contingent had agreed to come; more than a third had refused to take action against their former comrades.

Glassford ran from Bingham's office to the Capitol grounds to intervene. Any shooting could cause a revolt by the entire BEF and play directly into the Communists' hands.

The streetcars carrying the Marines stopped in the upper parking lot where the 60-man force jumped off and proceeded rapidly toward the Capitol grounds. They approached the marching veterans in a straight line, holding their rifles at arms.

One of the Death Marchers walking to the right of the Marines carried a large American flag. The lieutenant leading the Marines suddenly commanded, "Eyes right!" and the column stopped as one and snapped a salute to the flag.

At this a disabled veteran stepped out of line and started to cheer, "Hip-hip hurray! The Marines are here. Hip-hip hurray!" and the other marchers joined in.

The Marines then did a curious thing. First one officer stood his rifle stock down on the ground. One by one the other Marines came forward and did the same thing until 60 rifles were stacked there, the crossed blades of their bayonets glinting in the sunlight. The Marines had refused to move against the veterans.

* * *

Walter Waters returned to Washington, D.C. in his private plane on Thursday evening, July 14, concluding an exhilarating fundraising trip that had taken him to New York, Camden, New Jersey, and Pittsburgh. At each location he had received nothing but congratulations and encouragement.

While Waters had been away, rumors continued to fly that the BEF commander had been co-opted by the "Key Men Society." The secret group was supposedly closer than ever to overthrowing the government, perhaps assisted by a radical element within the American Legion. Rumors also persisted that the leader of the Key Men was Marine Major General Smedley D. Butler.

Butler, a ferocious cigar-chewing warrior in the Patton mold, had made several speeches and spent at least one night with the men at Camp Marks. During one speech Butler urged the formation of a permanent BEF camp in Washington.

The Marine had no use for Herbert Hoover. Butler delighted in telling his story of being in China when the bloody Boxer Rebellion broke out. Two thousand foreigners were trapped in Tientsin by the uprising, besieged by 30,000 Chinese fanatics. Every able-bodied man was at the walls defending the city, and in fairness to Herbert Hoover, who was there doing humanitarian work, it is well documented that he took the lead in organizing the defense of the city.

Still, Butler claimed that after his troops arrived to help with the evacuation, he asked where the women and children were and was directed to a cellar in a private home.

"When I arrived I found one man cowering among the frightened women," Butler said. "I kicked his ass into the street. I did not ask his name nor did I care who the coward was. Someone later told me it was an engineer named Hoover."

Years later when President Hoover was prepared to censure Butler for calling his then-ally Mussolini a "mad dog," Butler said that he sent a message to the White House that read "Remember Tientsin" and nothing more was heard of the censure.

* * *

The 72nd Congress was to adjourn on Saturday, July 16. According to tradition, the president would travel by car that evening from the White House to Capitol Hill where he would address Congress and sign any last-minute legislation.

This represented the best and perhaps only chance that the veterans would have to actually see Herbert Hoover. It was also a last opportunity to brace the congressmen who were eager to leave Washington and begin their campaigns for the November elections. Walter Waters had drafted a petition for the president that he intended to hand to him in person.

Pelham Glassford informed Waters that Royal Robertson had been given permission to hold a parade that same day and had called on men from Camp Marks to join him. Several thousand had indicated that they would. This was not a challenge that Waters could ignore. Neither, in fact, could Glassford.

* * *

Pelham Glassford was threatened with dismissal by the commissioners if he did not toughen his position toward the BEF. Sensing blood in the water, a "small but politically powerful faction" in the police department turned against Glassford and two senior officers began to actively petition for his removal.

Patrick Hurley got into the act as well and began to cast about for possible replacements for Glassford. He received a telegram in June from a man in Minneapolis identified only as "Cunningham" that read:

"Appoint John H. Hester Chief of Police, Washington, D.C. He will take care of so-called BEF. Answer requested."

After only seven months in the position, Glassford's days as police superintendent were numbered. But that did not stop him from carrying out the job he was hired to do.

* * *

At 10:30 a.m. on Saturday July 16, a crowd of about 3,000 veterans followed Walter Waters from Anacostia Flats up Maine Avenue to South Capitol Street and from there to the steps of the Capitol. Because Congress was in session, the men were not allowed to proceed beyond the barricades that Glassford's police had set up across from the Capitol steps.

The veterans crowded together ominously, watched over by only a dozen nervous Metropolitan policemen. Walter Waters strode to the front of the crowd and stood there, his arms crossed. Then Pelham Glassford drove up on his blue motorcycle. Pelham got off and turned to face Waters.

The BEF commander walked toward Glassford, up to the middle of the asphalt parking lot. The two men stared at each other for a few moments then Waters raised his right hand in the air. With an explosive yell, the 3,000 men of the BEF burst forward. They kicked aside the flimsy wooden barricades and surrounded Waters in a clamoring mass.

Glassford appeared non-plussed. To the shock of the crowd he stepped forward with two officers, handcuffed Waters, and hustled him through a lower door behind the Capitol steps.

This unprecedented action caused an immediate consolidation of the BEF behind their commander. *We want Waters!* the mob of men chanted over and over as they took possession of the front of the Capitol.

After fifteen minutes of heated protest, their handcuffed leader was brought outside. Waters climbed up several steps and raised his cuffed hands over his head.

"Men," he shouted, "let us try to work something out!" The veterans continued to shout and Waters was taken away again. The next time he was brought out, the handcuffs had been removed.

"We have achieved a concession!" Waters told them. "The Speaker of the House, John Nance Garner, has agreed to meet with me at noon."

But Waters had even more to say. As the men knew he had spent the last few weeks in very important meetings all up and down the East Coast. Now Waters could announce to them the creation of a new national political organization with the BEF as its nucleus.

Taken from *Veterans on the March*, Jack Douglas, Workers Library Publishers, 1934.

(Top) Waters being arrested at the Capitol, July 16, 1932. (Bottom) Veterans burst past police barricades and surged toward the Capitol when Waters raised his hand.

"This group will represent not just the veterans but poor people everywhere," Waters shouted. "It will be called the 'Khaki Shirts.'"

The meeting with Garner that afternoon yielded two further gains. First, veterans would be allowed to borrow a greater amount against their bonus vouchers. Secondly, Garner promised that the bonus bill would be reconsidered when Congress reconvened after the November elections.

That night a nervous Congress met for its adjournment. The traditional visit by the president did not take place. The congressmen set aside most of the formal ceremonies, notices, and resolutions and when the gavel sounded at 11:10 p.m., most of them rushed from the Capitol building via the underground tunnels that took them unobserved and unmolested to their office buildings.

Within the Capitol rotunda, the bright light went out.

* * *

Patrick Hurley called MacArthur and Van Horn Mosely into his office on July 20 to show them a memorandum from President Hoover regarding potential cuts in the military budget.

Attached to Hoover's memo was a strongly worded note from Senator David Reed, chairman of the Military Affairs Committee. Reed warned that if the Army did not significantly reduce its number of officers in the next budget, Hoover would have great difficulty getting support for his other key programs. (This assumed, of course, the re-election of Hoover and a Republican majority.)

Moseley said that the Army was already critically depleted. If it was weakened further, it might as well shut down altogether and allow the Communists to run wild in the streets. He also postulated that the bonus marchers had hurt the military's cause. Congress looked at them and said, "See what results from spending on the military? Just more veterans' demands."

MacArthur agreed. The country needed to see a military that protected them, not one that threatened them.

* * *

Trumped by Walter Waters and weary from his exertions, Royal Robertson left on a national tour to urge voters to reject those congressmen who had failed to support the bonus bill. Waving to the press he climbed alone into a chauffeured car on July 23.

As he had predicted, Robertson died within a few years.

* * *

That afternoon Walter Waters was summoned to the office of the District commissioners and handed an ultimatum. Treasury Secretary Ogden Mills had instructed the commissioners to clear the buildings and adjoining shelters occupied by approximately 200 veterans on lower Pennsylvania Avenue.

The BEF was given until the next day to leave or a forced evacuation would take place. To Waters this was just one more empty threat in a long series of huffs and puffs by the administration. The BEF commander did not respond, and no action was taken on the following day.

Waters felt certain that the Hoover Administration would not send Army troops against the BEF. He had even been told that by Glassford who said that he received similar reassurances in person from Douglas MacArthur.

* * *

Immense pressure was brought on John Pace by his Communist Party superior Israel Amter following Waters' Khaki Shirts announcement.

Amter feared that the veterans would withdraw from Washington without a fight. He told Pace that the Communists didn't care how many veterans were killed. Moscow wanted a bloody riot in the hope that it would set off a revolution.

Pace announced that the Communists would focus on the White House with daily picketing. Ogden Mills summoned even more Secret Service men to rush to Washington and serve as the president's human shields.

On the first day of the picketing, the men Pace sent were arrested immediately by Glassford's police. The next night John Pace himself led a delegation of 150 agitators to the front gate of the White House where he tried to make a speech.

The District police were forewarned and Inspector Albert Headley arrived at the White House just ahead of Pace. When Headley spotted Pace walking at the head of a large crowd of men, he ran up to him, grabbed Pace by the throat, and threw him back into the arms of the others. The Communists scattered as more police arrived.

The persistent Pace and his men tried again a few days later. This time they brought a communist speaker named Walter Eicker. Again the police and plainclothes officers descended on them. Pace later complained that the police used a new technique called "ju-jitsu" to throw them to the ground.

Eicker climbed a nearby tree from which he hoped to make his speech, but two policemen in white Panama suits followed him. Eicker climbed higher, alternately panting and yelling out his comments. Finally he was yanked down through the branches to the sidewalk below and arrested along with John Pace.

While these last-ditch efforts by the Communists had a Keystone-Kops quality, they provided Hurley and MacArthur with the final justification to implement the White Plan.

Communists had tried to attack the White House. Now they would have to be driven from their den—Camp "Marx."

CHAPTER TEN

The White Plan

"The White Plan is the official designation of the War Department...to be followed by the regular army in the quelling of serious internal disorders. It is applied under critical conditions when civil authority and all other normal sources of protection have failed."

Dr. Luther Reichelderfer, Chairman
District of Columbia Department of Commissioners

The day following their empty ultimatum to Waters, another series of confusing orders were issued from both the District commissioners and the Treasury department regarding the veterans who were billeted along Pennsylvania Avenue. Forced evictions by District police would occur within twenty-four hours, the notices said, starting with those residing in the half-demolished building.

That same day Ulysses S. Grant III, director of Public Buildings and Grounds, directed the commissioners to repossess all federal property from the veterans. U.S. Grant reported to Patrick Hurley.

Pelham Glassford consulted with legal counsel who assured him that the District commissioners did not have the authority to act on behalf of the Treasury nor could they command Glassford's police.

Acutely aware of the frayed patience of Patrick Hurley and the commissioners, Glassford knew that he had to hasten the veterans' departure from Washington. He notified Walter Waters that the BEF account had only $163 remaining. It was time for the veterans to leave.

Waters did not argue. He posted this bulletin at Camp Marks:

> Congress has adjourned. There is nothing more that we can hope to do in Washington at this time until Congress reconvenes...transportation is still available to your homes.

For those who did not have homes to return to, Waters offered a permanent camp in Washington where they would be fed and sheltered. The site that Waters had in mind was the 30-acre parcel of land that had been promised for the BEF's use by assistant postmaster John Bartlett.

Immediately after Waters' message was posted, Glassford reduced the meals at Camp Marks to one per day. It did not take long for the veterans to get the message. They began to leave Washington at the rate of about 1,000 people each day.

By July 26 the total BEF force in the District of Columbia was reduced by half to about 11,000 including 1,000 women and children. The number of new arrivals diminished as well. The gradual, peaceful disbanding that Glassford had envisioned was occurring and he felt certain that no military action would be taken.

* * *

Herbert S. Ward, volunteer attorney for the BEF, met with Treasury Secretary Mills to request more time to peacefully evacuate the Pennsylvania Avenue buildings.

Ward told Mills that the BEF needed time to arrange other shelter. He explained that Waters was meeting with John Bartlett about the construction of a permanent camp. Mills said that he understood but could only push the evacuation deadline back by twenty-four hours. He suggested that the BEF contact the Red Cross to obtain temporary tents.

Walter Waters approached Judge Payne, the chairman of the Red Cross. The relief organization had earlier turned down a BEF request for milk for children and rejected Waters down again. However, he suggested that Army Chief MacArthur might be able to provide tents and offered to call MacArthur to arrange an appointment.

* * *

Patrick Hurley's hatred of the veterans was visceral but his motivations for driving them away from Washington were many and complex.

First there was Hurley's erroneous conviction that the BEF was communist-led, reinforced by his knee-jerk reaction to the naming of Camp Marks. Secondly he was greatly influenced by Douglas MacArthur who felt that the veterans must be taught a public lesson in addition to other more complex motives.

The lessons that the Secretary of War drew from the downfall of Rome were also important, as were the promises that he had made at numerous social gatherings to rid Washington of the presence of the ragged and offensive men.

Hurley was also under great personal stress. His relationship with Ruth was collapsing and the president upon whom he had pinned his career hopes appeared certain to lose in a few months. To top it all off, Hurley had just about exhausted his personal assets.

When he arrived in Washington four years before, Patrick Hurley was enormously wealthy. He had placed his non-liquid investments and land titles into a private trust with a New York bank and had brought a substantial sum of cash with him to cover expenses not met by his government salary that was less than $20,000 per year.

Since then Hurley had purchased and renovated his 1,200-acre Virginia estate and spent lavishly in order to live up to the social expectations of a cabinet secretary.

The costs to maintain Belmont were substantial. Each night the Hurleys hosted a formal dinner for as many as eight people including Wilson's favorite Aunt Jo and the Hurleys' children and personal secretaries. There were salaries for housekeepers as well as thirty sharecroppers to whom Hurley paid $30 each per month.

(One day the local druggist stopped young Wilson on the sidewalk and said, "Please thank your father for me for paying his people. They are spending the only money that is in circulation in Leesburg.")

The Hurleys also sponsored a local hunt and fulfilled countless social obligations through large affairs at Belmont and private dinners in Washington. And then there were the clothes, the cars, the jewelry, the club memberships, and the gifts.

By July of 1932 Patrick Hurley found himself with only his trust investments to fall back upon. Unknown to Hurley, his trusts had been wiped out during the Depression.

* * *

Douglas MacArthur's determination to deal forcefully with the veterans accelerated considerably after his old friend George Patton arrived at Ft. Myer on July 8.

Patton, like MacArthur, was a warrior who accepted only total victory. He told the Army chief that Pelham Glassford "had a total misconception of mob psychology," and he agreed with Patrick Hurley that the Communists had taken control of the BEF.

Soon after arriving at Ft. Myer, Patton reportedly drew up a comprehensive military plan of action against the BEF for MacArthur (although he later denied having done so.) The Army chief began to make regular visits down the hall to Hurley's office where he used his typical method of persuasion—an unbroken torrent of words—to convince the Secretary of War to act.

The Communists have gained control of the veterans, MacArthur told him. "Revolution is imminent. My staff is in full accord. The Army has been ready for weeks and is growing impatient. You must allow MacArthur to act!"

After MacArthur left Van Horn, Moseley would come to Hurley with another round of arguments. President Hoover was barricaded behind a chained iron fence and a human ring of Secret Service men. Automobiles could not be driven within a block of the White House. The entire administration had been made to look foolish by the BEF.

Patrick Hurley—who from the beginning said that use of force against the veterans would be not only wise, but good politics—finally agreed. The last stages of the White Plan were put into motion even as the veterans were leaving the city on their own accord.

* * *

Alerted by his informers that military action against the BEF was imminent, Walter Waters, with the help of Judge Payne, arranged an emergency session at the office of the Secretary of War. This would be their first meeting and Waters hoped that they could resolve this matter man to man.

As Waters, Doak Carter, and Herbert Ward strode toward room 308 on the afternoon of July 26, the heels of their boots made sharp echoing sounds down the long, wide corridor of the War Department. The floor on which they walked was covered by large black and white tiles and the ceilings towered more than twenty feet above their heads.

Carter held open the slatted outer door to the secretary's office and Waters preceded the others into the anteroom. An aide, perhaps Eisenhower, led them to Hurley's office and Waters strode inside, no doubt slapping his riding crop lightly against his leg. The window curtains were pulled partially shut and the office was dark and gloomy.

Patrick Hurley was not alone. Standing to the left of his desk was a slim man in his early 50s with keen hawk-like features. Waters recognized him at once as Army Chief Douglas MacArthur and mistook him for being younger than the tired-looking Secretary of War.

Hurley remained seated behind his desk, illuminated by a table lamp. He was, as Waters had read, a natty dresser. That day Hurley wore a high-collared shirt, a silk tie and an expensive tailored suit. The secretary looked at Waters with a hooded expression, his face half-hidden behind steepled fingers.

Hurley's thick red hair was slicked back and he had dark circles under cold, pale blue eyes. He wore a thick western-style mustache and his handsome face was dominated by a square, imposing jaw.

The secretary's expression was set and stern. His first words were to inform Waters that the Hurleys had a dinner to attend that evening and he could not be late.

As Hurley spoke, MacArthur left his position by the side of the desk and moved behind Waters and his entourage where he began to pace. The Army chief walked back and forth during the entire meeting, his arms clenched behind his back.

Waters asked the secretary to provide more tentage for the veterans and their families who were about to be evicted. He said that he understood local Army warehouses were filled with tents and cots that could help solve his immediate problem.

Tentage! Hurley fell into an immediate rage. "What you need to do," he told Waters, "is to get these men out of Washington."

"You brought them here," Hurley said, "and they are a threat to the government. I implore you to lead them out!"

Waters said that he could not. The veterans would feel that he had betrayed them. Other aspiring leaders within the BEF would call him "yellow" and tell the men to stay.

Hurley looked at MacArthur. "Is there any tentage available?" he asked.

"No," MacArthur replied, clenching his pipe between his teeth.

"You and your Bonus Army have no business in Washington," Hurley said.

"We are not in sympathy with your being here. We will not cooperate in any way with your remaining here. We are interested only in getting you out of the District…and we have plenty of troops to put you out."

"Mr. Secretary, no one is seeking trouble in our ranks," Waters said. "The great bulk of the Bonus Army are honorably discharged veterans of the war and law-abiding citizens."

"I am aware of that," Hurley said. "But there are Communists in Washington as well."

"A small group," Waters protested, "that has been continually attempting to bring about trouble and disorders in the BEF."

Hurley waved him off. "Our agents know who every one of them is," he said, "and (we) are fully aware of every plan they make. Your problem," he told Waters ominously, "is that the BEF has been too orderly. Only a scratch of a pen is necessary to declare martial law," Hurley said, "if occasion arises."

The telephone on Hurley's desk rang. It was Ruth, confirming that he would be on time for their dinner appointment. After the secretary hung up, Doak Carter unwisely stepped into the conversation.

"On behalf of the veterans in Washington," he said, "I would like to convey to you that in case any serious upheaval develops in the capital from the activities of the Communists…the BEF would be proud to serve in the front line of defense."

"Under no circumstances would we accept such an offer!" Hurley roared. "We have plenty of troops to protect this government. We don't need you, and we don't want you. The American Army…can take care of that."

"Such a feeling did not exist toward us a few years ago," Carter replied.

"I wasn't Secretary of War in 1917," Hurley shot back. "I was one of you."

Waters stepped in to reassert his leadership.

"I am not only willing but anxious to bring about a gradual and orderly disintegration of the BEF," he told Hurley. "That is what is being done now and…it will soon be accomplished. Do you know that already more than 5,000 veterans have applied for transportation home?"

Hurley said that he had not understood that Waters felt that way and was glad to hear of it.

"Well, I'll call General Hines, of the Veteran's Bureau," Hurley said, "and see what can be done to help with the women and children." Frank Hines oversaw the various military installations in the Washington area.

When he had Hines on the line, Hurley asked if there was any chance the BEF could use Ft. Hunt as a temporary residence. No, Hines replied. The VA planned to close the fort on August first and was not willing to take on any BEF problems.

Hurley hung up the phone and shrugged. MacArthur continued to pace. The phone rang again. For the second time it was Ruth. When would he be home to pick her up? Hurley muttered a few words before he put the receiver down.

Suddenly the secretary's uncontrollable temper took over. Hurley's pale face infused with blood and his cold blue eyes bulged as he slammed his right fist down upon the surface of his desk. Waters and Carter flinched and moved back a step.

"Damn it, Waters!" Hurley shouted, half-rising to his feet. "By tomorrow night, you can either be a big man, or a broken one!"

Alarmed, Waters turned to MacArthur who had momentarily stopped his pacing. "If the troops should be called out against us," he asked, "will the BEF be given the opportunity to form in columns, salvage their belongings, and retreat in an orderly fashion?"

"Yes, my friend, of course!" MacArthur replied.

* * *

Walter Waters was told by Treasury officials that it was the pressure being brought by George Rhine, a salvage contractor, that was forcing the Pennsylvania Avenue eviction. They said that Rhine's company was losing money each day the buildings could not be torn down. Desperate to find a last-minute solution, Waters went to speak with Rhine himself.

"Frankly," Rhine told him, "I'm in no hurry to go on with this job. We have plenty of work at other sites to keep our men busy. If you evacuated those sites tomorrow, I wouldn't hire any additional labor to get to them."

What's more, Rhine said that the land the buildings occupied was not even needed for construction but would eventually be used for an open parkway much later in the development process.

Despite giving Water these reassurances, Rhine sent a demolition crew of workers with a crane to the Pennsylvania Avenue site the very next morning, July 27. When veterans surrounded the crane, Glassford and 70 police intervened and stopped the demolition.

(George Rhine later successfully petitioned the Roosevelt Administration for $27,500 in lost wages due to the veterans' "interference" with his work, citing Treasury Department correspondence with Ogden Mills.)

Glassford met with Commissioner Crosby and Treasury officials early that afternoon to try to resolve the situation. It was agreed that a limited eviction would take place the following morning involving one square block only.

That same afternoon Walter Waters called an emergency meeting with the 182 field commanders at Camp Marks. He told them to keep their men under tight control for the next day or two. "Something may be about to happen," Waters warned.

The BEF commander was then summoned by Pelham Glassford to a late-afternoon meeting with the commissioners to discuss the evacuation of the Pennsylvania Avenue buildings.

Although he had dealt with their staff, Waters had never actually met the commissioners. He only knew that they oversaw Glassford and reported to President Hoover. When Waters arrived at the commissioners' office for the 3:00 p.m. meeting, a curious pantomime took place.

Waters was prepared to offer to relocate up to 1,100 people from the District to Camp Bartlett over several days. But rather than be allowed to make his own case, the BEF commander was forced to sit in the waiting room while Pelham Glassford acted as a go-between. Back and forth the superintendent went, shuttling messages between Waters and the commissioners. At first Glassford said that the commissioners would wait until midnight on July 28 to begin the evacuation. Waters insisted on two weeks.

Glassford left with Waters' demand and then returned. "Now they will give you until Monday August 1, a total of four days," the superintendent said.

"Tell them I agree," Waters replied.

But upon returning to the commissioners, Glassford learned that the president had just agreed to evacuate the building the following morning.

For some reason Glassford did not give this information to Waters. Instead the BEF commander was dismissed and left the commissioners' building believing that he had four days in which to find an alternative site to house more than 1,000 people.

Months later Glassford wrote of this meeting in his memoirs:

"Waters was more than willing to be reasonable. The commissioners were not…they were being driven by pressure from higher up. The whole thing had an ugly aspect. The administration was forcing the issue, making a surprise attack."

* * *

At virtually the same time that Waters was trying to negotiate with the commissioners, Attorney General William D. Mitchell, Douglas MacArthur, Patrick Hurley, and Ogden Mills were all in a discussion with President Hoover.

Records show that at least one participant was attending the meeting "by telephone." It is not difficult to assume that this person was

Patrick Hurley, calling from the commissioners' office. Hurley's reluctance to be seen there could well have been the reason for the odd treatment given to Waters. The commissioners most likely had immediate knowledge of the president's decision because Hurley was on the telephone to the Oval Office while Waters was being kept in the waiting room.

Due to the demands of Hoover's campaign and the new Reconstruction Finance Committee, this was the first time in several weeks that the president had had a chance to focus on the veterans' issue. Rather than a simple briefing, however, Hoover found himself being pressured to authorize both an eviction and the possible use of Army troops.

Hoover supported the eviction but was greatly opposed to any use of the Army, despite assertions that the veterans would become violent when forced from their dwellings.

Patrick Hurley had drafted and sent to Hoover a presidential proclamation that authorized the use of federal troops if and when needed, but the president refused to sign it. Hurley's draft was dated "July" but did not specify a date.

"Maybe we could have the Army present but without arms, the president mused."

Not using my Army, MacArthur replied. At last Hoover reluctantly agreed to the "possible" use of troops but only if absolutely necessary.

Concerned that the eviction be handled in a balanced way, Hoover turned that responsibility over to Attorney General William Miller who in turn arranged for Ogden Mills' Treasury agents to be on the scene.

After the meeting ended at 4:00 p.m., Tom Henry, an enterprising reporter for the *Washington Star*, obtained details from a source and his story appeared in the July 27, 5:30 p.m. edition. It read in part:

> At a conference today…an agreement was reached on a plan of action to evict the Bonus Marchers who are billeted in partly demolished buildings along Pennsylvania Avenue…the question of martial law was discussed and the military in Washington is prepared to stand by in readiness to carry out any such orders for the Executive.

Although Walter Waters saw this story in the late edition of the *Star*, he spent the evening confident that he had four more days to relocate the veterans.

President Hoover continued to fret over the possible need to use the Army to control the veterans. Late that night he reportedly called Senator James Watson to discuss the matter. There was no love lost between Hoover and Watson, but the senator was a leader among Old Guard Republicans and the president wanted a sounding board from that constituency.

During the call, Hoover spoke at length about the illegal occupation of government-owned buildings and the stalled construction programs with contracts running into the millions. "All of this will require evicting the bonus marchers," Hoover said, "and the use of federal troops might be necessary."

"If you use troops," the sage old-timer replied, "it will be a colossal blunder. You will lose millions of votes in the upcoming campaign."

CHAPTER ELEVEN

Riot on Pennsylvania Avenue

After spending the night in his suite at the Ebbitt Hotel, Walter Waters awoke early. It was already stifling hot as a pewter-colored sun rose in the east.

First Waters planned to meet with the veterans at the Pennsylvania Avenue encampment, after which he would speak further with John Bartlett about the promised use of his land.

If everything went well, Waters hoped to move some families to Camp Bartlett that very day. Nevertheless he must have had some premonition of trouble, for Waters had sent his wife Wilma to a safe location in Baltimore the evening before.

By 9:30 a.m., as ordered by the commissioners, Pelham Glassford gathered a force of one hundred policemen near the Pennsylvania Avenue encampment. He sent another forty men to direct traffic and keep spectators away from the area.

Glassford had just called John Bartlett himself to confirm that he was willing to receive another thousand people at his 30-acre estate later in the day. Camp Bartlett was already home to 1,200 BEF members.

Bartlett agreed to do so but then began to have doubts. Later that morning, he sent letters by messenger to Glassford, Ogden Mills, and the local newspapers, stating that he would be glad to cooperate, but only if the "Government and the District" (ie, not Walter Waters) asked him to do so. Bartlett had read of the planned eviction in the morning newspapers and he left in his automobile to see what was going to happen.

* * *

The half-demolished four-story building that the BEF members from Texas occupied sat in the middle of acres of rubble and open lots. It looked much like the bombed-out structures that the veterans had seen in France years before. Dozens of families had lived there for two months. Ropes and boards were laid across the open spaces to keep people from falling and blankets were strung up for privacy.

This particular area on the south side of Pennsylvania Avenue had been known for decades as Murder Bay and was one of Washington's most notorious and unsanitary neighborhoods. In 1928, the National Capital Parks Authority obtained permission from Congress to raze Murder Bay and make room for the Federal Triangle project. Demolition began in 1930 but was soon slowed by the Depression.

At 8:15 on the morning of July 28, Walter Waters sat in a car with J.C. Wilford, the commander of the Pennsylvania Avenue camp. Wilford was adamant that his men, many former roughneck oil drillers, would not move to Camp Bartlett.

Waters climbed partway up one of the open stairwells to address about one hundred veterans gathered below him. When he introduced the idea of moving, he was jeered by several in the crowd. Waters told them, "You can sit there and...jeopardize the lives of women and children (but) if troops do come, you mugs will be the first ones to run. I've made an agreement which is the best thing for all of us." He was still speaking when two people pushed through the crowd to stand in front of him. Waters recognized one as Aldace Walker, a secretary from Glassford's office. Walker handed Waters a typed message.

The BEF commander read and re-read the brief message then turned back to the veterans. His face was pale.

"I have in my hand an order from the Treasury Department," Waters said. He then read aloud the notice, which gave them until noon to leave the area. Waters glanced at his watch as he spoke. It was already 9:50 a.m.

"There you are," Waters said. "You're double-crossed—I'm double-crossed."

Within minutes, 100 of Glassford's police officers arrived on foot from a block away. The police wore hats, white short-sleeved shirts with ties, and navy blue pants. Several officers carried wooden stakes and coils of rope that they quickly used to create a waist-high barrier 25 feet out from the building. The police took defensive positions between the rope and the building every eight feet or so.

Six Treasury agents arrived in hats and suits. Glassford's men could not enforce the eviction because the buildings were owned by the federal government. Accompanied by a dozen police, the agents climbed the open stairs of the building and started to lead the squatters out one by one.

Most of the veterans did not resist and were given time to gather their bedrolls and scant belongings. Some even joked with the officers. Several did refuse to leave and were dragged roughly down the concrete steps.

Waters and his bodyguards walked back and forth as the eviction took place, trying to calm any men who seemed upset. Glassford did the same thing and from time to time he nodded to Waters. Then the BEF commander abruptly left by car for Anacostia Flats where, curiously, he urged the men who were there to hurry to the eviction site. This was reported to Glassford who was agitated by Waters' actions.

The building was cleared within half an hour and the Treasury agents left, ending Ogden Mills' involvement for the day. The 200 evicted veterans stood around the building or walked across Pennsylvania Avenue to join a growing crowd of civilian onlookers. Dozens more veterans arrived from Camp Marks.

Waters returned and met briefly with Glassford. All was calm. Then precisely at noon a group of thirty-five men approached the eviction site at a trot from a grassy park at Third and Maine Streets. Police Private O. J. Patton recognized them as members of the communist-inspired WESL. As this group approached on foot, three trucks raced up to the building and came to a dusty stop, unloading another dozen thugs.

The two groups converged and moved quickly toward the police line. In the lead were two people. One carried an American flag like a lance and the other Waters recognized as Bernard McCoy, a ratty little man from Pace's Communist group.

When they reached the rope barricade, the men picked up broken pieces of brick and concrete from the many piles around the building. At a shout from McCoy, they began to heave the brickbats at Glassford and his policemen, some of whom ducked for cover behind the building walls while Glassman simply stood his ground, smiling.

When the police retreated, the agitators surged forward and broke down the rope barricade. McCoy attacked Pelham Glassford and ripped off his police badge. The man with the flag jabbed the point of the pole at another officer who grabbed it away from him.

One man in a gray cap wielded a piano leg that he used to club a policeman. Two other officers fell back under a second hail of brick and cement.

Taken from *Veterans on the March*, Jack Douglas, Workers Library Publishers, 1934.

*Top: A veteran is forcibly removed from the Pennsylvania Ave. encampment.
Bottom: Agitators attack police at the Pennsylvania Ave. eviction site
with bricks from the half-demolished building.*

About twenty police joined with the men and a fierce struggle began. Brick came flying from all directions. A chunk of concrete hit Glassford in the side and dropped him to one knee. Officer Edward Scott, a Medal of Honor hero from the war, ran across the rubble to stand over his fallen chief. He swung his billy club fiercely at the attackers as they closed.

Two men rushed him and battered the officer with pieces of brick. Scott collapsed to the ground, blood streaming from a fractured skull. A third man pounded on him with a club after he fell.

Waters' own bodyguards sprang forward. They threw the attackers off Scott and formed a circle around him. Eddie Atwell retrieved the superintendent's badge from the ground and handed it to him.

More police ran toward the scene from the other side of the building. For another minute or so the close-quartered battle raged on but then Glassford climbed upon a pile of rubble and shouted for the fighting to stop. As they ran from the site, several attackers climbed into waiting cars that sped away. The entire episode had lasted fewer than five minutes.

Police Lieutenant Ira Keck watched the attack from the crowd. Keck was a career officer who deeply resented Pelham Glassford. He had been secretly appointed by the commissioners to serve as their eyes and ears at the eviction site.

Glassford, his uniform torn and soiled, still managed to smile as he motioned Walter Waters aside.

"Well, what do you think?" he asked. "It's looking serious."

"What shall we do?" Waters replied.

"If I'm not asked to increase the area of evacuation, there will be no more trouble," Glassford said.

Waters frowned. The organized attackers had caused the riot, not the men who had been evicted.

"If things go ahead like this morning, then I can't control these men," Waters said, referring to the agitators.

Neither man noticed that Ira House Keck stood close behind them. The spy quickly raced the ten blocks back to the commissioners' office at 1350 Pennsylvania Ave. to make his report.

* * *

Ira Keck appeared breathless before Commissioner Crosby. There was a mad howling mob at the eviction site that was going to wipe up the police, he said. Federal troops were needed immediately. Waters said that he could not control his men.

Crosby ordered Keck to return to the scene and bring back Pelham Glassford. The informant raced back and found Glassford by the ambulances that were taking away Edward Scott and five other wounded officers. He told Glassford that the commissioners wanted him at once.

At 12:34 p.m., a disheveled and sweaty Glassford stood before Reichelderfer and Crosby. "Just give us the word," the chairman said, "and we will call for MacArthur and the troops."

Glassford said that he did not think such action was necessary because his men had things under control.

But there was a riot! Crosby said. Glassford reminded both commissioners that he had been there and it was no riot. If things were to get worse, they would still have time to call in the military.

"When would you call for troops?" Crosby pressed.

"If you have us carry out any more evictions, we may need them," Glassford said, "since we are so greatly outnumbered." At that, he returned to the eviction site on his blue motorcycle.

Unannounced, Crosby showed up a few minutes later and demanded a tour. Across Pennsylvania Avenue the crowd continued to build but remained orderly. After fifteen minutes of walking around the rubble, the commissioner returned to his office.

Five minutes later at 1:24 p.m., Patrick Hurley called President Hoover, apparently from his command post at the commissioners' office where he was personally overseeing the execution of a meticulously detailed plan to justify the Army's attack on the BEF. Hurley asked the president to sign the proclamation that he had left with him, authorizing the use of Army troops.

Hoover, who had been summoned by Hurley's call out of a late luncheon, was testy and he insisted on having a written request from the commissioners. Under the procedure that had been established, such a request could only be made after a formal appeal for help from Pelham Glassford.

At the same time that Patrick Hurley was on the telephone with the president, Commissioner Crosby was on another line with Douglas MacArthur, who was in his office at the War Department. Yes, Crosby no doubt assured the Army Chief, Hurley was asking the president to send in the troops. (Crosby later testified to a grand jury that unnamed "military authorities" had "evidently talked with the White House" before he alerted MacArthur.)

After he finished talking to Crosby, MacArthur called General Perry Miles at 1:30 p.m. and ordered him to put the troops on alert. Five minutes later he called again to put the White Plan into action. Miles was ordered to have Colonel Cootes dispatch all available cavalry and tanks from Ft. Myer to the ellipse and notify Ft. Washington to send the infantry by steamer and truck.

Both units were already on high alert awaiting the Army chief's call. As a result the 200-unit cavalry arrived at the Washington Monument ellipse just one hour later, fully outfitted and battle-ready.

Between 2:15 and 2:40 p.m., MacArthur and his officers exchanged four more calls, the last of which confirmed that all of the troops had departed. MacArthur then left his office to meet the soldiers at the ellipse.

MacArthur had summoned his troops for action even though the president—the only person with the authority to proclaim federal martial law—had yet to do so.

* * *

Tension continued to build at the eviction site as more veterans appeared by the minute from the various BEF camps. Perhaps 1,000 men were gathered at the site, many now taunting the police who still encircled the building. Several thousand spectators consisting of both civilians and veterans milled around across Pennsylvania Avenue. The temperature was in the 90s, there was little shade, and many people sat along the curb. Vendors had begun to flock, selling ice cream and cold drinks.

At 1:45 p.m., Pelham Glassford decided to climb to the roof of the building for a better look. He began to ascend the open stairs followed by several officers. Walter Waters moved to a place in the crowd where he could observe the superintendent.

William Hushka, a decorated veteran from the Great War, stood twenty feet from Waters with a jacket draped over one arm. A handsome man in his mid thirties, Hushka was an unemployed butcher who had come to Washington from Chicago because, as he told his brother in Illinois, "I might as well starve to death there as here." Standing beside Hushka was another veteran named Eric Carlson.

Metropolitan Police Officer George Shinault stood at the base of the stairs that Glassford had started to climb. In his later testimony, Shinault said that several veterans came running toward the stairwell to follow Glassford.

"You can't come in here," Shinault reportedly said.

"The hell we can't," a veteran replied and grabbed the policeman by the throat.

Other eyewitnesses said that before he fired Shinault was pelted with brickbats, jumped upon and throttled by several veterans including Hushka. Shinault then was said to have stumbled between two propped-up boards that were being used to climb into the stairwell. The photo of the dead Hushka shows him lying between the two boards and hospital records stated that Shinault was treated for a foot injury later that day.

Of what happened next there was no doubt. Officer Shinault unholstered his revolver and fired it twice at point-blank range at his attackers. William Hushka crumpled to the ground, killed instantly by a bullet through his heart. His death was captured in a dramatic photograph taken by Eddie Gosnell.

Photograph taken by Eddie Gosnell, Official Photographer of the BEF. Taken from *BEF*, by W. W. Waters and William C. White, John Day Company, New York, 1933.

William Huska minutes after being shot by Officer Shinault, July 28, 1932.

Seconds later, Officer Miles Znamenacek also fired into the crowd from the second floor. Erik Carlson, who was standing near Waters and turning away, was hit in the back. (He died in the hospital two days later.)

A third policeman, J.O. Fife, ran down the alley firing his gun as well. He hit a veteran named Will Boyd in the shoulder. Boyd spun around twice and fell to the ground.

At the sound of the gun shots, Pelham Glassford hurried to the edge of the second floor landing and looked down. From the street level Waters saw George Shinault raise his pistol and point it at the police superintendent.

"Stop that shooting!" Glassford shouted. Shinault fired again and Glassford ducked behind a column. Then Shinault slowly lowered his revolver.

"Come to my office this evening!" a furious Glassford yelled down to him.

The veterans who were grouped around Hushka stood perfectly still, shocked by the sudden violence. Only Gosnell was in action as he moved from place to place, furiously taking photographs.

Eddie Atwell and Doak Carter fought their way through the crowd to reach Walter Waters. They grabbed him by the elbows and rushed him away from the shooting scene to room 302 at the Ebbitt Hotel, two blocks away. Atwell told Waters that he had been targeted for assassination.

In the confusion following the shootings, Glassford looked in vain for Waters. He wanted the BEF commander to help him control the veterans who were beginning to clamor and mill about.

"When I needed his cooperation most," the superintendent later wrote, "Waters failed me."

* * *

Douglas MacArthur summoned Dwight Eisenhower from his small adjoining cubicle to tell him that they were going into action.

Eisenhower urged MacArthur not to participate. "This matter could easily become a riot," he said. "I think it would be highly inappropriate for the Chief of Staff of the Army to be involved in anything like…a street corner embroilment. Surely this does not require your presence."

"MacArthur has decided to go into active command in the field," his superior replied. "There is incipient revolution in the air."

Eisenhower cautioned that there were reporters everywhere. MacArthur said that he knew—he had called them so that this moment could be recorded for history. He told Eisenhower to go home and get into his uniform.

Eisenhower left at a half-trot for his DuPont Circle apartment, seven long hot blocks away.

* * *

Ira Keck rushed again to the commissioners' office at 1:59 p.m. to tell them of the shootings. This time Herbert Crosby called the White House to ask the president to send in the troops, probably because of Hoover's earlier insistance that the appeal come from the commissioners.

In his call, Crosby falsely assured the president that Pelham Glassford had asked for assistance. Again Hoover demanded that he receive the cmmissioners' request in writing.

Fifteen minutes later an envelope arrived by messenger at the White House with the following memorandum signed by L. H. Reichelderfer:

The President:

The Commissioners of the District of Columbia regret to inform you that during the past few hours, circumstances of a serious character have arisen in the District of Columbia which have been the cause of unlawful acts of large numbers of so called "Bonus Marchers" who have been in Washington for some time past.

This morning, officials of the Treasury Department, seeking to clear certain areas within the Government Triangle in which there were numbers of these Bonus Marchers, met with resistance. They called upon the Metropolitan Police force for assistance and a serious riot occurred. Several members of the Metropolitan Police were injured, one reported seriously. The total number of Bonus Marchers greatly outnumber the police, the situation is made more difficult by the fact that this area contains thousands of brickbats and these were used by the rioters in their attack upon the police.

In view of the above, it is the opinion of the superintendent of police, in which the commissioners concur, that it will be impossible for the police department to maintain law and order except by the free use of firearms, which will make the situation a dangerous one; it is believed, however, that the presence of federal troops in some number will obviate the seriousness of the situation and result in less violence and bloodshed.

The Commissioners of the District of Columbia therefore request that they be given the assistance of federal troops in maintaining law and order in the District of Columbia.

Oddly, the commissioners' request did not reference the fatal shootings that had just been reported to them even though it would have strengthened their position. To save time (no doubt having realized his error in unleashing MacArthur thirty minutes earlier), Crosby sent over the draft on which he and Hurley had been working for the past half hour. The formal wording of the request is distinctly that of the Secretary of War.

Even as Hoover read this request, the cavalry had departed Ft. Myer and were headed over the National Cemetery toward the Memorial Bridge into Washington. Six small M1917 tanks followed on trailers pulled by Army trucks.

Down-river at Ft. Washington, the 12th Infantry battalion had departed by steamer for the 18-mile journey upriver to debarkation near the War College. The trip from there by truck took them across the Anacostia River bridge, directly past Camp Marks.

* * *

Dwight Eisenhower arrived in a great rush at his three-bedroom apartment just off Connecticut Avenue at DuPont Circle at 2:25 p.m. The Wyoming was a popular address for War Department personnel— Van Horn Moseley lived there as well.

Ike's son John watched in amazement as his father, cursing, threw off his clothes and began to pull on his uniform. The major kept his uniform in a large closet in John's room. The boy had set up his electric train set on the floor, which caused Eisenhower to hop and stumble around the room as he dressed. Ike had particular difficulty with his stiff leather boots.

* * *

An hour after the troops were summoned, a newsman told Glassford that they were on their way. The superintendent had just returned from the emergency hospital where he had stood by Officer Scott as he lay on the operating table.

Things had quieted down at the eviction site even though the veterans outnumbered the police ten-to-one. Glassford left at once to find Douglas MacArthur.

Patrick Hurley called President Hoover at 2:37 p.m. to confirm that he had received the commissioners' written request and signed the order to declare martial law.

Hoover, still reluctant, told him that he had not done so. Three minutes later, the first of the 3rd Cavalry troops with Patton in the lead galloped onto the ellipse of the Washington Monument in clear view of the White House.

An agitated Patrick Hurley called MacArthur and instructed him to meet at Hoover's office—another sign that the Secretary of War was not at his own office just doors away from MacArthur's. Hurley had lobbied the president heavily at a White House luncheon that Sunday during which he stressed that the "remnants of the men in the BEF are Communists and criminals." When Hoover had agreed, Hurley felt certain that the president would accede to his request to summon the Army troops.

Now his assumption seemed less likely.

Hurley and MacArthur convened outside the Oval Office at 2:47 p.m. where the Secretary of War spoke urgently to the Army Chief of Staff. His whispered comments were overheard by George Drescher, the Secret Service agent who was stationed outside Hoover's door.

"Now listen," Patrick Hurley said, "you go in and tell the president that you're just back from the demonstration and that as the

Metropolitan Police cannot cope with the disorders, the president must send the troops in." MacArthur nodded.

Minutes later, the two men stood before Herbert Hoover. Although there is no transcript of their conversation, emotions were high and the conversation intense. Hurley undoubtedly told the president of the recent shootings and said that this was what the Communists had been waiting for. Soon the Reds would send word all across the country to start the revolution. The President had to send in the troops.

Hoover no doubt urged him to stay calm and he asked again whether the police superintendent agreed. Yes, Hurley assured him, Glassford had asked for their help.

MacArthur most likely told the president that every minute counted. The Army must be allowed to put down this menace before it spread to the very gates of the White House.

What about Winship's plan? Hoover asked. The Army's top lawyer, Major General Blanton Winship, had sent MacArthur several long memos suggesting a more cautious approach in which military trucks would carry the veterans away from the capital. Hoover was eager to avoid any further bloodshed.

MacArthur replied that they were beyond that. An overthrow of the federal government was imminent.

At last Hoover agreed to the use of troops but he told Hurley specifically that they could only use the Army to move the squatters on Pennsylvania Avenue back into the main camp at Anacostia. After that the Army was to surround the camp so that they could go in the next day to find out which of the men were Communists.

Although he gave them his verbal approval, Hoover still refused to sign the proclamation that gave total power to the military, feeling that it was too broad for the situation.

One more thing, Hoover said as they were leaving. "The soldiers are not to be armed."

Hurley returned to his office at the War Department where he had earlier drafted two handwritten versions of Hoover's verbal orders. He settled on the one that was more general in nature in order to give MacArthur greater latitude to act and changed the time on it from "2:15" to "2:55." He also duplicitly indicated carbon copies for "Walter W. Waters" and "John Pace." Hurley then sent the memo by messenger to the Army chief.

By 3:00 p.m., reporters were everywhere—outside Hoover's office, at Pennsylvania Avenue, on the ellipse, and at the War Department. Hurley had no choice but to report in an official press statement the odd facts that, "At 2:20 the commissioners requested assistance. Their request was approved by the president at 2:55 and at 3:00 the troops arrived."

Tom Henry of the *Washington Star* was handed this White House release in the press room at 4:22 p.m. just minutes before the troops began their attack. The statement also claimed that "several thousand men from different camps marched in and attacked the police." It went on to state that "A considerable part of those (BEF men) remaining are not veterans; many are Communists and persons with criminal records."

Although attempts to provoke the BEF to violence had failed, Hurley and MacArthur still managed to obtain Hoover's limited verbal approval to unleash the Army troops. The attack on the veterans could now begin.

CHAPTER TWELVE

Blue Tin Canisters

Pelham Glassford found General Douglas MacArthur sitting in his staff car at the ellipse below the Washington Monument at just past 3:00 pm.

MacArthur was still in his civilian clothes, awaiting the delivery of his freshly pressed uniform and medals from Ft. Myers. (Drew Pearson later reported that MacArthur's mother did the ironing.)

The Army chief invited Glassford to join him in the car and said that he had just received "orders from the Chief Executive to drive the veterans out of the city." He showed him Hurley's handwritten note that had been delivered to him from the nearby War Office. Dated July 28, 1932, 2:55 p.m., the memorandum read:

> The President has just informed me that the civil government of the District of Columbia has reported to him that it is unable to maintain law and order in the District.

You will have United States troops proceed immediately to the scene of disorder. Cooperate fully with the District of Columbia police force which is now in charge. Surround the affected area and clear it without delay. Turn over all prisoners to the civil authorities.

In your orders, insist that any women and children who may be in the affected area be accorded every consideration and kindness. Use all humanity consistent with the due execution of this order.

Patrick J. Hurley
Secretary of War

In his phrase regarding women and children, Patrick Hurley's Victorian manners shone through. These were the exact words that he had used eleven years before when he heroically led civilian volunteers to disperse a rioting mob of blacks in Tulsa, Oklahoma.

Hurley was experienced in this sort of action and he relished it.

Hurley's order did not instruct MacArthur to limit his attack to the Pennsylvania Avenue site and then simply surround Camp Marks, nor did it reference the president's dictate to not use weapons. In this way the Secretary of War left the door open for MacArthur to pursue a more aggressive approach than Hoover had anticipated.

"We are going to break the back of the BEF," MacArthur said. "The operation will be continuous. It will all be done tonight."

MacArthur asked Glassford to notify the BEF leaders that the Army was coming and that all 27 camps must be evacuated before nightfall, and then to set up police barricades to block off any traffic that might try to enter those camp sites. Any BEF camps on private land such as those at the Seventh Street wharves and Camp Bartlett would not be cleared.

MacArthur said that the Army would first do a "demonstration of force down Pennsylvania Army to let them know that we mean business and resistance would be futile."

Glassford told MacArthur that there would be women and children involved and the general said that he understood. He also told the superintendent that he did not relish the assignment but he had "received orders direct from the president" and the Army had a job to do, "no matter how distasteful" it was to MacArthur personally.

To those closest to the situation, whose public opinions would later count, Douglas MacArthur skillfully avoided any blame for the routing of the BEF. For Hurley, those responsible were the Communists and he spent the rest of his life believing and seeking, in vain, to prove their responsibility.

Now, in his comments to Glassford, MacArthur assigned the blame to the hapless Herbert Hoover. All of Glassford's public comments going forward would claim that the attack on the veterans was politically motivated, just because MacArthur suggested that it was so.

Glassford returned to the eviction site and informed reporters that "General MacArthur will soon be here with troops."

* * *

While General MacArthur cried crocodile tears in his staff car and the two hundred cavalry troopers rested on the ellipse, George Patton used the extra time to reconnoiter by "trotting stonily down Pennsylvania Avenue to Third Street." There he found thousands of people crowded along both the north and south sides of the wide avenue.

When he rode into sight they greeted him with both cheers and jeering. Patton trotted his horse along further as he tried to locate the mob, but the crowd appeared to be in a holiday mood. People sat on the curb, stood in small groups, and talked with one another.

Taken from The Bonus March and the New Deal, *John Henry Bartlett; M.A. Donohue and Company, Chicago, 1937.*

Third Cavalry approaches the crowd on Pennsylvania Avenue.

It was very warm and hundreds of sidewalk vendors were doing a brisk business selling lemonade, snowballs, ice cream bars, and souvenirs. Sun-baked veterans hawked the *BEF News*. It looked very much like a scene from a county fair.

Patton turned his horse and rode back to the ellipse.

General Perry L. Miles who nominally commanded the operation was surprised to see MacArthur at the ellipse. The Army chief told him that he had come at the suggestion of President Hoover and Patrick Hurley to "take the rap" should any unfavorable repercussions occur. Miles was very impressed by the general's consideration.

After the infantry under Lieutenant Colonel Louis Kunzig arrived at the ellipse by truck, the soldiers were called to assembly at 4:05 p.m. Miles conferred with MacArthur and then raised a bullhorn to his mouth.

First he said they were to clear the eviction site and other camps near the Capitol building. Next they would push the rioters in a southwesterly direction away from the White House and the Capitol, down Maine Avenue toward the Anacostia River. There they would complete the operation at Anacostia Flats.

* * *

When the crowd of 10,000 people saw the armed horsemen approach in close quarters down the width of Pennsylvania Avenue, they began to applaud. The large crowd grew excited, even joyous. Then as they saw that the troops were armed, the veterans among them grew silent. Most had never believed that the U.S. Army would actually move against them.

Troop E of the cavalry was under Captain Lucian K. Truscott, Jr. Behind the prancing horses lined up twelve across came the 12th Infantry Battalion. The soldiers carried rifles with bayonets. A scout plane from Bolling Field buzzed overhead. This was serious business. All of the implements of modern warfare were on display.

After the infantry came four-wheeled caissons with mounted machine guns, and behind those rumbled the six small MI917 tanks, their treads higher in the front than the back. The purpose of the tanks, MacArthur later explained, was to inspire terror.

From inside one of the small two-man tanks an arm emerged and waved a white handkerchief. The crowd cheered again.

At the rear of this small army came the staff cars, one of which carried MacArthur and Miles. The heat inside the car was unbearable yet MacArthur did not even break a sweat. He was busy explaining to Miles how much he regretted doing this.

"It was clearly evident that the operation was as distasteful to him as it was to all of us," Miles later wrote.

* * *

From his suite at the Ebbitt Hotel, Walter Waters called Doak Carter at BEF headquarters and told him to contact Mayor Eddie McCloskey in Johnstown, Pennsylvania.

McCloskey had visited Camp Marks just the week before, reportedly at the invitation of the Key Men. While there, he made a fiery speech about patriotism, and in an unguarded moment McCloskey promised the veterans, "If you are ever driven out of Washington there will be a place for you in Johnstown."

Given John Bartlett's about-face, it now occurred to Waters that Johnstown offered the only sanctuary large enough to accommodate all of his people.

Carter spoke with McCloskey and called back to tell Waters that the mayor's offer was still good. Waters then sent a messenger to the disbelieving commanders at Camp Marks: "Prepare for an attack by the troops and fall back to Johnstown, Pennsylvania, if necessary," the note said.

Johnstown was 174 miles away.

* * *

From the perspective of crowd control, the attack at 5:00 p.m. could not have occurred at a worse time. It took place just as thousands of federal workers came streaming out of nearby office buildings at the end of the work day. Because the streetcars on Pennsylvania Avenue had been halted, the crowd quickly grew in size to more than 10,000.

Dozens of reporters jogged down the street alongside the cavalry, their notepads out to record the story. Movie cameramen sat atop automobiles and peered through their mounted viewfinders. Police on motorcycles buzzed in and out of the path of the advancing troops like angry hornets.

When the cavalry reached the Third Street block, the horsemen turned their mounts to face the several thousand people who were grouped across the street from the eviction site.

The young infantrymen moved into position to the left of the horsemen and advanced on the crowd. They held their rifles across their chests to push the people back. The veterans stepped forward, some of them laughing, and pushed back at the soldiers.

The infantrymen retreated behind the cavalry where they opened the canvas kits that hung around their necks and donned their gas masks—pointed devices with perforated shields that made them look like predatory insects. Each infantryman carried six metallic blue tear gas canisters the size of a small canteen affixed to a webbed belt.

Each horseman also carried six tear gas canisters tucked under his saddle blanket. Alongside the leather saddles hung three-foot sabers in bronze scabbards. The soldiers' olive-drab shirts were soaked with sweat from the intense heat.

At a command from Truscott, the 200 horsemen reached down as one, unsheathed their sabers and held them high over their heads. Then the riders yelled in unison and urged their horses forward at a steady pace directly into the crowd.

The infantry advanced at double-time to the left of the cavalry. This time they pulled the pins from their tear gas canisters and hurled them into the crowd.

The plan devised by MacArthur and Patton was to disable and disorient the veterans with the sickening gas, cower them with the cavalry and tanks, and then drive them back toward Anacostia Flats. They would be pressed by the mounted cavalry on one side and by the bayonets of the infantry on the other, the two forces coming together like pincers.

A wind blew from the south toward the troops, thus dispersing the tear gas faster than was desired. Altogether, more than 1,500 canisters of gas were used. The soldiers had been trained to cradle the blue tin canister in their non-throwing hand, pull the pin, and then wait a few seconds until the metal felt warm before throwing it.

When the canister landed on the pavement, it spun around like a dust devil, going "PFUT-PFUT-PFUT" as it discharged a thick cloud of noxious blue-gray gas twenty feet high and forty feet wide and deep.

By waiting those few seconds, the soldiers could ensure that the canisters would be red-hot on delivery and therefore could not be picked up and thrown back. But because the troops were young and anxious, most failed to follow their training and threw the canisters as soon as the pins were pulled.

As a result, the first wave of attack featured a volley of tear gas canisters that flew back and forth and created a thick haze of purplish gas that floated over all of Pennsylvania Avenue. The gas had a sickly sweet odor as it drifted into nearby apartment rooms and stores. Doors and windows were quickly slammed shut despite the oppressive heat.

Urged onward, the horses began to twist and edge their massive haunches sideways against the crowd. The veterans cursed and shoved back and the horsemen leaned down and sliced at them with their sabers. One veteran, Otto Breen of Nashville, screamed and fell away, his ear severed. Another black veteran was stabbed in the back and fell under the prancing feet of the horses. Dozens of people suffered scalp lacerations from the swinging sabers.

The first group to be attacked included hundreds of civilians, among them Senator Hiram Bingham and the veterans' benefactor John Bartlett. When Bartlett had arrived several hours earlier, he found the crowd saddened and whispering about the shooting of the veterans. There had been no violence of any kind. Now he was in the phalanx of the attack, which he later described as follows:

"Into the crowd they ruthlessly drove, scattering us like sheep, knocking down many…Following the cavalry came four companies of infantry, six hundred strong, with their khaki uniforms and iron hats, armed with rifles and bayonets, all set for battle."

Most of the civilians wore jackets with ties, which made it easy for the cavalrymen to distinguish them from the more ragged veterans. The horsemen cut the veterans out and herded them onto Pennsylvania Avenue.

There was a chorus of loud boos from the crowd. "Yellow! Yellow!" someone shouted. Bartlett watched in horror as an old man raised his hand and had a saber thrust through it by an oncoming horseman. Tears caused by the gas streamed from his eyes as Bartlett stumbled from the crowd to his car. Once he had recovered, Bartlett drove quickly back to his estate. Later he denied ever having offered the use of his land for a BEF camp.

Around the same time that the cavalry attack began, Walter Waters left the Ebbitt Hotel after two hours of "being kept...by my bodyguards." He hurried to BEF headquarters where he changed from his commander's uniform to civilian clothes in order to look like any other federal employee. Dressed in a brown suit with a hat pulled low over his eyes, Waters merged into the crowds to watch the attacks take place.

* * *

Army Chief Douglas MacArthur stood calmly in the middle of Pennsylvania Avenue where he straddled the trolley tracks. He posed in his trademark fashion, long arms out and bent like wings with his hands tucked into his rear pants pockets. Major Dwight Eisenhower was at his side as he would be all night long.

MacArthur was immaculate in his tailored uniform with its tunic and three-inch black belt. The general's left chest was festooned with gleaming medallions and ribbons. He wore his military hat with its oak leaf and crisp brim at eye level. His khaki whipcord trousers ballooned out at the thigh then tapered into shiny black boots. His riding crop was by his side.

MacArthur stared fiercely at the scene in front of him, nostrils flared beneath his long aquiline nose. His mouth twisted in fury as he barked out commands and he smiled thinly when they were carried out. Although tears ran down his face from the clouds of gas that floated overhead, he did not flinch. After more than fourteen years, MacArthur was finally back in battle.

* * *

Waiting in his office, room 308 at the War Department, Patrick Hurley was kept abreast of events by a series of telephone calls from Ira Keck. Keck called him when the troops moved down Pennsylvania Avenue, then when they were in "fighting order" with rifles and sabers mounted. He called again when they attacked the veterans at 4:50 p.m. After a few anxious minutes, Hurley was told that there was "no resistance." Not by the veterans—not against their own.

Finally Hurley could not stand it any longer. He rushed from the office to his car and drove the few blocks down Pennsylvania Avenue where he joined MacArthur to observe the battle.

* * *

When the hot blue tin canisters exploded at their feet, the veterans tore off their shirts and held them against their faces as they ran doubled-over out of the reach of the gas. There were instances of resistance, such as when a man grabbed a horse's reins to unseat the rider, and a shower of bricks at C Street, but for the most part the veterans retreated in eerie silence, many of them simply walking ahead of the soldiers' bayonets.

Patton, who was briefly unseated by a brick that grazed his face, was in a fury and drove his troops relentlessly. Later he wrote: "Bricks flew, sabers rose and fell with a comforting smack and the mob ran. Two of us charged at a gallop and had some nice work at close range with the occupants of a truck, most of whom could not sit down for a few days."

Forced onto Maine Avenue, about 1,000 veterans faced a line of infantrymen who pressed them backwards with their pointed steel bayonets—sharp 16-inch MI905s designed to impale the enemy. Up close the veterans saw that the soldiers were young enough to be their sons.

The infantry advanced as they were taught, crouching and stepping forward one foot at a time while jabbing with their bayonets to force the enemy back. In this manner the U.S. Army soldiers and the veterans inched slowly down the thoroughfare like a mirrored image. The one side thrust its weapons and advanced as the other yelled taunts and retreated, their wives and children huddled behind them.

The veterans greatly outnumbered the soldiers and could have counter-attacked at any time, but they did not.

* * *

Two trolley cars became trapped among the infantry at the intersection of Maine and Fourth. A dense cloud of tear gas rolled over the cars and the riders, many of them women, buried their faces in handkerchiefs. Several men rushed to lower and close the windows of the street cars, which only trapped the hot gas inside. They quickly pushed them up again.

* * *

Franklin Delano Roosevelt sat on his porch at Hyde Park on the afternoon of July 28 and listened to radio reports of the violent surprise attack on the veterans. With him was his closest advisor, Harvard law professor Felix Frankfurter.

"Well, Felix," Roosevelt said to the diminutive future Supreme Court chief justice, "this will elect me."

Roosevelt made the same observation to Rexford Tugwell the next morning as he sat in his bed with the Friday newspapers strewn around him. FDR expressed anguish for the state of the veterans and described the newspaper photos as "scenes from a nightmare." After that, during the entire campaign Roosevelt never spoke Herbert Hoover's name again.

* * *

Once the Pennsylvania Avenue eviction site was cleared, Douglas MacArthur called a sergeant over and gave him brief instructions. A few minutes later, the officer directed several soldiers to the shacks at the base of the building. They balled up newspapers and set them aflame; soon all of the shelters were on fire. (General Perry Miles later blamed the initial fires on tear gas bombs. He said the soldiers who were photographed torching the shacks had mistakenly thought that they had been given an order to do so.)

The troops spread out to other encampments as they made their way south. First they went to C Street between 12th and 14th Streets, SW, to clear out the communist encampment, which was a priority; then to Maryland and Maine Avenues near the wharves, then to a camp near the Congressional Library. At each location most of the veterans had already left.

The soldiers encountered two more brief flurries of resistance. At 3rd and Missouri, Captain Lucian Truscott's P181 cavalrymen were "heckled and bombarded with bricks" then pelted with a "severe shower of rocks" at Maryland and C Street. By the end of the operation, four soldiers were listed with facial wounds from thrown bricks; another four were injured due to their mishandling the burning hot tear gas canisters.

Several veterans were chased by a cavalryman under the low roof of a gas station where they huddled together for protection. The horseman ducked his head and rode in after them. He chopped at the men with his saber until they ran back out into the street.

A reporter from the *Daily News* watched in horror as a soldier impaled a civilian in the buttocks with his bayonet. "Forget you saw that," the soldier snapped at him.

"How could you do that?" the reporter yelled.

"We've been cooped up so much—I guess we're just losing our heads," the soldier said.

* * *

MacArthur's main body of troops proceeded relentlessly toward the Navy Yard.

With the sidestreets blocked by the infantry, the large body of veterans and their families retreated on foot to Anacostia Flats. They looked very much like a horde of European refugees fleeing an attacking enemy. As they rounded the corner of the Navy Yard and started down the cobblestones of Eleventh Street, the veterans saw hundreds of their comrades on the other side of the Anacostia drawbridge, urging them on to the temporary safety of Camp Marks.

CHAPTER THIRTEEN

Anacostia Flats

Inside Camp Marks there was pandemonium. The water supply had been cut off and word spread quickly that MacArthur and the troops were coming. Thousands of veterans had already grabbed their meager belongings and left and several thousand more were in the process of doing so. But a core group of about 1,000 people refused to flee—they planned to stay and fight.

At 5:30 p.m. the first Army troops arrived at the Navy Yard side of the Anacostia River. MacArthur ordered that they be rested and fed supper before completing the operation. From both sides of the river more than 2,000 spectators flooded onto the 11th Street Bridge, many well-dressed in white linens. They were there to watch the eviction.

* * *

Still eager to be part of the action, Patrick Hurley followed the troops down Maine Avenue in his personal automobile. Soon his car was surrounded by a mob of angry veterans who rocked the vehicle back and forth and pounded it with rocks and iron rods. Hurley managed to back his damaged sedan away and return to the War Department.

Taken from From the Crash to the Blitz, 1929-39, Cabell Phillips, The New York Times Company, 1969.

General Douglas MacArthur and Major Dwight D. Eisenhower oversee the attack made on the BEF.

At the White House, a worried President Hoover received regular communique as the attack against the veterans proceeded, brought to him by a soldier who was allowed the use of one of MacArthur's staff cars.

When the troops reached the 11th Street Bridge, a newspaper reporter who was sympathetic to the veterans called Senator Borah and urged him to intervene with the president, which he tried to do. Hoover assured Borah that no attack on Camp Marks was planned. Then, disturbed by the senator's call, Hoover contacted Van Horne Moseley at the War Department where the deputy chief had been stationed throughout the day. The president instructed Moseley to re-confirm to MacArthur that the troops should not cross the drawbridge.

MacArthur, Eisenhower, and other officers and newsmen were relaxed and chatting when Moseley arrived. Moseley conferred privately for several minutes with MacArthur who appeared greatly annoyed.

After Moseley returned to the War Department, Hoover called again to make certain that MacArthur had been told. Yes, Moseley said, he had gone in person and the mission was completed.

"Send the message once more," Hoover replied.

This time Moseley gave the assignment to Colonel Clement B. Wright, secretary of the general staff. (The next day, laughing, Moseley claimed that he told Wright to "get lost.")

According to Dwight Eisenhower, Wright did get to the 11th Street Bridge just before troops were deployed, although it took him nearly two hours to do so. MacArthur told Eisenhower to meet with Wright and when the second message was finally conveyed to him, the Army chief said, "I do not have time for people pretending to carry messages from the president, and I will not have my men bivouacked under enemy guns."

Wright later testified that he told Moseley that when he arrived the troops were already advancing on the bridge.

* * *

Taken from *The Bonus March and the New Deal*, John Henry Bartlett;
M.A. Donohue and Company, Chicago, 1937.

Camp Marks, prior to the evacuation and fire.

As the troops prepared for the final attack at 6:45 p.m., Eddie Atwell, the BEF military police commander, ran across the field from the camp toward the river waving a white flag. He worked his way through the people on the bridge and insisted on being taken to MacArthur.

Atwell told the Army chief that there were a large number of women and children still in the camp and he pleaded for more time. MacArthur agreed to give Atwell one more hour to evacuate. At their own initiative, National Guard troops had already taken position on the Anacostia side of the river and mounted powerful floodlights atop local fire truck ladders around the perimeters of Camp Marks.

Although they could see the armed forces massed across the way, a core group of hardened veterans refused to leave Camp Marks and stood around in confused, angry groups. Earlier Walter Waters had entered the camp and pleaded with the men not to use the guns they had supposedly hidden there. "These are Army troops," Waters stressed. "They have tanks. They will massacre you."

The wives of the recalcitrant veterans stood nearby wringing their hands. "If he's going to be killed, I'm going to stay here and be killed with him," one woman cried.

* * *

The staged nature of the entire affair starting with the faux "riot" that morning was inadvertently disclosed by Commissioner Reichelderfer as he and Crosby left their office that night.

Ira Keck had called to tell them that Camp Marks was about to be set afire. Their work done, the two men left after spending fourteen hours at the District office command post. A reporter waiting outside asked why the eviction notice that was signed by Ogden Mills on Wednesday night had not been made public until that morning.

"You wouldn't expect us to tip the enemy off in advance as to our tactics, would you?" the chairman of the District commissioners responded.

* * *

The attack on Camp Marks began at 9:22 p.m., more than two and one-half hours after Atwell made his plea to MacArthur. The first task that the Army faced was to clear the 11th Street Bridge. They did this by tossing tear gas into the crowd of astonished spectators who quickly ran off the bridge onto either side of the river.

The infantry crossed first with a fire truck behind them, throwing its floodlights as far as the first row of tents and hovels. There was no sign of life. The remnants of the BEF army had retreated to the center of the camp.

The soldiers advanced cautiously in single file along the riverbank. There was a rumor that a band of heavily armed veterans were waiting in the shadows of the drain pipe at the rear of the camp. Out of the darkness came two representatives of the remaining veterans. Cigarettes were exchanged and the men were taken by a messenger to speak with MacArthur. They asked if they could leave now but return tomorrow for their belongings. MacArthur said that he would consider their request.

The young soldiers advanced into the darkness of Camp Marks, tossing tear gas canisters ahead of them. The National Guard floodlights followed their progress and illuminated an alien scene. The sulfurous gas, yellow from the floodlights, drifted in a thick haze over the camp and just above the Anacostia River on which Old Ironsides sat like a ghost ship. Mounted cavalry led by Patton moved in and out of the clouds of gas as they encircled the camp and began to move inward.

Suddenly a tower of flame shot skyward. Someone had set fire to the camp platform where so many performances had been put on for the veterans. Nearby rose another pillar of flames. The big gospel tent had been fired. The wind had died and the flames sizzled straight upward like a red-hot saber.

Men and women screamed in panic and scrambled down the streets of the camp ahead of the masked troops. There was the sound of sirens from approaching fire trucks and the fierce whinnying of frightened horses; the roar of motorcycles and Army trucks; the yelling of the soldiers; and everywhere the thick, choking sulfur gas and the pungent odor of burning tar paper.

Out on the Potomac River, two teenaged sisters were returning with their dates on an excursion boat. One of the young men was an Army captain named Bender who had been at Ft. Myer for several months. As the boat docked at Water Street, they saw a red haze near the mouth of the Anacostia. The whole bank of the river appeared to be burning. Bender realized what was happening and asked if they could drive to Camp Marks.

Once there, Bender talked his way across the 11th Street Bridge into the camp. It was like a descent into hell. Camp Marks was a maze of dusty streets filled with ragged people. Angry men pummeled their car when they saw Bender in his uniform. The sisters panicked and ducked behind the seats. Tear gas hovered above them like cumulus clouds, yellow on top and red underneath from the reflected flames. Garbage was everywhere and the odor of the burning camp was "vile."

At last they reached MacArthur. The older sister wrote: "I will never forget the staunch outline, the erect figure of MacArthur in the middle of the melee as he gave orders and saluted Captain Bender."

The soldiers advanced block by block and permitted the evacuees limited time to gather their belongings. One father, Charles Ludlow, stumbled ahead of the advancing soldiers. He carried his one-year-old daughter in one arm and pulled his wife by the hand. She was French, a war bride; they had driven to Washington from Toledo, Ohio.

Even though a soldier kept prodding him with a bayonet, Ludlow stopped every few yards to blow air down his child's throat. The little girl was asthmatic and had inhaled a lungful of tear gas. She was taken to Providence Hospital later that night and survived thanks to Ludlow's efforts. Another small child would not.

Pressed on by the soldiers, the Meyers family of Ephrata, Pennsylvania, hurried out of the camp. Like the other refugees, they were being herded toward the rear. Louisa Meyers carried her baby Bernard while her husband John and another man pulled along the child's heavy wooden crib.

As they scrambled over the ridge toward Anacostia, a woman called to them from a nearby farmhouse. Louisa Meyers rushed into her yard with a cavalryman on her heels.

She pulled herself and her infant onto the woman's porch just as the soldier threw a tear gas canister at her feet.

The thick, noxious cloud of gas filled the house and the owners provided wet towels for everyone to put over their faces. An hour later the Meyers' baby began to vomit. The next morning Bernard Meyers, 11 months old, died. His small body had turned black and blue.

* * *

Pelham Glassford crossed the 11ᵗʰ Street Bridge on his motorcycle. Looking pale and troubled, he followed the troops into Camp Marks. A woman he knew as Mrs. Davis hurried up to him. "They are burning my house," she sobbed.

"I am sure they did not mean to do that," Glassford said, comforting her.

They watched silently as other shacks around them went up in flames. Just a day before the veterans had been leaving and everything had been arranged for a happy ending.

"This is such a shame that this would happen," Glassford said quietly.

* * *

Altogether nearly 7,000 people were forced out of Camp Marks. Many had left earlier in the evening because of Glassford's warnings. About 1,500 of those walked up-river to Camp Bartlett where they stayed through the night and departed early the next day.

Thirty men went to the Benning freight yards where they tried to hitch a ride to Johnstown. Others made their way north on Wisconsin Avenue to Rockville, Maryland, where they slept in the Cabin John Park and on the old Court House lawn. (Residents fixed them a meal of hot dogs.) One thousand people camped in the woods near the Bladensburg Jail.

Those 1,000 or so who were forced away at bayonet point were less fortunate. Their only way out of camp was over the high ridge at the back of the Flats and into the town of Anacostia. Some spent the night there sitting on curbstones with their backs against lightposts. Others stumbled through the darkness, many sick and injured from the tear gas, into southern Maryland and from there north to Pennsylvania.

Walter Waters moved largely unnoticed through Camp Marks during the eviction, urging restraint where he could. He tried to speak with a group of veterans but they booed and threatened him. At midnight, Waters made his way back to BEF headquarters where an urgent telephone message from Baltimore awaited him. When he returned the call, an unidentified man told him that the keys to a Baltimore armory were his if the BEF wanted arms. Would he send a truck?

Waters indignantly refused the offer and hung up. This was no longer his battle.

Several BEF officers were stunned. They had been waiting for Waters to organize a marauding party to storm nearby government warehouses where guns were reportedly stored. Instead Waters left BEF headquarters, walked to the nearby garage where he kept his car, and drove to join Wilma in Baltimore.

* * *

The Army and some of the fleeing veterans set thousands of dried wooden huts afire and the flames rose hundreds of feet into the sky. The blaze could be seen for miles around, including from the Lincoln Study where Herbert Hoover was meeting with a wealthy supporter from Los Angeles, banker Henry M. Robinson, and Assistant Attorney General Seth Richardson.

Richardson called to the others as the glow intensified in the southeast and the three men gathered at the window. The wall of flames rose and spread until the entire sky over Anacostia was blood red.

* * *

The military operation was completed by 10:30 p.m. and sentries were placed around Camp Marks to keep any of the veterans from returning, even though there was little but burned ash to come back to.

As they left Anacostia Flats, Major Dwight Eisenhower again urged General MacArthur to be cautious. "There are certain to be reporters back at the War Department," he said. "Let Hurley handle the explanations."

The Army Chief of Staff disagreed. "MacArthur will report himself."

The press conference that Douglas MacArthur had called began promptly at 11:00 p.m. with a statement by the general.

"Most of you saw what happened," MacArthur began. "That mob down there was a bad-looking mob. It was animated by the essence of revolution. Those men misconstrued the gentleness and consideration shown them in the past as a sign of weakness."

MacArthur said that "beyond a shadow of a doubt" the BEF was "about to take over the direct control of the government. Had the president not acted today...he would have been faced with a grave situation...had he let it go on another week...the institutions of our government would have been very severely threatened."

A reporter asked who had fired the camp, and MacArthur said that the veterans must have fired it themselves. "There were...few veteran soldiers in the group we cleared out today...few indeed. If there was one man in ten who is a veteran it would surprise me," the Army chief replied.

Then MacArthur swelled his chest and made one of the strangest pronouncements of the day:

"I have never seen greater relief on the part of the distressed populace than I saw today. I have released in my day more than one community which had been held in the grip of a foreign enemy. I have gone into villages that for three and one-half years had been under the domination of the soldiers of a foreign nation. I know what gratitude means along that line. I have never seen, even in those days, such expressions of gratitude as I heard from the crowds today."

Patrick Hurley made the point that the military had not initiated the attack.

"The commissioners and the District asked the president for this support when they felt that they could no longer maintain law and order."

Taken from *The Bonus March and the New Deal*, John Henry Bartlett; M.A. Donohue and Company, Chicago, 1937.

Camp Marks on July 28, 1932.

MacArthur added, "We haven't taken over any functions of the government and the commissioners are in complete control of the city now as they were this morning, except that when they call on us, we are going to help them."

* * *

In the pre-dawn hours of July 29, Colonel George Patton sat on a bale of hay with several other soldiers, drinking coffee and watching the smoke from the dying fires at Camp Marks twist skyward. A tall infantry sergeant wove his way through the rubble, yanking along a dirty veteran.

"This man says he knows you," the sergeant said as he pushed Joe Angelo forward. The little veteran turned his large brown eyes hopefully toward Patton. The colonel looked down at Angelo, his thin face flushed with fury.

"Sergeant, I do not know this man!" Patton replied. "Take him away and under no circumstances permit him to return!"

As Angelo was hauled away, Patton turned to a small group of officers and said, "That was my batman in France. Can you imagine the headlines if the paper got wind of our meeting here?"

"I'll take care of him later," he added.

In another part of the camp, Douglas MacArthur and Patrick Hurley returned to look over the smoking ruins.

As reported by Lee McCardle of the *Star*, "The dapper Secretary of War was attired in white sport shoes and pants and a flapping felt hat, and he smoked his cigarette in a debonair fashion."

* * *

At 10:30 the night before, Hurley and MacArthur had returned in person to Herbert Hoover before they met with the press. The following description of that meeting has been pieced together from various accounts.

The president was equal parts bewildered and furious. He demanded to know why MacArthur had acted against his orders.

MacArthur told Hoover that intelligence reports had showed that the Communists had taken over Anacostia Flats and that there were arms in the camp. He could not allow his men to be targets for subversives who intended to fire upon them.

Hoover said that he had sent specific orders twice not to proceed into the camp. MacArthur replied, with some visible discomfort, that the troops had already been committed when Hoover's messengers arrived.

Hoover asked whether they had found weapons in the camps. MacArthur assured him that they had found rifles and machine guns. In his opinion, had they waited one more day, the Communists would have stormed the White House.

Hoover dismissed them and went to bed immediately afterwards. The next morning, his anger fully returned, the president summoned both men again.

This time MacArthur said, "You may have my resignation if you wish it, sir."

"Good God!" Hoover exclaimed. "You've just praised me to the heavens before the press. How am I to fire you now?"

Hurley emphasized to Hoover that the press was on his side. The morning editorials had largely praised the president for saving the country from a Communist revolution. *The Boston Herald* wrote: "The only criticism that lies against the president is that he did not act sooner." The *Columbus (Ohio) Evening Dispatch* said, "President Hoover was entirely within his right to insist that order be maintained and to lend the services of Army troops."

"Sir," Hurley told him, "you are a hero."

* * *

A small airplane circled slowly over Camp Marks later that morning. In it were a father and son. They had taken off from Bolling Field for the express purpose of showing the young boy what remained of the "Communist camp."

The pilot, Gene Vidal, dipped the right wing and pointed down. Anacostia Flats looked like an enormous garbage dump with thin lines of gray smoke drifting up from dozens of smoldering piles of rubble.

"Remember that, son," he yelled over the airplane engine. "That was where General MacArthur stopped the revolution!"

Young Gene looked down and nodded. He remembered the boner men who had frightened him so. Now the power of his grandfather and the other strong men he knew had driven them away.

Gene Vidal felt safer, more free, and more privileged than ever before.

CHAPTER FOURTEEN

The Cover-Up

Although Camp Marks had been destroyed, there was still much follow-up work for Patrick Hurley and Douglas MacArthur to oversee.

During the night, scores of veterans had crept back into the District and holed up in some of the shacks that remained. Some were trying to find family members who were lost during the attack. They had to be rounded up and sent by truck to Johnstown.

The remaining encampments also needed to be cleared out, including the "family encampment" at 14th and B Streets, SW. Those squatters would be sent to Pennsylvania as well, even though Pelham Glassford had urged women and children not to go there.

One hundred and fifteen members of the Communist Party had been picked up the night before as they left a meeting at an abandoned church at 5th and Virginia Avenue, SW, and seventy-five of those were taken to the Maryland state line via Bladensburg Road.

Forty others including Emanuel Levin, John Pace, and James Ford, the Communist presidential candidate, were arrested without formal charges and held in the miserable District jail. Patrick Hurley personally arranged for this to be done. In doing so, the Secretary of War went over Pelham Glassford's head.

Then there was the need to shore up the various lies and distortions that were involved in justifying the routing of the veterans. There were so many—the unnecessary eviction, the staged "riot," the claim of communist infiltrators, the premature call for the troops, Glassford's non-existent request for help, Moseley's "lost" messenger, the lie that soldiers had not fired the camps—all of these minor conspiracies were compounding and soon would come down like a house of cards.

* * *

At 9:00 a.m., John Bartlett called BEF headquarters to re-confirm that his permission to permanently house the veterans had been withdrawn given the violent turn of events. Bartlett also said that federal troops were on their way to drive out the remaining veterans who were encamped there.

Walter Waters, who had just returned from Baltimore, was giving an interview to the New York Times in which he said that the Khaki Shirts would "clean out the high places of government on behalf of the inarticulate masses of the country." When he received Bartlett's call, he dramatically raced by car across the Memorial Bridge into Virginia, past barricades manned by soldiers to stop veterans from returning to the city. On his way, Waters passed the troops that were en-route to Camp Bartlett.

Many of the refugees who had spent the night there had already left due to the camp's lack of food. Waters and Camp Commander Charles Mugge quickly assembled the several hundred remaining veterans into formation. John Bartlett watched timidly from inside his house as the veterans marched off on their 174-mile trek to Johnstown, just ahead of the Army troops.

Another large contingent had escaped up Wisconsin Avenue toward Maryland. These miserable families were blockaded by Maryland State Police at the District line just yards from Evalyn Walsh McLean's property. After pressure from Patrick Hurley, Maryland Governor Ritchie relented and allowed U.S. Army trucks to haul the refugees across his state to Johnstown.

Yet another group of veterans received permission from the commissioners to march out of the city in military formation. These several hundred men passed by the White House carrying torn American flags that they had salvaged. Impressed by their dignity, residents and office workers lined the streets to cheer and applaud them.

Among this group were several of the original Oregon marchers. Asked if they were heading to Johnstown, one marcher shouted, "We are heading for the United States, wherever that is!"

* * *

Mamie Eisenhower wrote of these turbulent hours in a letter to her parents, the Douds:

> "Well, if we didn't have excitement here Thursday with Bonus men. I had taken Helen G. and Bess Mc to Commissary and…when I reached Apt. at 3:10 there were clothes from front door back…at 5:30, Gen McA's sec called and saidMajor E didn't know when he would be home. Then did I get excited…we rode downtown to see sights B everything that could turn a wheel was out. At 9:30 streets were cleared by tear gas and marchers pressed across Dis. Line.

The big camp we had seen from Old Ironsides was in flames...Ike got home at 1 o'clock and was out again at 7 Fri...It was such a terrific day for heat. When he came in he didn't have a dry rag on and his good uniform soaked. Everyone gathered over here last nite (Friday) to greet the returned "hero" Ha ha and get all the dope first hand...Ike is fine except the tear gas started his eye off again. Everything is quiet now although city still under "martial law." But talk about a compliment to one Dwight D., only officer taken with Gen Mc except Davis. I'll bet there was some gnashing of the teeth in some quarters..."

* * *

On the morning of July 29, President Hoover released a letter that he had just sent to the District commissioners. This letter's purpose was to establish Hoover as a man with backbone. For the first time it introduced a phantom "organized attack by several thousand men." Obviously authored by Patrick Hurley, the document set forth the official line of the administration and subtly placed blame for the entire matter on Pelham Glassford. The letter read:

Honorable Luther H. Reichelderfer
Commissioner, District of Columbia
Washington, D.C.

In response to your information that the police of the District of Columbia were overwhelmed by an organized attack by several thousand men, and were unable to maintain law and order, I complied with your request for aid from the Army to the police. It is a matter of satisfaction that, after the arrival of this assistance, the mobs which were defying the municipal government were dissolved without the firing of a shot or the loss of a life.

I wish to call attention of the District Commissioners to the fact that martial law has not been declared; that responsibility for order still rests upon your Commission and the police. The civil government of Washington must function uninterrupted. The Commissioners, through their own powers, should now deal with the question decisively.

It is the duty of the authorities of the District at once to find the instigators of this attack on the police and bring them to justice. It is obvious that, after the departure of the majority of the veterans, subversive influence obtained control of the men remaining in the District, a large part of whom were not veterans, secured repudiation of their elected leaders and inaugurated and organized this attack.

They were undoubtedly led to believe that the civil authorities could be intimidated with impunity because of attempts to conciliate by lax enforcements of city ordinances and laws in many directions. I shall expect the police to strictly enforce every ordinance of the District in every part of the city. I wish every violator of the law to be instantly arrested and prosecuted under due process of law.

There is no group, no matter what its origins, that can be allowed either to violate the laws of this country or to intimidate the Government.

Yours faithfully,
Herbert Hoover

From his cell at the District jail, Emmanuel Levin was more than willing to take responsibility for the violence. "Yes," he said eagerly, "the Communist Party had been in full control of the BEF, especially in the later weeks. We hoped to turn Washington into another Petrograd."

* * *

That same afternoon, July 29, a tired-looking Pelham Glassford appeared at the Office of the Commissioners to make a statement to the press.

Glassford's demeanor was dour and serious. The superintendent had been stung by Hoover's accusations of "lax enforcement" of the District's laws and he believed with some justification that he was being set up to take the blame for the persecution of the very veterans he had struggled so hard to protect.

"I would like to make the following statement," Glassford said. "I was never asked, nor did I request, the intervention of federal troops against the veterans. There was, to my knowledge, no communist plot being hatched to control the government. The veterans were under control at all times.

"Although it is true that a riotous condition did exist, I had maintained complete control and at no time requested troops. At no time did we face incipient revolution.

"If anything, it was extremely unwise to drive the men out of their buildings and into the streets, where they were far more difficult to control."

Glassford's statement was picked up by the late edition of the *Evening Star* and the following morning it made front-page news nationwide.

The next day an anxious Herbert Hoover summoned MacArthur and Hurley to his office once again. If Glassford had not requested the troops, he said, then Hurley and MacArthur must tell the press about their own roles in what had happened.

But MacArthur's web had been spun and the president had already been pushed forth as the savior. The Army chief said that for them to take credit "would be bragging." The Secretary of War said that they had no desire to be the "heroes." The communist threat was a serious one and support for the president's actions was "99 percent." Hurley encouraged the president to simply enjoy the glory of what had occurred.

There was no need to be defensive, Hurley said. In days to come they would be able to prove that the veterans had posed a dangerous threat and that the president was fully justified in taking the steps that he took.

* * *

For the first few days the nation's mostly conservative press accepted the administration's claims that the country had been saved from revolution at the hands of a violent mob. Only a few publishers were not supportive. William Randolph Hearst wired his New York bureau chief that the attack was "the most stupid thing the government had ever done," and an "excellent way to encourage Communism and fascism."

Patrick Hurley basked in the positive attention and the apparent success of their plan. He emerged from a cabinet meeting on July 30 and spoke expansively to the press about his great pride in the Army.

"And I want to tell you," he said, "Mac was there. He was there like four aces and a king."

To blunt any negative reaction and to reinforce their claims, Hoover instructed Attorney General William Mitchell to prepare a report on the BEF episode. A grand jury was also convened that very day. The grand jury inquiry lasted from July 29 to August 15 and featured mostly interviews with friendly witnesses such as the commissioners and police officers hostile to Glassford who willingly testified as to the need for Army intervention.

The white-wash nature of the inquiry was clear from the start when Judge Oscar Luhring instructed the jurors that "the mob, guilty of violence, included few ex-servicemen and was made up mainly of Communists and other disorderly elements. I hope you will find that this is so."

* * *

After Glassford's statement, Herbert Hoover sensed public opinion swinging against him. Hundreds of telegrams, letters, and phone calls poured into the White House, most of them highly critical of MacArthur's attack on the veterans. American Legion posts across the country passed resolutions to censure the president and called him a sadist and a frightened, brutal cynic.

In his radio broadcast, reporter Floyd Gibbons compared the fleeing veterans to refugees and said, "The only difference was that the members of the BEF were American refugees, fleeing from the fire and sword of the Great Humanitarian."

* * *

Walter Waters continued to man the BEF headquarters in Washington, primarily to keep his fledgling "Khaki Shirts" organization alive. His final order as BEF commander was for all veterans to leave the capital by Saturday noon, July 30.

Waters received a letter from a family named Edgell in Catonsville, Maryland, that offered up to 50 acres of land for him to use as a camp for the veterans. He drove to their farm that same day to meet with the Edgells, letter in hand.

The land was heavily wooded and Waters felt that it would make an ideal protected camp. He secured a deed for the property in his name (to revert to the Edgell family if the BEF could not use the land) and made an appointment to see Governor Ritchie in Annapolis, Maryland.

* * *

Patrick Hurley's campaign of misinformation grew in proportion to the mounting national criticism. He released a statement at mid-day on August 3 that amplified the earlier letter sent by President Hoover, which read, in part:

> The marchers refused all overtures to vacate the premises (at Pennsylvania and C Streets). During the morning of July 28, the police again appeared and asked the marchers to vacate…the marchers refused. The police then attempted to oust them (and) the marchers then attacked the police.
>
> From the Camp on the Anacostia River, a mass of veterans together with the radical agitators marched into Washington and…a definite organized attack of several thousand men was then made upon the police. The veterans participating in the attack…were entirely controlled by Red agitators whose sole purpose was to bring about disorder, riots, bloodshed and death.

His statement also re-spun the tale that "the huge riot was still in progress at 2:55 p.m." when the president ordered in the troops.

During the Army's actions, Hurley maintained, no property was destroyed, no shacks set on fire by the Army, and no women or children were evicted. In fact, he said, care was taken to transport home all of the families of the BEF.

In response to these distortions, local newspapers printed lists of the dozens of seriously wounded people, including women and children, who had received treatment at local hospitals. They also ran photographs of federal troops setting fire to the veterans' pathetic wooden shacks.

Patrick Hurley's carefully orchestrated deceit began to fall apart because one man whose cooperation he had automatically assumed— former Brigadier General Pelham Glassford—had broken rank.

CHAPTER FIFTEEN

Johnstown

Five thousand men, women, and children of the BEF somehow found their way to Johnstown, Pennsylvania. Many walked the entire 174 miles in darkness and rain.

BEF officers set up assistance stations along the way at Frederick and Hagerstown, Maryland, and at McConnelsburg and Bedford, Pennsylvania, to direct and feed the long line of sick and exhausted people.

Mayor Eddie McCloskey was at first delighted by the positive national publicity that he received as the "savior" of the BEF, but he soon became dismayed by heavy local criticism from the Johnstown American Legion, city council, and local residents.

McCloskey had been wooed by Smedley Butler to have Johnstown become the headquarters of the new Khaki Shirts organization. Too late, McCloskey realized that Johnstown did not have the resources to deal with such a large influx of needy people.

The site that the mayor made available for the veterans was the "Ideal Amusement Park." The park's owners allowed him to do this in return for the right to sell tickets to see the Bonus Marchers. Within just hours, the speculators placed billboards along the main road into Johnstown reading "Come Out and See the Bonus Marchers!"

The Amusement Park was a terrible choice for 5,000 sick, wounded, and exhausted people. There was only one water line, few toilets, and no shower. What's more, no one had arranged food or bedding for the marchers. The swimming pool at the park was closed by the owners out of fear of "contamination."

Walter Waters still had his supporters, for the airplane remained at his service. On Sunday, he drove past the still-smoking ruins of Camp Marks and flew from Bolling Field to Johnstown.

At the rough camp Waters found his people hungry, despairing, and sick. Many had slept on the ground in the open air. The park was surrounded by Pennsylvania state troopers deployed by Governor Pinchot.

Dozens of refugees had been taken to the Johnstown Hospital. For years after, hundreds of those who had been gassed suffered skin blisters that would never close, lung scarring, and permanent eye damage.

Waters tried to make one of his rousing speeches but no one seemed interested. He assured McCloskey that he would move the marchers to a permanent camp in Catonsville, Maryland, within two weeks.

When word filtered through the refugees that a rioting army of "red insurrectionists" had been driven out of the nation's capital, the marchers were confused. They had just been in Washington and had seen no such army.

The veterans did not realize until later that the news reports were about them.

* * *

William Hushka, winner of the Distinguished Service Cross, was buried in a veterans ceremony at Arlington Cemetery the following

Tuesday, August 2. The service for Eric Carlson followed two days later. Several of the troops who had just driven the BEF from Washington took part in the honor guards for both ceremonies.

After attending Hushka's funeral, Walter Waters drove to Annapolis to meet with Maryland Governor Albert Ritchie.

Waters' plan, devised in discussions with Smedley Butler, was to secure approval for the BEF to use the Catonsville land and then establish similar Khaki Shirts encampments in every state, with Key Man support. A second possible site had already been found in Huntington, West Virginia.

Ritchie until recently had been a Democratic presidential candidate and he enjoyed national visibility. While he was willing to see Waters, the governor had no intention of making the BEF's problem his own.

"It is unfeasible," Ritchie told him. He could not allow thousands of people from other states to come to Maryland to collect unemployment benefits there.

"How can you prevent it?" Waters asked. "It is my property and I shall break no law."

"Yes you will," Ritchie said, and the meeting disintegrated into angry words.

Out of options, Waters called Doak Carter who had taken the most expensive room at a hotel in Johnstown. Waters ordered Carter to have the veterans disband and to go home. Governor Pinchot of Pennsylvania had pledged to provide transportation.

Carter, who had assumed more and more authority of the BEF during Waters' frequent absences, dramatically refused to obey the BEF commander. For the next two days Carter tried to generate enthusiasm among the beaten veterans for a new plan that would take them to Mexico.

Faced with Carter's mutiny, Waters sent Eddie Atwell to Johnstown to read his official disbanding notice that included a vague promise that he would "make definite plans to carry on."

Free passage out of Johnstown was provided, ironically, by the B&O Railroad on August 4. Within two days, all 5,000 marchers had departed.

Unfortunately the trains, called the "Bonus Special," took the veterans only as far as the B&O lines went, and no other railroads had been enlisted to help. Nine dismal days after their expulsion from Washington, the stragglers of the veterans' army were deposited, largely penniless, at the Chicago and St. Louis terminals.

Forty-three men from the original Oregon contingent of 250 arrived home in Portland on August 10. Although dusty and road weary, they formed a column and marched with military bearing from the railroad depot where the BEF had begun almost three months before.

The BEF name continued for two more years. A convention of former marchers was held in Uniontown, Pennsylvania, that fall and a second much smaller march on Washington was undertaken by the Communists in 1933. BEF camps existed as late as 1934—but as of August 6, 1932, the Bonus Expeditionary Force was essentially dead.

* * *

Back in Washington a coroner's jury found Metropolitan Police Officer George W. Shinault, 38, innocent of misconduct in the shooting at the eviction site. It was revealed at his hearing that Shinault had actually carried two guns—one his regular service revolver, and the other a "personal" gun.

George Shinault was the father of five children, one of them a newborn. He was reinstated to active duty but refused to return to foot duty. Shinault acted as though he were in constant danger and demanded to be assigned to a radio patrol car.

On August 14, two weeks after the veterans' eviction, Officer Shinault's scout car was summoned to a family disturbance at 39 P.

Street, NW. His partner, who drove, stayed with the police car while Shinault approached the open front door of the darkened row house. When he reached the door, three shots were fired. Shinault was hit twice in the chest and fell to his side on the ground.

Shinault shouted a warning to his partner who chased the shooter down an alley.

As the policeman lay dying, someone robbed George Shinault of his revolver.

The police identified a suspect—a black man named Bullock.

* * *

Assistant Attorney General Nugent Dodds was assigned by Hoover to recruit the grand jury witnesses and coordinate their testimony.

When they testified, both Ira Keck and Commissioner Reichelderfer essentially lied. Using the same exact language, they both said that Pelham Glassford had stated that "the police could no longer control the situation and it was necessary to call for troops."

As the grand jury hearings continued, Attorney General Mitchell called together the heads of all the intelligence agencies who had been involved with the BEF. These included the Secret Service, the Bureau of Investigation, and the War Department's Military Intelligence, as well as the U.S. District Attorney, the Metropolitan Police, and representatives from the Veterans Administration and the Immigration Service.

The various agencies were charged with finding evidence that the Communists and other criminal elements had gained control of the BEF.

None were able to do so.

J. Edgar Hoover was particularly unhelpful, perhaps because Herbert Hoover was on the ropes. The BI director provided only one report to the grand jury based upon hearsay that the appearance of the Renault tanks had discouraged the veterans from using weapons.

The president insisted that the BI search its fingerprint files to see which of the veterans who had been in Washington had prior criminal records. (Personal information from 5,091 veterans had been obtained when they applied for free fares home and 4,384 of them had agreed to be fingerprinted.)

The administration was elated to learn that 24.4% of those 4,384 men had arrest records. Extrapolated to the 30,000 or so people who had come through Washington as part of the BEF, this could mean that 7,300 were criminals.

Upon closer examination, the Bureau of Investigation determined that most of the arrests were for minor offenses like vagrancy and panhandling and only 829 had been convicted. Still, this provided Hurley and MacArthur with a hard statistic that they would use for years to come as "proof" that a large criminal element existed among the BEF.

The grand jury asked where the communists had been during the Army's attack upon the veterans. They were told that the 200 men under Emanuel Levin were in a meeting in the basement of the abandoned Pythian Temple from 9:00-11:00 p.m., singing revolutionary songs and completely unaware of what was transpiring.

When the communists emerged from their meeting and saw the flames from Anacostia Flats Levin had been ecstatic. Soon thereafter, most of the group were rounded up by the police and marched out of the District.

* * *

Major Dwight Eisenhower, the War Department's detail man, was assigned the delicate job of preparing MacArthur's official report on the Bonus March episode. Ike's thoroughness is evident in the carefully worded document that was issued on August 15 under MacArthur's name.

The report is replete with observations meant to color, spin, and excuse the War Department's handling of things. In describing Camp Marks, Eisenhower wrote of the "deplorable conditions under which these people were compelled to live, entailing an ever-present danger of disease and epidemic."

Eisenhower repeated the administration's unsubstantiated claim that by mid-July the later arrivals to Camp Marks were "of radical tendencies." He wrote that "Former leaders of the Bonus Army lost, to a considerable degree, the authority they had so far exercised…and the subversive element gradually gained in influence."

After expanding the five-minute attack by agitators at the Pennsylvania Avenue site into a full-blown riot involving large numbers of veterans, radicals and "hot-heads," Eisenhower further reconstructed events by writing that "The president promptly directed the Secretary of War to cooperate with the civil authorities in restoring law and order in the District of Columbia."

Eisenhower then delivered a coupe de grace to Walter Waters by writing (for MacArthur): "Unfortunately, the leader of the bonus movement had apparently lost all control of the situation. According to reports made to me, he had stated he was no longer able to handle his men and had withdrawn from the scene of operations. I vainly sought him during the entire operation so that I might utilize his influence toward pacification of the situation."

The Army chief's self-congratulatory report concluded with a three-page dissertation on how to put down civil disturbances, followed by this statement: "Within a few hours, a riot rapidly assuming alarming proportions was completely quelled."

* * *

By the middle of August the Khaki Shirts movement had lost its momentum. After Walter Waters failed to secure support from Governor Ritchie, coupled with the desertion of Waters' closest aides and his inability to start a second camp in West Virginia, Smedley Butler conceded that (the BEF) "has become a disorganized group that can neither aid their cause nor themselves."

Butler also noted that the 1932 Presidential election was only a few months off. The election could result in sudden, even violent change that could require a different, more militaristic Khaki Shirts organization. That, of course, would require a highly respected military leader, not a Walter Waters.

The Khaki Shirts' (former BEF) national office in Washington was closed in the fall of 1932.

* * *

The national convention of the American Legion took place in Portland, Oregon, on September 13 with Patrick Hurley as a featured speaker.

The day before the convention began, Attorney General William Mitchell released his official report on the Bonus March episode. Mitchell telegraphed a copy of the 25- page document to Hurley at the resort where he was staying. While factual in part, the section of the report that dealt with communist influence on the BEF was greatly distorted.

Mitchell's report concluded that "the Bonus Army brought into Washington the largest aggregation of criminals that had ever been assembled in the city at any one time." The report also criticized Pelham Glassford for failing to circulate detectives among the residents at Camp Marks or at the Pennsylvania Avenue eviction site.

Glassford retaliated again. The police superintendent called a press conference at which he identified by name the detectives who had been at both sites. He also released a copy of his confidential grand jury testimony in which Glassford had maintained that the character of the bonus marchers was deliberately misrepresented by Hoover's White House.

There was no communist conspiracy that warranted the use of such force, Glassford declared. Nor had the veterans been criminals. In fact, only twelve serious crimes were committed by veterans during the entire two months of their encampment. The city, he said, had actually been safer because of their presence.

Glassford's statements again made front-page news nationwide. Combined with the disbelief generated by Mitchell's report, a fresh wave of opposition to Herbert Hoover swept across the country. No criticism of the thin-skinned president was deemed too harsh. Editorials screamed that Hoover had dishonored the presidency and should be run out of Washington just as MacArthur had run out the veterans.

Glassford's statement was the last straw for many dispirited members of the Hoover Administration who began to admit publicly that the president was headed for certain defeat. Hoover's friend, journalist Mark Sullivan, predicted that the veterans' route would be the determining factor in the upcoming election.

In appreciation of his character and honesty, 55 of Washington's leading reporters and editors held a dinner in Pelham Glassford's honor at the National Press Club on September 17.

* * *

Eddie Gosnell, the "official" photographer of the BEF, was at the Pennsylvania Avenue eviction site when Hushka was shot. Gosnell took the graphic, close-up photographs of the fallen veteran within minutes of his killing that appeared in Hoover's grand jury report. Gosnell also took numerous photographs of the eviction "riot" and of the people who surrounded the building that day.

After the BEF was driven out, Gosnell remained in Washington in order to set up a photography business. In mid-October, the popular photographer was discovered dead in his photo lab.

An autopsy determined that Gosnell had drunk acid that was used for mixing chemicals needed to develop photographs. The official explanation was that Gosnell, an experienced photographer, had been drunk and had consumed the wrong container of liquid by mistake.

According to his many friends, Eddie Gosnell was a staunch non-drinker.

Whether by coincidence or purpose, two of the men closest to the shootings that launched the veteran's "riot" and justified the Army attack—first Officer George Shinault and now Eddie Gosnell—had now been killed under mysterious circumstances.

* * *

No longer welcomed at Don Zelaya's home and without any Khaki Shirt supporters to pay for his suite at the Ebbitt Hotel, Walter Waters sent Wilma back to Oregon and moved to a small apartment in New York City. The former commander was feeling his brief fame and future opportunities evaporate day by day. During his nine months at the Times Square Hotel, Waters never visited the former BEF men who had built a winter encampment under Riverside Drive.

Perhaps during his last weeks in New York City, Walter Waters finally caught a glimpse of Herbert Hoover as the former president walked along the sidewalk like any other man, on the way to his new rooms at the Waldorf-Astoria Hotel.

Small counterfeit "BEF" chapters sprung up in cities across the country still raising money for the "cause." In a desperate attempt to reclaim his fading influence, Waters used the last of his funds to launch a veterans' publication called the *BEF Crusader*. He printed 25,000 copies and took them to the New York State American Legion Convention. Only 5,000 copies were sold and the magazine was discontinued.

Waters was asked to make a speech at the New England American Legion convention where he was well-received but soon after that his money ran out. By September 1932, the former BEF commander could not even afford the train fare to return to Portland for the national American Legion convention where Patrick Hurley was scheduled to speak.

A conciliatory but defiant Hurley attended the convention despite threats to his life. During his speech, Hurley said, "Now you talk about who was there (at Camp Marks). Why some men were there for whom I would lay down my life tonight…(but) by the eternal…I recognize in this broad land of ours but one Army and that Army is the Army of the United States."

Even though his speech was drowned out numerous times by heckling from the 18,000 legionnaires, Hurley claimed to have been "well received." His friend Will Rogers reported that "Pat got away with his life, but no votes."

At the convention, the officer-dominated legionnaires reversed their former position and demanded that the veterans' bonus be paid at once. They also voted to censure Patrick Hurley but that was withdrawn after Hurley's loud protest. He was, after all, a former American Legion post commander.

* * *

Walter Waters got a break when the publisher John Day Company asked him to produce a book about the BEF. Waters and co-author William C. White spent several months in Florida during the winter of 1932 where they completed the manuscript for the book simply titled *BEF*.

The book featured a striking photo of Waters that conveyed his charismatic nature and included a sweeping if rambling defense of his actions. Within 18 months of MacArthur's attack on the veterans, nine books were written about the infamous event.

By April of 1933, the former BEF commander was working as a gas station attendant in Omaha, Nebraska. Two years later an interesting event occurred. As one of his final acts before President Roosevelt sent Douglas MacArthur to the Philippines, the Army chief arranged for a menial office job for the former BEF commander at the War Department.

* * *

Under pressure, Pelham Glassford resigned his duties as superintendent of police on October 20, 1932. As rationale for his dismissal, the commissioner pointed to unrest among the police due to Glassford's demotion of two officers who had gone around him, under orders by Patrick Hurley, to arrest Emanuel Leven and other Communists.

During his eleven months of service as police superintendent, Pelham Glassford had never personally met Herbert Hoover. In fact, Hoover had often confused the superintendent with Commissioner Herbert Crosby. Now Hoover's poor instinct in allowing the commissioners to fire the police superintendent just prior to the November elections proved to be the president's final undoing.

The first in a series of eight articles written by an angry and defensive Pelham Glassford appeared on the front page of 20 Hearst newspapers in major cities across the country on October 30, 1932. The series for which Glassford was paid $600 was arranged by his friend Cissy Patterson. In the last of the sensational articles, Glassford, the former reporter, contended that Hoover had set the troops upon the veterans in order to create a law-and-order issue for his campaign.

As part of his proof, Glassford noted that the troops had been standing on alert, just awaiting Hoover's order. The damning series concluded the day before the presidential election.

These widely read articles, coupled with personal appearances by Glassford in a number of major cities, drove the public's resentment of Herbert Hoover to a fever pitch and ensured not only the president's defeat, but that of his entire party.

Hoover made a last desperate radio broadcast on November 6 during which observers felt he was on the point of collapse. Insensitive to the end, Hoover cried, "Thank God you still have a government in Washington that knows how to deal with a mob!"

On election day, Cissy Patterson's *Washington Herald* ran the dramatic photo taken by Eddie Gosnell of Hushka lying dead on the ground.

* * *

Prior to his election, Roosevelt was told that he had the opportunity to "go down in history as the nation's greatest president."

"If I fail," FDR replied, "I shall be the last one."

In November, Herbert Hoover lost to Roosevelt by seven million votes and 158 members of the 72nd Congress were thrown out with him. Nearly 50% of the senators who had voted against the bonus lost their seats. It was the greatest clean sweep without any prior "trending away" from the dominant party of any election in American voting history.

Herbert Hoover left the White House as one of the most embittered of ex-presidents, the transition to FDR's Administration marked by rancor and a complete lack of cordiality. As he rode in the car with Roosevelt to the inauguration, Hoover refused to speak. He slumped in his seat and scowled the entire way. He sat on the inaugural platform at the Capitol in sullen bitterness as Roosevelt was sworn in, declared war against the Depression, and asked for sweeping power from the new Congress to institute the reforms needed to restore national prosperity.

Roosevelt entered office armed with Democratic majorities of 59 to 36 in the Senate and 313 to 117 in the House of Representatives.

During those anxious days, the newly elected candidate was forced to wait four months until March of the following year to be sworn in. Senate leader Burton Wheeler predicted, "Whatever laws the president thinks he may need to end the Depression, Congress will jump through a hoop to put them through." Congress began a special session on March 9 and proceeded to do just that. Fifteen major new laws were passed that gave Roosevelt virtual dictatorial authority over the country.

For Roosevelt, every moment counted. Just weeks before he took office, Adolph Hitler looked down in glee from his suite in Berlin as Nazi Storm Troopers marched through the Brandenburg Gates.

CHAPTER SIXTEEN

Final Chapters

It has been said that the course of history turns on the smallest of events. For many of those involved in the Anacostia Flats episode, this is certainly true.

Herbert Hoover anguished for years over the unfair blame assigned him as the result of Douglas MacArthur's attack on the veterans. That event, coupled with Hoover's lasting identity as the "Depression president," caused him to be disenfranchised by the public and by his political party. Hoover retired to the Waldorf-Astoria Hotel in New York to write his memoirs and was never again a deciding force in American life.

All of Patrick Hurley's trust fund investments were lost in the Depression. He managed to regain his fortune through shrewd oil negotiations and a surprising friendship that he forged with Franklin Roosevelt for whom he served as a roaming ambassador and, later, ambassador to China.

(When he resigned from that post, following Roosevelt's death, Hurley made a startling accusation of Communists in the State

Department—a charge that some historians believe opened the door to Joseph McCarthy's reign of terror soon afterwards.)

Shortly before his death, Roosevelt supposedly asked Hurley to be his vice presidential nominee during the upcoming election. Hurley claimed to have turned it down and the position (and the subsequent presidency) went instead to Harry Truman. Hurley lost in three close Senatorial bids—the last due to local radio broadcasts made by a vengeful Drew Pearson, reminding the voters of New Mexico of Hurley's role in the expulsion of the BEF. Hurley retired to Santa Fe where he reunited with his family before his death in 1963 at age 80.

His son Wilson became an Air Force pilot, a bank president and finally, today in his 80s, the successful landscape painter that he always wanted to be.

Douglas MacArthur stayed on as Army Chief of Staff under Franklin Roosevelt until he was made U.S. Advisor to the Philippines. A reluctant Dwight Eisenhower joined him there for five unhappy years until he returned to the U.S. to help prepare for World War II, where he was swiftly promoted by Army Chief of Staff George Marshall.

MacArthur's own subsequent achievements in World War II, his brilliant success as supreme commander in Japan, and his tragic misjudgments in Korea have all been well-documented.

MacArthur ran for the vice presidency in 1952, but he and Robert Taft lost the Republican nomination to Dwight Eisenhower after MacArthur made a shrill, bizarre speech during the convention. Ironically, Taft died soon after Eisenhower took office. Had circumstances been different, MacArthur—like Hurley before him—could have inherited the presidency. MacArthur died on January 26, 1964, in New York. Neither Eisenhower nor Truman attended his massive funeral.

Dwight Eisenhower's attention to detail and his ability to work with difficult people were essential qualities when he was made supreme commander by George Marshall during World War II. Following brief post-war service with NATO and Columbia University, Ike became one of America's most popular presidents. He oversaw the end of the Korean War, the launch of America's space program, the paving of 41,000 miles of super highways, inoculation programs to end childhood diseases and the rules of engagement for the Cold War. After a less eventful second term he and Mami retired to Gettysburg, Pennsylvania, where Ike died on March 28, 1969.

Young Gene Vidal changed his first name to Gore at age 14 and became one of America's most prolific authors. His body of work shows a lifelong fascination with Depression-era Washington, D.C.

George Patton's impetuous nature created much controversy during his World War II commands. At one point he was disciplined and pulled out of combat by his commanding officer and old friend, Dwight Eisenhower. Once back in battle, however, Patton played a key role in the decisive defeat of Hitler's troops at the Battle of the Bulge.

After the war's end, on the day before his return home for Christmas leave, Patton's chauffeured limousine collided with a U.S. Army truck in Germany. Patton's neck was broken and he was paralyzed. He died on December 21, 1945, his faithful wife Bea by his side.

Following the 1932 elections, Pelham Glassford turned down the position of baseball commissioner and briefly served as chief of police in Phoenix, Arizona. He failed in a bid for Congress then re-enlisted in the Army where he served as Chief of Internal Security for the Provost Marshall General during World War II, helping to oversee the internment of Japanese-Americans in the infamous relocation camps.

Glassford retired to a golf course home in Laguna Beach, California, with his second wife in 1943. He was briefly active in the "Draft MacArthur" movement in 1948. In 1951 he authored a response to a Reader's Digest article that suggested that Communists were behind the Bonus Army. In his rebuttal, Glassford wrote:

"An incident involving violence was necessary in order to justify calling out the troops which for several weeks had been in training."

Walter Waters left his clerical job at the War Department after less than a month. He enlisted in the Navy during WWII and then retired with Wilma to Nevada where he wrote poetry.

In 1959 there was a one-line obituary in a Walla Walla, Washington, newspaper that noted the passing of a "Walter W. Waters."

THE END

CHAPTER NOTES

Chapter One
The Witness

9.   The witness sat: R.J.W., "Defeat of the Bonus Marchers,"
       Progressive America, by J.W., Unit 6, p. 676 n/d; Martin
       Blumenson, *The Patton Papers*, (Boston: Houghton Mifflin Co.,
       19 by 72), p. 954.

       At first glance: William Manchester, *The Glory and the Dream*
       (Bantam Books, 1975), p. 36.

10.   Nothing. I am nothing: *Progressive America*, pp. 677-78.

       Angelo forged ahead: Talcott Powell, *Tattered Banners* (New
       York: Harcourt, Brace & Co., 1933), pp. 223-24.

11.   For more than two years: Manchester, *The Glory and the Dream*,
       pp. 35-36.

12.   Despite such widespread: Ibid, p. 39.

Two million people were on the road: Ibid, pp. 17-19.

The guards were often members: Studs Terkel, *Hard Times* (New York: Pocket Books, 1970), p. 47.

In Washington, D.C., Patrick Hurley: Ibid, p. 59.

Tall, robust: Allen, Pearson, *More Merry-Go-Round* (New York: Liveright, Inc., 1932), p. 156; 161.

...complex and ill-tempered: Dwight D. Eisenhower, ed. Daniel D. Holt and James W. Leyerzapf, *Eisenhower: the Pre-War Diaries and Selected Papers, 1905-1941* (Baltimore: The Johns Hopkins University Press, 1998), p. 228

13.   ...young men in their teens: Powell, p. 172.

    ...that was passed into law: Geoffrey Perret, *Old Soldiers Never Die* (Massachusetts: Adams Media Corp., 1996) p. 76.

14.   ...the plaza squares: Roger Daniels, *The Bonus March* (Connecticut: Greenwood Publishing Corp., 1971), pp. 74-75.

    That spring had brought: Manchester, *The Glory and the Dream*, p. 42.

    Alman's activism: Walter W. Waters and William White, BEF (New York: John Day & Co., 1933), p.15.

    It is time: Jack Douglas, *Veterans on the March* (Workers Library Publishers, 1934), p. 26.

    His speech: Waters and White, pp. 13-15

15. Born in 1898: Waters & White, p. 4.

The next year: Daniels, p. 77; Waters and White, 4.

In Great Britainonly six weeks: Meirion & Susie Harries, *The Last Days of Innocence* (New York: Random House, 1997), p. 215.

The job faced by Waters: Laurence Stallings, *The Doughboys* (New York: Harper & Row Publishers, 1973), pp 113; 173.

Within the year: Daniels, 77.

16. During this time: Harries, pp. 400-01.

…airplanes with synchronized: Richard Hollian, *Rise of the Fighter Aircraft*, 1914-1916 (National Aviation Publishing. 1984), pp. 45; 59.

As a medic: Stallings, p. 186.

Upon his return home: Waters and White, pp. 4-5.

"Eager to begin completely anew": Ibid, p. 6.

17. Wilma and "Bill": Daniels, p. 78.

By December of 1931: Waters and White, p. 6.; Douglas, p. 27

Within a few days, 250 men: Ibid, p. 26.

Chapter Two
Springtime in Washington

18. The president had just addressed: interview with Richard Baker, Historian of the Senate, May 2000.

19. In the meantime: Arthur M. Schlesinger, Jr., *The Crisis of the Old Order* (Boston: Houghton Mifflin Co., 1957), p. 1

     The first elected office: Robert Allen and Drew Pearson (anonymous), *Washington Merry-Go-Round* (New York: Horace Liveright, Inc., 1931), p. 53

20. Most things of importance: Manchester, The Glory and the Dream, p. 45.

     Wright Patman: Studs Terkel, *Hard Times* (New York: Pocket Books, 1970), p. 325.

     ...and a pyramid of holding companies: John Kenneth Galbraith, "Why the Money Stopped," *A Sense of History, the Best Writing from the Pages of American Heritage* (Boston: Houghton Mifflin Co., 1985), p. 672.

     Even when taxes seemed to be unavoidable: Schlesinger, p. 253.

     The veterans bonus bill: Daniels, p. 53.

     One person: Manchester, *The Glory and the Dream*, p. 27.

21. The bonus had been thought up: Daniels, p. 4.

     Bonuses for soldiers: Powell, pp. 4-5.

During 1932, Southern Pacific: Manchester, *The Glory and the Dream*, p. 21.

After two days of stalemate: Walter W. Waters and William White, *BEF* (New York: John Day & Co., 1933), pp. 23-26.

22.   It was 6 p.m. on May 12, 1932: Douglas, p. 27.

...chances for H.R. 1: Lisio, p. 49.

...other major legislation: Ibid, p. 46.

Andrew Mellon was an emaciated: Allen and Pearson, p. 273.

23.   During twelve years: Ibid, p. 244; Schlesinger, p. 253

Wright Patman called Mellon: Daniels, pp. 49-50

Mellon pulled the whistle: Harris Gaylord Warren, *Herbert Hoover and the Great Depression* (New York: W.W. Norton & Co., 1967), p. 230.

An avid collector: Irving Bernstein, *The Lean Years* (Baltimore: Penguin Books, 1966), p. 313.

Patman put the dour Mellon: Terkel, pp. 326-27.

...who had become an embarrassment: Allen and Pearson, *More Merry-Go-Round* (New York: Liveright, Inc., 1932), pp. 34-35.

Hoover was determined: Samuel Hopkins Adams, "The Timely Death of President Harding" (*The Aspirin Age*, 1919-1941, 1949), as reprinted in *Katharine Graham's Washington*, p.482: "Mr. Secretary, there's a bad scandal brewing..."

The timing of Mellon's ouster: Daniels, p. 35, 44.

24.   ...of the 500,000 people who resided: Arthur Herman, *Joseph McCarthy* (New York: The Free Press, 2000), p. 42.

... paid an average of $3,600 a year: Jay Franklin, "Main Street on Potomac," *Katharine Graham's Washington* (New York: Alfred A. Knopf, 2002), p. 24.

While some 18,000 residents: David Brinkley, *Washington Goes to War* (New York: Alfred A. Knopf, 1988), p. 19.

Members of Congress enjoyed: Allen and Pearson, *More Merry-Go-Round* (New York: Liveright, Inc., 1932), p. 185.

During the depression: Ibid, p. 431.

Fueled by the growing Democratic revival: Allen and Pearson, *Washington Merry-Go-Round*, p. 185.

Chapter Three
The Secretary of War

26.   Then in 1917: John Keegan, *The First World War* (New York: Alfred A. Knopf, 1999), p. 373.

When the survivors returned: Meirion & Susie Harries, *The Last Days of Innocence* (New York: Random House, 1997), p. 453.

27.   The Secretary of War: William Manchester, *The Glory and the Dream* (Bantam Books, 1975), p. 7.

The Oregon veterans' advance man: Jack Douglas, *Veterans on the March* (Workers Library Publishers, 1934), p. 28; Walter W. Waters and William White, *BEF* (New York: John Day & Co., 1933), p. 27.

... where they confronted: Douglas, p. 28.

... arrested by the local police: Walter W. Waters and William White, *BEF* (New York: John Day & Co., 1933), p. 27-28.

Quiet-mannered George Alman: Donald J. Lisio, *The President and Protest* (New York: Fordham University Press, 1994), p. 102.

28. His father Pierce: Telephone interview with Wilson Hurley, March 6, 2000; Parker LaMoore, *Pat Hurley: The Story of an American* (New York: Brewer, Warren & Putnam., 1932), p. 10.

29. One of the few bright spots: LaMoore, pp. 171-20.

When farming failed: Don Lohbeck, *Patrick J. Hurley* (Chicago: Henry Regnery Co., 1953), p. 19.

The year that Patrick turned thirteen: telephone interview with Wilson Hurley, June, 2000

Following this tragedy: Buhite, p. 9.

While working on a ranch: LaMoore, pp. 23-25

30. Believing that he was an Indian: Telephone interview with Wilson Hurley, June 2000.

Armed with his law degree: Lohbeck, p. 39

Fortunes were being made: Ibid, p. 47.

When the United States entered World War I: Lohbeck, pp. 70-73.

On his return to the states: Ibid, p. 75.

"Why I don't even know you!": Telephone interview with Wilson Hurley, July, 2000.

31.   The newlyweds returned: LaMoore, pp. 78-79.

When Hoover formed: Lohbeck, p. 83.

...under Secretary James Good: Buhite, p. 41.

In the spring of 1929: LaMoore, p. 138.

A few months later: Telephone interview with Wilson Hurley, June, 2000.

Upon Good's death: Lohbeck, pp. 85-86.

...one of Hoover's closest aids: Robert Allen, Drew Pearson (anonymous), *More Merry-Go-Round* (New York: Liveright, Inc., 1932), p. 138.

32.   Because Herbert Hoover: Roger Daniels, *The Bonus March* (Connecticut: Greenwood Publishing Corp., 1971), p. 132; Robert Allen, Drew Pearson (anonymous), More Merry-Go-Round (New York: Liveright, Inc., 1932), p. 211.

33.   Hurley had briefly seen the famous soldier: Telephone interview with Wilson Hurley, July, 2000.

The bantam Pershing resented: Geoffrey Perret, *Old Soldiers Never Die* (Massachusetts: Adams Media Corp, 1996), p. 127

The final straw: William Manchester, *American Caesar* (Boston: Little, Brown & Co., 1978), pp. 121-24.

34.   After three years: Manchester, *American Caesar*, p. 134.

Upon their return: Allen and Pearson, *More Merry-Go-Round*, p. 194.

MacArthur was next appointed: Ibid, pp. 136-141.

Instead MacArthur played up: LaMoore, pp. 117-118.

35.   ...who just recently had criticized: Allen and Pearson, *More Merry-Go-Round*, p.   167.

When Hurley put MacArthur's name forward: Perret, p. 143; Lohbeck, p. 101.

Chapter Four
Battle of the B&O

36.   Although he worked diligently: Dwight D. Eisenhower, *At Ease* (New York, Doubleday & Company, 1967), p. 195.

It was Eisenhower's misfortune: Robert Allen and Drew Pearson (anonymous), *More Merry-Go-Round* (New York: Liveright, Inc., 1932), pp. 189-90.

An outstanding football player: Merle Miller, *Ike the Soldier* (New York: G. P. Putnam's Sons, 1987, pp. 30-35.

The Eisenhowers lived: Ibid, p. 248; Susan Eisenhower, *Mrs. Ike* (New York: Farrar, Straus and Giroux, 1996), p. 122.

37. From Leavenworth: Ibid, 169.

Eisenhower was next assigned: Ibid, 186.

In 1928, Eisenhower: Allen and Pearson, 188; Dwight D. Eisenhower, 211-23; 216.

…meticulous preparation: Miller, p. 246.

38. Veterans from an earlier war: Walter W. Waters and William White, *BEF* (New York: John Day & Co., 1933), pp. 39-40; Roger Daniels, *The Bonus March* (Connecticut: Greenwood Publishing Corp., 1971), p. 80.

Returned to Washington: Geoffrey Perret, *Old Soldiers Never Die* (Massachusetts: Adams Media Corp, 1996), p. 149; : Don Lohbeck, *Patrick J. Hurley* (Chicago: Henry Regnery Co., 1953), p. 98.

(The report never made it): Oral history interview: Raymond Henle with General Dwight D. Eisenhower, July 13, 1967: Gettysburg, Pennsylvania. Herbert Hoover Presidential Library, West Branch, Iowa.

Although he had been an average student: Miller, pp. 249, 257.

This new assignment was important and enjoyable: Interview with Wilson Hurley, July, 2000.

39. Eisenhower worked diligently: Ibid.

MacArthur placed Ike: Dwight D. Eisenhower, 213.

"About 49 years old...": Dwight D. Eisenhower, ed. Daniel D. Holt and James W. Leyerzapf, *Eisenhower: the Pre-War Diaries and Selected Papers, 1905-1941* (Baltimore: The Johns Hopkins University Press, 1998), p. 228.

40.   The week before: Arthur M. Schlesinger, Jr., *The Crisis of the Old Order* (Boston: Houghton Mifflin Co., 1957), pp. 242-43.

(King Tut spent): Presidential Pet Museum, Lothian, MD, "President Herbert Clark Hoover," 2002.

...including Patrick Hurley: Parker LaMoore, *Pat Hurley: The Story of an American* (New York: Brewer, Warren & Putnam, 1932), p. 138.

... celebrated as a hero: Irving Bernstein, *The Lean Years* (Baltimore: Penguin Books, 1966), p. 248.

41.   In private: Arthur Krock, *Memoirs* (New York: Funk and Wagnalls, 1968), p. 122.

A joke making the rounds: Schlesinger, p. 245.

Another rumor claimed: William Manchester, *The Glory and the Dream* (Bantam Books, 1975), p. 23.

One evening: Interview with Wilson Hurley, May 9, 2000.

Patrick Hurley received a letter: Schlesinger, p. 179.

42.   After Woods resigned in frustration: Allen and Pearson, p. 39.

Gifford was subsequently called to appear: Schlesinger, p. 173; Harris Gaylord Warren, *Herbert Hoover and the Great Depression* (New York: W. W. Norton & Co., 1967), p. 201.

... Waters' transportation committee: Waters and White, pp. 42-44..

43. Waters arranged with: Waters and White, pp. 46-56.

44. Willard appealed for local help: Daniels, p. 81.

For the first time in his life: Ibid, p. 80.

Next in line: Ibid, pp. 30; 66.

45. At the top of this pyramid: Robert S. Allen and Drew Pearson, "Boiled Bosoms, "*Katharine Graham's Washington* (New York: Alfred A. Knopf, 2002), p. 127.

While not a classic beauty: Carol Felsenthal, *Alice Roosevelt Longworth* (New York: G.P. Putnam's Sons, 1988), p. 61.

Alice, the daughter of Teddy Roosevelt: Margaret Truman, *First Ladies* (New York: Random House, 1995), p. 313

One evening a mentally ill man: Ibid, p. 100.

Alice rejected her cousin: Gore Vidal, *The Second American Revolution* (New York: Random House, 1976), p. 210.

The young couple married: Felsenthal, p. 105.

46. When Alice's cousin Franklin came to town: Felsenthal, p. 137.

...pulled his blue Harley-Davidson motorcycle: Daniels, 90.

Attending this particular meeting: Ibid, 88.

47. Glassford had already handled: Donald J. Lisio, *The President and Protest* (New York: Fordham University Press, 1994), pp. 61-62.

Crosby told him: Jack Douglas, *Veterans on the March* (Workers Library Publishers, 1934), p. 36.

Acting on behalf of the commissioners: Ibid, p. 39

The city had long been managed: Lisio, p. 53; Robert S. Allen and Drew Pearson, "The Capital Underworld,"*Katharine Graham's Washington* (New York: Alfred A. Knopf, 2002), p. 204.

48. The job of reforming: Daniels, p. 88.

... a pair of anonymous authors: Oliver Pilat, *Drew Pearson* (New York: Harper's Magazine Press, 1973), 125, 127.

49. Hurley then used his influence: Ibid, 131; "More Merry Go Round," *Time Magazine*, September 19, 1932.

Later that year: Drew Pearson, edited by Tyler Abell, *Drew Pearson Diaries 1949-59* (New York: Holt, Rinehart and Winston, 1974), p. 228.

...Pearson and Allen began the infamous: Pilat, p. 133.

By 1949 Pearson could name: Abell, pp. 53-54.

Drew Pearson never forgot an enemy: Russell D. Buhite, *Patrick J. Hurley and American Foreign Policy* (Cornell University Press, 1973), p. 321.

50.	Glassford was made the youngest: Lisio, p. 52

	After the war: Allen and Pearson, p. 28.

	After his father died suddenly: Lisio, p. 53.

	Glassford visited the District office: Paul Dickson and Thomas B. Allen, *The Bonus Army* (Walker & Co., 2004), p. 43.

	Glassford accepted the position: Bernstein, p. 443.

51.	As Glassford readily admitted: Daniels, p. 89.

	Glassford enjoyed living in Washington: Miller, P. 263

	...the 6'3 tall, handsome general: Allen and Pearson, p. 28.

	Glassford's watercolors: Daniels, p. 90.
	The Oregon veterans: Ibid, p. 81.

	"I'm through." :Douglas, p. 32.

52.	The veterans arrived in Caseyville: Waters and White, pp. 52-56.

	Frustrated by the situation: Douglas, p. 34.

	There at Washington, Indiana: Waters and White, pp. 56-57.

	Pelham Glassford met early: "MacArthur and the Bonus Army," Pelham D. Glassford. Article accompanied letter to Joseph Choate, May 14, 1948. Pelham Glassford Collection, University of California, Los Angeles, Young Research Library, Box 14: Folder 4.

53.   But the wily MacArthur...Paul Dickson and Thomas B. Allen, *The Bonus Army* (Walker & Co., 2004), pp. 73-74.

       Although they opened: Schlesinger, p. 222.

       Now the biggest opportunity of all: Warren, p. 60.

       Party leader Emanuel Levin: Lisio, p. 117.

54.   Browder demanded to know: Daniels, p. 109; Lohbeck, p. 105.

       ...at 905 Eye Street: Douglas, p. 87.

Chapter Five
The Blind Opponent

55.   The senator was sightless: Gore Vidal, *Palimpsest* (New York, Random House, 1995), p. 49.

       Gore worked with a young Patrick Hurley: Don Lohbeck, *Patrick J. Hurley* (Chicago: Henry Regnery Co., 1953), p. 56-59.

56.   The blind senator lived with his wife: Vidal, 43.

       ...a former West Point football star: Ibid, 12, 41.

       ...he was well-acquainted: Fred Kaplan, *Gore Vidal* (New York: Doubleday, 1999), 28-29.

       When he was not spending hours: Vidal, 57.

57.   The sexually adventurous Nina: Vidal, 14.

...romancing his co-worker: Kaplan, 52.

He formed an airmail company: Ibid, pp. 50-51.

It went instead to a rival airline: Robert S. Allen and Drew Pearson, *Washington Merry-Go-Round* (New York: Horace Liveright Co., 1931), p. 258.

Among the first to arrive: Jack Douglas, *Veterans on the March* (Workers Library Publishers, 1934), p. 48.

58. In this picturesque Ohio town: Walter W. Waters and William White, *BEF* (New York: John Day & Co., 1933), pp. 59-60.

59. ...understandably, since the president of France: *Time Capsule/ 1932* (New York, Time-Life Books, 1968), p. 99, 108.

The Portland veterans: Waters and White, p. 61.

Waters and his men: Douglas, p. 39.

60. ...whose only prior: Allen and Pearson, pp. 52-53.

While a young boy: Allen and Pearson, pp. 69-70.

Others believed that Hoover's: Arthur M. Schlesinger, Jr., *The Crisis of the Old Order* (Boston: Houghton Mifflin Co., 1957), p. 52.

As a young man in the Harding Administration: Ibid.

61. Even at age 38: Waters and White, pp. 62-64.

62. With the Depression: Robert Allen and Drew Pearson (anonymous), *More Merry-Go-Round* (New York: Liveright, Inc., 1932), p. 201; Geoffrey Perret, *Old Soldiers Never Die* (Massachusetts: Adams Media Corp, 1996), p. 151.

Missouri Democrat Ross Collins: Allen and Pearson, pp. 201-204.

Hurley had converted: Interview with Wilson Hurley, July, 2000.

63. Walter Waters, the unintended: Waters and White, pp. 62-64.

64. Gene had recently discovered: Gore Vidal, *The Second American Revolution* (New York: Random House, 1976), p. 56; Kaplan, p. 48.

65. J. Edgar Hoover got his start: Richard Powers, *Secrecy and Power: The Life of J. Edgar Hoover* (New York, The Free Press, 1987), pp. 55, 151.

In Detroit and New York City: Irving Bernstein, *The Lean Years* (Baltimore: Penguin Books, 1966), [[. 421-22; 437.

66. Pelham Glassford saw: Douglas, p. 55.

The next morning he brought: Waters and White, p. 65.

Glassford informed Waters that: Douglas, p. 49; Roger Daniels, *The Bonus March* (Connecticut: Greenwood Publishing Corp., 1971), pp. 96-97.

When Herbert Hoover campaigned: Telephone interview with Wilson Hurley, March 9, 2000.

67. Herbert Hoover toweled: Parker LaMoore, *Pat Hurley: The Story of an American* (New York: Brewer, Warren & Putnam., 1932), p. 138.

68. One early June morning Glassford ushered: Douglas, p. 63; Letter from Harold Foulkrod to Pelham Glassford, August 4, 1932. Pelham Glassford Collection, U.C.L.A., Box 14: Folder 7.

69. This gave Eisenhower: Oliver Pilat, *Drew Pearson* (New York: Harper's Magazine Press, 1973), p. 226.

   For nearly 50 years: "The Guns of Anacostia," *Washington Post*, Section F-1, March 12, 2000.

70. The legendary Navy Yard Commander John Dahlgren: "The Waterline," Comprint Military Publications, July 26, 2002.

   Ever the military strategist: Waters and White, p. 82.

   Anacostia Flats was fronted: John D. Weaver, *Another Such Victory* (New York: Viking Press, 1948), p. 37.

71. Across the drawbridge: Daniels, p. 101.

   Glassford detailed these advantages…Paul Dickson and Thomas B. Allen, *The Bonus Army* (Walker & Co., 2004), p. 94.

   Grant and MacArthur: William Manchester, *American Caesar* (New York: Little, Brown & Co., 1978), p. 53; Allen and Pearson, *More Merry-Go-Round*, p. 207.

72. But Anacostia Flats had not been chosen for comfort: Daniels, p. 102.

Most likely unknown: Louise Daniel Hutchinson, *The Anacostia Story* (Washington, D.C.: Smithsonian Institution Press, 1977), p. 5.

Chapter Six
Welcome to Anacostia Flats

73.   Nearly 1,000 veterans preceded: "Bonus Trek Started Here in May" (*Evening Star*, July 29, 1932), p. A-10.

Walter Waters was either…Paul Dickson and Thomas B. Allen, *The Bonus Army* (Walker & Co., 2004), p. 85; Jack Douglas, *Veterans on the March* (Workers Library Publishers, 1934), pp. 58-59.

Pelham Glassford asked: Ibid, pp. 51-52

74.   Glassford convinced a friend: Roger Daniels, *The Bonus March* (Connecticut: Greenwood Publishing Corp., 1971), p. 98.

When funds ran low: Talcott Powell, *Tattered Banners* (New York: Harcourt, Brace & Co., 1933), p. 232.

Finally overwhelmed by the number: Walter W. Waters and William White, *BEF* (New York: John Day & Co., 1933), pp.105-06.

Almost every shack: John Henry Bartlett, *The Bonus March and the New Deal* (Donohue & Co., 1937), p. 63.

After Glassford sent him a scolding telegram: Glassford to Hurley, May 30, 1932: "Failure of the War Department to furnish…;" Pelham Glassford Collection, U.C.L.A., Box #48: Folder #1.

Sanitation soon became an issue: Douglas, p. 140.

Walter Waters later remarked…Paul Dickson and Thomas B. Allen, *The Bonus Army* (Walker & Co., 2004), p. 107.

75.   After their temporary homes: Ibid, p. 133.

The veterans were visited: Waters and W hite, p. 106.

Impressed by his kindness: Bartlett, p. 120; Daniels, p. 101.

Each new arrival: Donald J. Lisio, *The President and Protest* (New York: Fordham University Press, 1994), p. 93; Waters and White, pp. 67-68.

76.   If a man had no papers: Daniels, p. 106.
The final enrollment requirement: Waters and White, p. 92.

When they were discovered: Douglas, p. 85.

During the eight weeks: Lisio, p. xv; Russell D. Buhite, *Patrick J. Hurley and American Foreign Policy* (Ithica, N.Y.: Cornell University Press, 1973), p. 55.

Once accepted into camp: Waters and White, p. 67.

77.   Glassford came to the camp: Handwritten recollection written on BEF stationary by Pelham Glassford, p. 3. Pelham Glassford Collection, U.C.L.A., Box #14: Folder #2.

Most were from: Waters and White, pp. 112-22.

Walter Waters also met: Bartlett, p. 115

…began to swelter: Ibid, p. 109.

Another involved a convoluted: Robert S. Allen and Drew Pearson (anonymous), *More Merry-Go-Round* (New York: Liveright, Inc., 1932), pp. 179-182.

79.   Donations of food and money: Daniels, 113, 104.

Clark Griffith: Douglas, p. 76.

80.   One elderly woman wrote: Waters and White, p. 141.

Some letters included suggestions: Weaver, p. 142, 187.

There were so many requests: Ibid, p. 112.

81.   President Hoover still refused: Ibid, p. 82.

But when Hoover heard: Lisio, pp. 80-81

Activity surrounding HR 1: Waters & White, pp. 80-81.

Waters appointed Harold Foulkrod: Douglas, p. 59.

82.   Their approach was blunt: Lisio, p. 99.

The next morning: Douglas, p. 96.

The famed populist Will Rogers said: (delete "MacArthur" reference)Pelham D. Glassford. P. 3. Article accompanied letter to Joseph Choate, May 14, 1948. Pelham Glassford Collection, University of California, Los Angeles, Young Research Library, Box 14: Folder 4.

Scores of veterans also watched hawk-like: Lisio, p. 98.

Six of the thirty-four Republicans: Ibid, p. 99.

83. Emanuel Levin's office on Eye Street: Daniels p. 108.

85. In addition to Camp Marks: Lisio, p. 76.

   ... approximately 30,000: Daniels, p. 204.

   As reporter Tom Henry wrote: Ibid, p. 276.

86. Pelham Glassford was in a no-win: Glassford handwritten recollection, p. 5.

87. On June 8 he received: Memorandum George Paddock to Patrick Hurley, June 6, 7, 8, 1932. Patrick Hurley Collection, University of Oklahoma, Box 48: Folder #2.

88. Two of Hurley's young children: Telephone interview with Wilson Hurley, October, 2000.

89. More fuel: Lisio, p. 87.

   Soon afterwards Allen Straight: Ibid, p. 95.

   A similar report came from: Douglas, p. 101.

   This warning: Lisio, p. 90.

90. With the Communists reportedly: Daniels, p. 112.

   Waters now had a personal adjutant: Waters and White, pp. 66-67.

   To further maintain control: Irving Bernstein, *The Lean Years* (Baltimore: Penguin Books, 1966), p. 475.

Although the stated purpose of these agents: Waters & White, p. 66.

91. The relationship between: Ibid, p. 73.

At their meeting: Douglas, p. 98.

When they were told of this plan: Lisio, pp. 104-05.

92. When he visited Camp Marks: Ibid, p. 101; Waters & White, p. 83; Douglas, p.101.

It was dusk when the parade started: Douglas, p. 101

93. Now even though the oldest: Waters & White, pp. 83-85.

The signs that the marchers carried: Weaver, p. 57; Douglas, p. 109.

...Hurley's War Department had issued : Waters and White, p. 75.

In Gibbons' words: Douglas, p. 106.

94. The next morning: Ibid, p. 112.

Chapter Seven
Learning to Salute

95. ...a half-demolished: Roger Daniels, *The Bonus March* (Connecticut: Greenwood Publishing Corp., 1971), p.140.

...the largest secondary camp: John Henry Bartlett, *The Bonus March and the New Deal* (Donohue & Co., 1937), p. 88; "News from Camp Bartlett," (*The BEF News*, July 27, 1932), p. 2.

96.   Bartlett several times told Waters: Ibid, pp. 20-22.

Of the six: Ralph G. Martin, *Cissy* (New York: Simon and Schuster, 1978), p. 315, 319.

Further complicating things: Ibid, p. 176.

97.   The treasury of the BEF: Jack Douglas, *Veterans on the March* (Workers Library Publishers, 1934), p. 116.

For a few days in early June: Walter W. Waters and William White, *BEF* (New York: John Day & Co., 1933), p. 87.

Some veterans did leave: Douglas, p. 149.

98.   Another new arrival was : Douglas, p. 69.

It was Angelo, Patton and 15 men: Martin Blumenson, *The Patton Papers*, 1885-1940 (Boston: Houghton Mifflin Co., 1972), pp.764-66; Carlo D'este, *Patton, A Genius for War* (New York: HarperCollins Publishers, 1995), p. 261.

99.   As he walked to his father's office: Telephone interview with Wilson Hurley, June, 2000.

100.   Charles Frederick Lincoln: Douglas, p. 67.

Various ways to take money: Bartlett, p. 109.

101.   Many congressmen came: Bartlett, p. 48.

Mark Sullivan, a reporter: Donald J. Lisio, *The President and Protest* (New York: Fordham University Press, 1994), p. 169.

102. The debate was all for show: Ibid, p. 93.

Even should a bonus bill pass the Senate: Daniels, p. 115.

…the death of Representative Edward Eslick: Waters and White, p. 88.

Speaker John Nance Garner: Ibid, p. 145.

Following the vote: Daniels, p. 117.

103. As they made their way to the Senate galleries: "Works of Art in the Capitol Complex," The Architecture of the Capitol, (Web Site: Office of the Curator, June 2002).

…the American history murals of Constantino Brumidi: Harold Helfer, "The Case of the Forgotten Genius": *Coronet*, April, 1952.

104. The social lions spoke: Telephone interview with Wilson Hurley, March 9, 2000.

Cabinet positions in 1932: Robert S. Allen and Drew Pearson (anonymous), *More Merry-Go-Round* (New York: Liveright, Inc., 1932), pp. 161, 166, 167.

They were especially busy: Katharine Graham, *Katharine Graham's Washington* (New York: Alfred A. Knopf, 2002), p. 68.

For the extroverted and ambitious Patrick Hurley: Telephone interviews with Wilson Hurley, June and August, 2000.

The Hurleys' former neighbors: Katharine Graham, *Personal History* (New York: Alfred A. Knopf, 1997), pp. 48, 55-56.

105. Ruth Hurley was also appalled: Ibid.

On June 16 the rain finally stopped: Douglas, pp. 137-38.

106. Inside the Senate chambers: Waters and White, p. 145.

Elmer Thomas of Oklahoma: Ibid, p. 146; Douglas, p. 151.

Prior to the Senate debate: Douglas, p. 97.

107. After Waters climbed down: Waters and White, p. 147.

Just before noon: Douglas, p. 151.

109. Within the Capitol: Ibid.

Dawe had served: Arthur M. Schlesinger, Jr., *The Crisis of the Old Order* (Boston: Houghton Mifflin Co., 1957), p. 238; Waters and White, p. 124.

Walter Waters stood: Ibid, p. 149.

110. At his estate: Fred Kaplan, *Gore Vidal* (New York: doubleday, 1999), p. 46.

When the car approached: Ibid, p. 48.

…the senators rehashed: Daniels, pp. 119-21.

111. Senator Brookhard emerged: Waters and White, p. 147; Douglas, p. 152.

By eight-thirty it was dark: Ibid, 149-50; Douglas, 153.

From time to time: Waters & White, pp. 148-49.

112.   Conservative Democrat Burton Wheeler: Daniels, p. 119.

An occcasional current of anger: Douglas, p. 153.

...and make a brief speech: Bartlett, p. 97.

113.   As the night wore on: Douglas, p. 153-54.

"This is only a temporary set-back": Waters and W hite, pp. 151-52.

A dozen reporters: Daniels, p. 121.

Elsie Robinson: Douglas, p. 156.

114.   Pelham Glassford watched with pride: Handwritten recollection written on BEF stationary by Pelham Glassford, p. 8. Pelham Glassford Collection, U.C.L.A., Box #14: Folder #2.

Chapter Eight
Aftermath

115.   The morning after: Walter W. Waters and William White, BEF (New York: John Day & Co., 1933), p. 152.

Soon after this episode: Roger Daniels, *The Bonus March* (Connecticut: Greenwood Publishing Corp., 1971), p. 105.

... and helped pay for: Receipt of money received from Zelaya to Glassford dated October 3, 1932. Pelham Glassford Collection, U.C.L.A. Young Library, Box #15: Folder #1.

116. Those who did fall out: Jack Douglas, *Veterans on the March* (Workers Library Publishers, 1934), p. 157.

118. Only three governors responded: Donald J. Lisio, *The President and Protest* (New York: Fordham University Press, 1994), p. 84; Douglas, p. 143.

Glassford placed another call to Daniel Willard: Waters and White, pp. 159-60.

President Hoover finally: Ibid, p. 161; John Henry Bartlett, *The Bonus March and the New Deal* (Donohue & Co., 1937), p. 95.

Glassford printed flyers: Roger Daniels, *The Bonus March* (Connecticut: Greenwood Publishing Corp., 1971), p. 125.

These offers led: Bartlett, p. 47.

119. Cissy Patterson and her best friend: Evalyn Walsh McLean, "Depression Days," *Katharine Graham's Washington* (New York: Alfred A. Knopf, 2002), pp. 293-96.

Then in April: "More Sideshow," *Time Magazine*, May 16, 1932.

Even Evalyn's fabulous 75-acre estate: David Brinkley, *Washington Goes to War*, New York: Alfred A. Knopf, 1988.), p. 159.

...site of a former monastery: Paul Dickson and Thomas B. Allen, *The Bonus Army* (Walker & Co., 2004), p. 97.

120. This was not the first time that Cissy: Ralph G. Martin, Cissy (New York: Simon and Schuster, 1978), p. 315-16.

The two friends drove: Ibid, p. 318.

... dubbed "The Hut": Paul Dickson and Thomas B. Allen, The Bonus Army (New York: Walker & Company, 2004), p. 111.

The two had met as geology majors: Margaret Truman, First Ladies (New York: Random House, 1995), p. 264.

121. The Hoovers were both intellectuals: Ibid, p. 269.

(Few knew that...): Oral history interview by Raymond Henle with Katurah and Phillips P. Brooks; p. 12, September 1, 1970, Washington, D.C.: Herbert Hoover Presidential Library, West Branch, Iowa.

...after being elected President: William Manchester, The Glory and the Dream (New York: Bantam Books, 1975), p. 23.

Some BEF officials: Waters and White, p.154

122. The commander-in-chief was subjected: Douglas, pp. 166, 171; Lisio, p. 120.

...who immediately cut off all food and water: Douglas, p. 164.

"Any man who disobeys my orders": Waters and White, p. 158.

"To hell with civil law...": Lisio, p. 121.

To help re-establish discipline: Douglas, pp. 175, 166.

123. "We made no finer friend in Washington": Waters and White, p. 69.

...who was the son of Jose Santos Zelaya: Harold Norman Denny, *Dollars for Bullets* (New York: The Dial Press, 1940), pp. 63-67; 83.

...despite severe dyslexia: Carlo D'este, *Patton, A Genius for War* (New York: HarperCollins Publishers, 1995), p. 79.

Patton fondly recalled: Herbert Molloy Mason, Jr., *The Great Pursuit* (New York: Smithmark Publishers, Inc., 1970), pp. 185-87.

124. Patton met Douglas MacArthur: William Manchester, *American Caesar* (Boston: Little, Brown & Co., 1978), pp. 101-02.

Although the War College: D'este, pp. 349-50.

Nicaragua was actually two countries: Forrest D. Colburn, *Post-Revolutionary Nicaragua* (Berkeley: University of California Press, 1986), pp. 25-27.

125. In 1901 Zelaya's father: Denny, pp. 14-32.

Now Sandino: Ibid, pp. 225-26; 313-316.

126. A rumor was circulating: Waters and White, p. 158; Douglas, pp. 217-19; Weaver, p. 184.

(The Key Men actually existed.): Letter from Thomas Jarrell to Pelham Glassford, June 25, 1932. Pelham Glassford Collection, U.C.L.A. Young Research Library. Box #14: Folder #4.

Butler confirmed: Studs Terkel, *Hard Times* (New York: Pocket Books, 1970) p. 328.

MacArthur, a staunch supporter: Manchester, p. 185.

127. Soon after Pace's arrival: Douglas, p. 224; Bernstein, p. 445.

128. In ten weeks' time: Lisio, p. 122.

"Letters received by hundreds assured me...": Waters and White, p. 173.

In a July article: Dickson and Allen, p. 152.

"What matters...if I go down fighting!": Douglas, pp. 225-26.

129. Pelham Glassford again offered: Harris Gaylord Warren, *Herbert Hoover and the Great Depression* (New York: W. W. Norton and Co., 1967), p. 232.

Each new group was infiltrated: Lisio, p. 123.

As early as June 3: Daniels, p. 102.

130. The infantry troops were barrackaded: Ibid, p. 232

About 600 soldiers: Douglas, pp. 227-31.

A new officer: Brig. Gen. Perry L. Miles, *Fallen Leaves* (unpublished). Source: MacArthur Memorial, Norfolk, Virginia.

Hurley approved Miles' request: Douglas, p. 229; William Manchester, *The Glory and the Dream*, p. 14.

Measures were quietly taken: Douglas, p. 229.

131. Six small M1917 tanks: Ibid, p. 230.

Farriers had to tap: "Old Guard Solemnly Ready for Role in History," Susan Kinzie: *Washington Post*, p. A11, June 9, 2004.

A new worry whispered: Ibid, p. 231.

132. ...Ernie Pyle had just been named: David Nichols, editor, *Ernie's America* (New York: Random House, 1989) .p. xxiii.

Ernie Pyle and his wife Jerry: Pyle and Nichols, p. xxiv. Conversation with Margie Elsberg, March, 2004.

Chapter Nine
The Death March

133. Few top Republicans: Arthur Krock, *Memoirs* (New York: Funk and Wagnalls, 1969), p. 141.

... known as the cheapest man: Arthur M. Schlesinger, Jr., *The Crisis of the Old Order* (Boston: Houghton Mifflin Co., 1957), p. 227.

134. ...Herbert Hoover was relieved: William Manchester, *The Glory and the Dream* (New York: Bantam Books, 1975), p. 49.

To counter rumors: Manchester, p. 47.

Harold Foulkrod: Jack Douglas, *Veterans on the March* (Workers Library Publishers, 1934), p. 182.

135. Many in the administration: Don Lohbeck, *Patrick J. Hurley* (Chicago: Henry Regnery Co., 1953), pp. 133, 136.

On his first night of travel: William Manchester, *The Glory and the Dream* (Bantam Books, 1975), pp. 23, 53.

Traditionally, Washington wives: Carlo D'este, Patton, *A Genius for War* (New York: HarperCollins Publishers, 1995), pp. 18, 24; Margaret Truman, *First Ladies* (New York: Random House, 1995), p. 274.

136.   Ruth Hurley was the exception: Telephone interview with Wilson Hurley, January, 2001.

For weeks military intelligence reports: Walter W. Waters and William White, *BEF* (New York: John Day & Co., 1933), p. 164.

Before the war, Robertson: Paul Dickson and Thomas B. Allen, *The Bonus Army* (New York: Walker & Co., 2004), p. 145.

Other sailors had tied: "Robertson Voices His Opinion" (*BEF News*, Vol. 1, No. G-B, July 27, 1932), p. three, courtesy MacArthur Memorial.

Surgeons kept Robertson alive: Donald J. Lisio, *The President and Protest* (New York: Fordham University Press, 1994), p. 126.

Inspired by the Oregon: Roger Daniels, *The Bonus March* (Connecticut: Greenwood Publishing Corp., 1971), p. 85.

137.   The event's carnival-like atmosphere: Douglas, p. 194.

By the time he left: Ibid, pp. 186-89.

When Robertson finally marched: Waters and White, p. 165.

138.   ...Patrick Hurley's boyhood friend Will Rogers: Telephone interview with Wilson Hurley, June, 2000.

Despite his compassion for the unemployed: John Henry Bartlett, *The Bonus March and the New Deal* (Donohue & Co., 1937), pp. 93-94.

When Patrick Hurley tried: Telephone interview with Wilson Hurley, June, 2000.

When he was met by BEF men: Douglas, p. 191.

139.   The next morning: Waters and White, p. 165.

Robertson asked if there were any laws: Lisio, p. 128.

In his role as secretary: Daniels, p. 99

140.   ...dissatisfaction with Walter Waters: Douglas, p. 176; Waters and White, p. 156.

To many of the men: Daniels. P. 120.

Both George Alman and Mike Thomas: Douglas, p. 174.

The counterfeit *BEF News*: Daniels, p. 138.

141.   A single line of 250 gray and weary men: Douglas, pp. 198.

Although Pelham Glassford's jurisdiction: Ibid, p. 130.

"You'd better have ambulances": Ibid, p. 192.

Robertson himself "collapsed": Talbott Powell, *Tattered Banners* (New York: Harcourt, Brace and Co., 1933), p. 233.

The Capitol Police turned on the lawn sprinklers: Douglas, p. 196.

142.   Using his authority: Waters and White, pp. 166-67.

Pelham Glassford was summoned: "MacArthur and the Bonus Army," Pelham D. Glassford. P. 5. Article accompanied letter to Joseph Choate, May 14, 1948. Pelham Glassford Collection, University of California, Los Angeles, Young Research Library, Box 14: Folder 4.

Glassford rushed to: Douglas, p. 199.

"Do you want to take personal responsibility …": Lisio, p. 131; Robert S. Allen and Drew Pearson (anonymous), *More Merry-Go-Round* (New York: Liveright, Inc., 1932), p. 47.

Only 60 members: Lisio, p. 160; Daniels, p. 132.

The streetcars carrying the Marines: Powell, pp. 235-36.

143.   The lieutenant leading the Marines: Douglas, pp. 161, 199.

Walter Waters returned to Washington: Ibid, p. 200.

During one speech: Douglas, p. 219.

144.   Two thousand foreigners were trapped: George Seldes, *Witness to a Century* (New York: Ballantine Books, 1987), pp. 337-38.

The 72nd Congress: Allen and Pearson, p. 47.

Waters: Douglas, p. 207

145.   "…a small but politically powerful": Glassford, pp. 3-4.

"Appoint John H. Hester...": Copy of telegram, June 28, 1932 from Cunningham to Patrick Hurley, War Department. Patrick Hurley Collection, University of Oklahoma; Box #48, Folder #6.

At 10:30 a.m. on Saturday: Daniels, p. 133.

146. Walter Waters strode: Daniels, pp. 133-34.

This unprecedented action: Waters and White, pp. 168-70.

"We have achieved a concession!": Douglas, pp. 209-10.

148. "This group will represent not just the veterans...": Powell, p. 244.

The meeting with Garner: Waters and White, p. 170.

That night a nervous Congress: Daniels, p. 136.

... when the gavel sounded at 11:10 p.m.: Douglas, p. 214; Lisio, p. 138.

Patrick Hurley called: Ibid, p. 91.

149. Trumped by Walter Waters: Douglas, p. 216.

As he had predicted: Daniels, p. 346.

That afternoon: Waters and White, pp. 181-83.

150. Immense pressure was brought on John Pace: Lisio, pp. 140-42.

...the Communists didn't care: Howard Rushmore, "Ex-Red Tells How 'Smear' of Hoover M'Arthur Started," (*New York Journal-American*, Thursday, Aug. 30, 1949.)

On the first day of the picketing: Douglas, p. 213.

The District police were forewarned: Ibid, p. 220.

This time they brought: Ibid, p. 222.

151.   Communists had tried: Lisio, p., 149.

Chapter Ten
The White Plan

152.   "The White Plan is...": Jack Douglas, *Veterans on the March*
(Workers Library Publishers, 1934), p. 236.

...another series of confusing orders: Roger Daniels, *The Bonus
March* (Connecticut: Greenwood Publishing Corp., 1971), pp.
141-43.

That same day Ulysses S. Grant III: Donald J. Lisio, *The President
and Protest* (New York: Fordham University Press, 1994), p. 144.

153.   Pelham Glassford consulted: Ibid, p. 145; Daniels, p. 142.

He notified Walter Waters: Douglas, p. 169.

Congress had adjourned: Walter W. Waters and William White,
BEF (New York: John Day & Co., 1933), pp. 176-79.

Immediately after Waters' message: Daniels, pp. 138-39.

The gradual, peaceful disbanding: Handwritten recollection
written on BEF stationary by Pelham Glassford, p. 7. Pelham
Glassford Collection, U.C.L.A., Box #14: Folder #2.

154. Herbert S. Ward: Lisio, p. 150.

Mills said that he understood: Ibid, p. 151.

Walter Waters approached Judge Payne: Waters and White, p. 191.

Patrick Hurley's hatred: Telephone interview with Wilson Hurley, June, 2000.

155. By July of 1932: Telephone interview with Wilson Hurley: November, 2000.

156. ...George Patton arrived at Ft. Myer: Martin Blumenson, *The Patton Papers*, 1885-1940 (Boston: Houghton Mifflin Co., 1972), p. 975.

The Army Chief MacArthur began: Carlo D'este, *Patton, A Genius for War* (New York: HarperCollins Publishers, 1995), p. 353.

157. ...with the help of Judge Payne: Lisio, p. 151.

As Walter Waters, Doak Carter and Herbert Ward: Letter from Herbert Ward to Patrick Hurley, August 31, 1932, confirming all details of this meeting. Patrick Hurley Collection, University of Oklahoma: Box #48, Folder #19.

157-160. ...Waters strode into the office: Waters and White, pp. 192-200. Waters' recollections agree with those of Herbert Ward.

Walter Waters was told: Ibid, p. 186.

161. George Rhine later successfully: Lisio, p. 157. Letter from Perry Heard, assistant secretary of the Treasury, to Attorney General

William Miller, Aug. 3, 1932. (Hoover Institution of War, Revolution and Peace, Stanford, CA.), Exhibit B, SA-L, "D.C. Building Program."

That same afternoon: Waters and White, p. 202.

The BEF commander was then summoned: Daniels, p. 145.

Waters had never actually met the Commissioners: Lisio, pp. 163-64.

But rather than be allowed to make his own case: Waters and White, pp. 202-04.

162.   Back and forth the superintendent went: Daniels, p. 145.

For some reason, Glassford did not give: Ibid, p. 146.

Months later, Glassford wrote: Douglas, p. 224.

At virtually the same time: Lisio, p. 159.

Records show that at least: Ibid.

163.   Due to the demands: Ibid, pp. xiv; 168.

Hoover supported the eviction: Ibid, p. 159.

Concerned that the eviction be handled: Ibid, p. 161.

After the meeting ended at 4:00 p.m.: Ibid, p. 172.

164.   President Hoover continued to fret: Gene Smith, *The Shattered Dream: Herbert Hoover and the Great Depression* (New York, William Morrow & Co., 1970), p. 16

Chapter Eleven
Riot on Pennsylvania Avenue

165. It was already stifling hot: Talbott Powell, *Tattered Banners* (New York: Harcourt, Brace and Co., 1933), p. 241.

Glassford had just called John Bartlett: John Henry Bartlett, *The Bonus March and the New Deal* (Donohue & Co., 1937), p. 20.

The half-demolished four-story building: Walter W. Waters and William White, *BEF* (New York: John Day & Co., 1933), p. 207; Bartlett, p. 9.

166. This particular area on the south side: Donald E. Press, "South of the Avenue: From Murder Bay to the Federal Triangle," *Records of the Columbia Historical Society of Washington, D.C.* (The University Press of Virginia, 1984), Vol. 51, pp. 53-54.

167. "You can sit there...": Waters and White, p. 208.

"I have in my hand..." Roger Daniels, *The Bonus March* (Connecticut: Greenwood Publishing Corp., 1971), p. 147.

...which gave them until noon: Waters and White, p. 264.

Within minutes one hundred of Glassford's: Waters and White, pp. 212-13.

Glassford's men could not: "MacArthur and the Bonus Army," Pelham D. Glassford. P. 6. Article accompanied letter to Joseph Choate, May 14, 1948. Pelham Glassford Collection, University of California, Los Angeles, Young Research Library, Box 14: Folder 4.

Several did refuse to leave: Weaver, p. 224.

168.   Then the BEF commander: Daniels, p. 148.

Precisely at noon: Waters and White, pp. 214-15; Daniels, pp. 149-50.

When they reached the rope: Donald J. Lisio, *The President and Protest* (New York: Fordham University Press, 1994), pp. 178-79.

Glassford simply stood his ground: "Glassford Calm Through-Out Riots," *Evening Star*, July 29, p. A-4.

170. A chunk of concrete hit Glassford in the side: Lisio, pp. 178-79; Daniels, p. 150; Powell, p. 241.

Waters' own bodyguards: Waters and White, p. 215

Glassford climbed upon a pile: Ibid

Police Lieutenant Ira Keck watched from the crowd: Lisio, p. 181.

Keck was a career officer who deeply resented: Daniels, p. 152.

Glassford, his uniform torn: Waters and White, pp. 215-16.

171.   At 12:34 p.m.: *Evening Star*, July 29.

Glassford said that he did not: Ibid, 182-83; Daniels, 151.

Unannounced, Crosby showed up: Lisio, p. 196-97.

172. At the same time that Patrick Hurley: Lisio, p. 184; Daniels, p. 163.

After he finished talking: Ibid, p. 332.

Both units were already on high alert: Martin Blumenson, *The Patton Papers*, 1885-1940 (Boston: Houghton Mifflin Co., 1972), p. 976; Daniels, p. 161.

Between 2:15 and 2:40, MacArthur: Daniels, p. 332.

173. Perhaps 1,000 men were gathered: Daniels, p. 154.

At 1:45 pm, Pelham Glassford: Daniels, p. 153.

…Hushka was an unemployed butcher: "Riot Victim Left Work at Chicago," *Evening Star,* July 29, P. A-10xx.; Waters and White, p. 217..

Metropolitan Police Officer George Shinault: Lisio, p. 185; Daniels, pp. 153-55.

Other eyewitnesses said: Harris Gaylord Warren, *Herbert Hoover and the Great Depression* (New York: W. W. Norton & Company, Inc., 1967), p. 233; "List of BEF Riot Victims," *Washington Herald*, July 29, 1932, p. 1.

…jumped upon and throttled: Oral history interview by Raymond Henle with Byron Price, p. 28; March 21, 1969, Chestertown, MD: Herbert Hoover Presidential Library, West Branch, Iowa.

174. Of what happened next: Waters & White, p. 217.

Officer Shinault unholstered: Bartlett, p. 45.

175. Seconds later: "Second Outbreak Brings Out Army," *Evening Star,* July 29. p. A-4.

"Stop that shooting!": Ibid; Daniels, p. 154.

Eddie Atwell and Doak Carter: Waters and White, p. 222.

In the confusion following the shootings: Daniels, p. 149.

176. Eisenhower urged him not to lead the troops: Lisio, p. 193.

"There is incipient revolution in the air": William Manchester, *The Glory and the Dream* (Bantam Books, 1975), p. 13.

He told Eisenhower: Susan Eisenhower, *Mrs. Ike* (New York: Farrar, Straux and Giroux, 1996); p. 119.

Ira Keck rushed again: Lisio, p. 186

177. "The President: The Commissioner…" : Daniels, p. 163.

178. Oddly, the commissioners' request: Lisio, p. 188.

Even as Hoover read: Daniels, p. 332.

Down-river…Paul Dickson and Thomas B. Allen, *The Bonus Army* (New York: Walker & Company, 2004), p. 171.

Dwight Eisenhower arrived: *Eisenhower,* pp. 119-20; conversation with John Eisenhower, Easton, Maryland; May, 2001.

179. …from the Emergency Hospital: *Evening Star,* July 29, p, 2.

Patrick Hurley called President Hoover: Lisio, p. 197.

Hurley had lobbied the president: Oral history by Raymond Henle with James H. Douglas, Jr., pp. 18-19; October 13, 1969, Chicago, Ill.: Herbert Hoover Presidential Library, West Branch, Iowa

Hurley and MacArthur convened...at 2:47: Ibid, pp. 197-98.

180. Although there is no transcript: Ibid, pp. 198-99.

What about Winship's plan? Daniels, p. 162.

One more thing: Theodore Joslin, *Hoover Off the Record* (New York, 1934), p. 268.

181. Hurley returned to his office: Lisio, p. 201.

...and changed the time: Paul Dickson and Thomas B. Allen, *The Bonus Army* (New York: Walker & Co., 2004), p. 328.

Hurley had no choice: Patrick Hurley memo to General Douglas MacArthur, Chief of Staff, U.S. Army, July 28, 1932, 2:55 pm. R6-14: Papers of Jean MacArthur; Personal Corresp., "March, 1971," courtesy of MacArthur Memorial, Norfolk, Virginia.

Tom Henry of the *Washington Star*: Daniels. P. 165.

Chapter Twelve
The Blue Tin Canisters

182. Pelham Glassford found: Roger Daniels, *The Bonus March* (Connecticut: Greenwood Publishing Corp., 1971), p. 167.

The president has just now informed me: Patrick Hurley memo to General Douglas MacArthur, Chief of Staff, U.S. Army, July 28, 1932, 2:55 pm. R6-14: Papers of Jean MacArthur; Personal Corresp., "March, 1971," courtesy of MacArthur Memorial, Norfolk, Virginia.

183.   In his phrase: Donald J. Lisio, *The President and Protest* (New York: Fordham University Press, 1994), p. 200.

"We are going to break the back...": Ibid, p. 204.

184.   "...a demonstration of force": "MacArthur and the Bonus Army," Pelham D. Glassford. P. 8. Article accompanied letter to Joseph Choate, May 14, 1948. Pelham Glassford Collection, University of California, Los Angeles, Young Research Library, Box 14: Folder 4.

"...received orders from the president": Ibid.

...and he spent the rest of his life: In 1948 Patrick Hurley asked Bonner Fellers at the Republican National Committee to look into what the Communists who had been leaders during the Bonus March were up to in recent years. Walter Eicher (who climbed the tree) could no longer be found; John Pace renounced Communism in 1935 and was a deputy sherrif in Centerville, Tennessee; Emanuel Leven ran unsuccessfully for the state senate and Congress from New York, moved to California and fell out of sight. Samuel Stember left to fight with the Loyalists in Spain and disappeared. Only James Ford was still listed as an active member but it was reported that the Party could not persuade him to attend meetings. Telegram Fellers to Hurley: "Research Division unable as yet to identify Communists in Bonus Army with present or later Communist activities but research being continued." September 18, 1948. Patrick Hurley Collection, University of Oklahoma Western History Collections, Box #47, Folder #3.

Glassford returned to the eviction site: Jack Douglas, *Veterans on the March* (Workers Library Publishers, 1934), p. 5.

...and the two hundred cavalry: Martin Blumenson, *The Patton Papers*, 1885-1940 (Boston: Houghton Mifflin Co., 1972), p. 977.

...the crowd appeared to be in a holiday: "Veterans Ouster Drama to Crowd," *Evening Star*, July 29, 1932, p. A-4.

185. General Perry L. Miles: Brig. Gen. Perry L. Miles, *Fallen Leaves: Memoirs of an Old Soldier* (Wuerth Publishing Co, 1961), p. 307.

186. When the crowd of 10,000: William Manchester, *The Glory and the Dream* (Bantam Books, 1975), p. 15.

He was busy explaining: Miles, p. 307.

From inside one of the tanks: "Tanks Are Surprise," *Evening Star*, July 29, 1932, p. A-4.

187. From his suite at the Ebbitt: Walter W. Waters and William White, *BEF* (New York: John Day & Co., 1933), pp. 239-40.

From the perspective of crowd control: Daniels, p.168.

Dozens of reporters: *MacArthur*, PBS documentary.

188. When the cavalry reached the Third Street block: Douglas, pp. 7-8.

...the 200 horsemen reached down: *MacArthur*, PBS Documentary

189. The soldiers had been trained: Ibid, p. 240; Miles, p. 308

As a result, the first wave: John Henry Bartlett, *The Bonus March and the New Deal* (Donohue & Co., 1937), p. 38; Miles, p. 308

The gas had a sickly sweet odor: Douglas, p. 238.

The veterans cursed and shoved: Bartlett, p. 65.

Dozens of people: *Washington Herald*, July 29, p. 1.

…among them Senator Hiram Bingham: Manchester, p. 14.

Now he was in the phalanx: Bartlett, p. 33.

190. There was a chorus of loud boos: Lisio, p. 206.

Around the same time: Waters and White, p. 227.

Army Chief Douglas MacArthur: *MacArthur*, PBS documentary.

191. Waiting in his office, room 308: Waters and White, p. 227.

192. Patton, who was briefly unseated: Blumenson, p. 978; Carlo D'este, *Patton, A Genius for War* (New York: HarperCollins Publishers, 1995), p. 353.

The infantry advanced as they were taught: Douglas, p. 8.

Two trolley cars: "Trolly Riders Trapped in Gas," *Washington Herald*, July 29, 1932, p. 2.

193. Franklin Delano Roosevelt sat: Donald J. Lisio, *The President and Protest* (New York: Fordham University Press, 1994), p. 285.

Roosevelt made the same observation: Daniels, P. 218.
FDR expressed anguish: Manchester, p. 18.

(General Perry Miles later...): Miles, p. 308.

Once the Pennsylvania Avenue: *MacArthur*, PBS Documentary.

The troops spread out: Miles, P. 309.

194. Several veterans were chased: Douglas, pp. 237-38.

A reporter from the *Daily News*: Waters and White, p. 230.

MacArthur's main body of troops: Manchester, p. 15.

Chapter Thirteen
Anacostia Flats

195. In Camp Marks: Walter W. Waters and William White, *BEF* (New York: John Day & Co., 1933), p. 231.

At 5:30 p.m.: Donald J. Lisio, *The President and Protest* (New York: Fordham University Press, 1994), p. 209-10.

Still eager to be part of the action: Telephone interview with Wilson Hurley, May 9, 2000.

197. Hoover assured Borah: Waters and White, p. 232.

MacArthur, Eisenhower and other: Daniels, p. 171.

This time Moseley: Roger Daniels, *The Bonus March* (Connecticut: Greenwood Publishing Corp., 1971), p. 171.

The next day, laughing: Oral History interview, Tape 256, Side A., F. Trubee Davison, A. Henle interviewer. Herbert Hoover Presidential Library. Also, in his unpublished memoirs, *One*

Soldier's Story, p. 142, Moseley later wrote: "As I now recall, Col. Wright reported to me that the troops had not crossed but were advancing on the bridge." Patrick Hurley Collection, University of Oklahoma Western History Collection, Box #48, Folder #6.

MacArthur told Eisenhower to meet: Dwight Eisenhower, *At Ease* (Doubleday, 1967), p. 217

Wright later testified: Paul Dickson and Thomas B. Allen, *The Bonus Army* (New York: Walker & Company, 2004), p. 180.

198.   ...ran across the field: Handwritten recollection written on BEF stationary by Pelham Glassford, p. 8. Pelham Glassford Collection, U.C.L.A., Box #14: Folder #2.

199.   "If he is going to be killed: "Flame and Sword Wipe Out Hovels," *Evening Star*, July 29, 1932, p. A-2

"You wouldn't expect us..." "D.C. Chiefs Keep 14-Hour Watch," *Evening Star*, July 29, 1932, p. A-4. Also, in his unpublished memoir *One Soldier's Story*, p. 143, George Van Horn Moseley wrote that the order from Hurley "resulted in putting in operation a plan which had been carefully worked out." Hurley Collection, Box #48, Folder #6.

The attack on Camp Marks: "From Riot to Rout," Evening Star, July 29, 1932, p. A-4.

The infantry crossed first: Ibid.

200.   The big gospel tent: John Henry Bartlett, *The Bonus March and the New Deal* (Donohue & Co., 1937), p. 51.

Out on the Potomac: Article by Mrs. Elbridge C. Purdy, Dec. 29, 1975—RG-15: Contributions from the Public, Box 11, F. 7. MacArthur Memorial, Norfolk, Va.

201. Pressed on by the soldiers: Ibib, p. 234; Jack Douglas, *Veterans on the March* (Workers Library Publishers, 1934),, pp. 246-47.

202. ...everything had been arranged for a happy ending: Glassford, handwritten recollection, p.

...where they stayed the night: "Veterans Start for Pennsylvania," *Evening Star*, July 29, 1932, p. A-2xx.

...on the old court house: "Veterans Go on Northward Trek, Still Dazed by Defeat," *Evening Star*, July 29, 1932, p. A-2.

203. Instead, Waters left BEF: Douglas, p. 243.

...including from the Lincoln study: Robert S. Allen and Drew Pearson (anonymous), *More Merry-Go-Round* (New York: Liveright, Inc., 1932), p. 51.

204. As they left Anacostia Flats: Dwight D. Eisenhower, *At Ease* (New York: Doubleday & Company, Inc., 1967), pp. 217-18.

"Most of you saw...": Herbert Hoover Archives, Presidential File, Box 23: "Bonus March—D. MacArthur." C. of Press Release from Press Section, War Department, 11:00 p.m., July 29, 1932. Hoover Institution, Stanford, CA.

A reporter asked who had fired the camp: Ibid

206. ...Colonel George Patton sat: Carlo D'este, *Patton, A Genius for War* (New York: HarperCollins Publishers, 1995), p. 354; Paul Dickson and Thomas B. Allen, *The Bonus Army* (New York:

Walker & Company, 2004), p. 194.

In another part of the camp: Lisio, p. 221.

...Hurley and MacArthur had reported: Ibid, pp. 217-18; Davison interview, p. 3.

207. ...with some visible discomfort: Oral history by Raymond Henle with F. Trubee Davison, p. 2; Locust Valley, N.Y., September 14, 1969: Herbert Hoover Presidential Library, West Branch, Iowa.

The next morning: Ibid, pp. 227-28; summary of press reports on bonus march episode, *Evening Star*, July 29, 1932, p. A-5.

208. A small airplane droned: Fred Kaplan, *Gore Vidal* (New York: Doubleday, 1999), p. 48.

Chapter Fourteen
The Cover-Up

209. During the night: Roger Daniels, *The Bonus March* (Connecticut: Greenwood Publishing Corp., 1971),, p. 177; Jack Douglas, *Veterans on the March* (Workers Library Publishers, 1934), p. 252.

Those squatters would be sent: "Troops Renew Their Gas Attack," *Evening Star*, July 29, 1932, P. A-2; "Veterans Start for Pennsylvania," Ibid.

210. At 9:00 a.m., John Bartlett called: Walter W. Waters and William White, *BEF* (New York: John Day & Co., 1933), p. 229.

Walter Waters, who had just: Ibid, p. 240-41; Paul Dickson and Thomas B. Allen, *The Bonus Army* (New York: Walker & Company, 2004), p. 186.

Yet another group of veterans: Donald J. Lisio, *The President and Protest* (New York: Fordham University Press, 1994), p. 223-24.

211. Mamie Eisenhower wrote of these: Susan Eisenhower, *Mrs. Ike* (New York: Farrar, Straus and Giroux, 1997), pp. 121-22.

212. On the morning of July 29: Letter from Herbert Hoover to Commissioner Luther Reichelderfer, "The Depression Papers of Herbert Hoover.

214. That same afternoon: Lisio, p.
Glassford's statement was picked up: "Glassford Denies He Asked Army Aid," *Evening Star*, Friday, July 29, 1932.

215. "...would be bragging...": Lisio, pp. 233-34; Russell D. Buhite, *Patrick J. Hurley and American Foreign Policy* (Cornell University Press, 1973), pp. 52-53.

For the first few days: Buhite, p. 57.

Patrick Hurley basked in the positive attention: Lisio, p. xiv.

To blunt any negative: Daniels, pp. 187-88.

216. ...Herbert Hoover sensed: Buhite, p. 58.

Walter Waters continued: Douglas, p. 254.

Waters had received a letter: Waters and White, pp. 243-44.

217.   Patrick Hurley's campaign of misinformation: Daniels, p. 176.

218.   In response to these distortions: Ibid, p. 180.

Chapter Fifteen
Johnstown

219.   Many walked: Donald J. Lisio, *The President and Protest* (New York: Fordham
University Press, 1994), p. 222; Jack Douglas, *Veterans on the March* (Workers Library Publishers, 1934), p. 183.

Mayor Eddie McCloskey:: Lisio, p. 224.

McCloskey had been wooed: Jack Douglas, *Veterans on the March* (Workers Library Publishers, 1934), p. 259-61.

The site that the Mayor made available: Ibid, p. 258.

220.   Walter Waters still had: Walter W. Waters and William White, *BEF* (New York: John Day & Co., 1933), pp. 245-46.

At the rough camp Waters found: Roger Daniels, *The Bonus March* (Connecticut: Greenwood Publishing Corp., 1971), p. 183.

For years after: John Henry Bartlett, *The Bonus March and the New Deal* (Donohue & Co., 1937), p. 117.

When word filtered: Daniels, p. 185.

William Hushka, winner: Waters and White, pp. 246-48.

221. Waters' plan: Douglas, p.: 263.

Out of options: Waters and White, p. 249.

Carter, who had assumed: Daniels, p. 186.

Faced with Carter's mutiny: Waters and White, pp. 254-55.

222. Nine dismal days: Lisio, p. 225.

Forty-three men: Daniels, p. 186-87.

Back in Washington: Waters and White, 218-19.

...and the other a "personal" gun: Daniels, p. 189.

Shinault acted as though: Waters and White, pp. 218-19.

223. As the grand jury's hearings: Lisio, pp. 241, 148.

J. Edgar Hoover was particularly: Richard Gid Powers, *Secrecy and Power, The Life of J. Edgar Hoover* (New York: The Free Press, 1987), pp. 167-68.

224. The president insisted that the Bureau: Lisio, p. 250.

The Administration was elated to learn: Daniels, p. 198.

The grand jury asked: Lisio, p. 249.

Major Dwight Eisenhower: Daniels, p. 276.

225. The report was replete: Daniels, pp. 291-307.

226. ...the Khaki Shirts' movement: Douglas, p. 283.20

The election could result: Arthur Krock, *Memoirs* (New York: Funk and Wagnalls, 1968), p. 138.; Clayton E. Cramer, "An American Coup d'Etat?" (*History Today*, November, 1995).

The national convention of the American Legion: Daniels, pp. 199-200.23

Mitchell telegraphed a copy: Patrick Hurley Collection, University of Oklahoma Western History Collections, Norman, OK. Box #48, Folder #15

227.   Glassford retaliated again: Lisio, pp. 254-55.

Nor had the veterans been criminals: Daniels, p. 204.

In appreciation of his character: *Washington Post*, Sept. 17, 1932.

Eddie Gosnell, the "official" photographer: Douglas, p. 235.

228.   … and moved to a small apartment: Douglas, 281.

During his nine months: Ibid, p. 280; Talbott Powell, *Tattered Banners* (New York: Harcourt, Brace and Co., 1933), p. 244.

229.   …cities across the country: Waters and White, p. 253.

In a desperate attempt to reclaim: Daniels, p. 335.

Waters was asked to make a speech: Douglas, p. 281.

A conciliatory but defiant Hurley: Ibid, p. 206.

"Now you talk about…" Patrick Hurley Collection, Box #48, Folder #20.

At the convention: Powell, pp. 247, 257.

230.   Walter Waters got a break: Douglas, p. 281.

As one of his final acts: Lisio, p. 193; *Evening Star*, January 22, 1935.

Under pressure, Pelham Glassford: Daniels, p. 208

During his eleven months of service: Ibid, p. 271.

231.   The first in a series of eight: Lisio, p. 265..

...for which Glassford was paid $600: Lisio, p. 266.

...arranged by his friend Cissy Patterson: Daniels, p. 208

These widely read articles: Daniels, p. 209.

Hoover made a last desperate: Lisio, p. 276.

On election day... Paul Dickson and Thomas B. Allen, *The Bonus Army* (New York: Walker & Company, 2004), p. 201.

231.   In November: Interview with Richard Baker, Senate Historian, April 14, 2000.

Prior to his election: William Manchester, *The Glory and the Dream* (New York: Bantam Books, 1975), p. 80

Nearly 50% of the senators: Waters and White, p. 131

232.   Herbert Hoover left the White House: William Manchester, p. 14; Arthur M. Schlesinger, Jr., *The Crisis of the Old Order* (Boston: Houghton Mifflin Co., 1957), p. 444.

He sat on the platform: Manchester, p. 77.

Senate leader Burton Wheeler: Ibid, p. 80.

Chapter Sixteen
Final Chapters

233. That event: Margaret Truman, *First Ladies* (New York: Random House, 1995), p. 273.

All of Patrick Hurley's: Telephone interviews with Wilson Hurley, June, 2000; November, 2000.

...and a surprising friendship: Don Lohbeck, *Patrick J. Hurley* (Chicago: Henry Regnery Company, 1956), pp. 147-48; 153.32

(When he resigned from that post): Arthur Herman, *Joseph McCarthy* (New York: The Free Press, 2000), pp. 48, 51, 96-97. Telephone interview with Wilson Hurley, June, 2001.

Roosevelt supposedly asked: Russell D. Buhite, *Patrick J. Hurley and American Foreign Policy* (Ithica, N.Y.: Cornell University Press, 1973), p. 175.

234. His son Wilson: Telephone interview with Wilson Hurley, November, 2000.

Douglas MacArthur stayed on: William Manchester, *American Caesar* (Boston: Little, Brown and Company, 1978), p. 159. William Manchester, *The Glory and the Dream* (New York: Bantam Books, 1975). p. 50; Dwight D. Eisenhower, *At Ease* (New York: Doubleday & Company, Inc., 1967), p. 223.

MacArthur ran: Manchester, p. 682.

Ironically, Taft died: Herman, p. 209.
...helping to oversee the internment...: Paul Dickson and Thomas B. Allen, *The Bonus Army* (New York: Walker & Company, 2004), p. 293.

MacArthur died: Manchester, p. 706; Perret, p. 586.

Dwight Eisenhower's attention to detail: Stephen E. Ambrose, *The Victors* (New York: Simon and Schuster, 1998), p. 36.

235. George Patton's impetuous nature: Martin Blumenson, *Patton* (New York: William Morrow, 1985), pp. 181, 198; Carlo D'este, *Patton, A Genius for War* (New York: HarperCollins Publishers, 1995), p. 551-52. Charles M. Province, *The Unknown Patton* (New York: Bonanza Books, 1983), pp. 71-74.

Young Gene Vidal: Fred Kaplan, *Gore Vidal* (New York: Doubleday, 1999), p. 137.

After the War's end: Martin Blumenson, *Patton* (New York: Wiliam Morrow, 1985), p. 271; 279-86; 292.

Following the 1932 elections: Daniel, p. 285.

236. Walter Waters: Dickson and Allen, p. 299.

Printed in the United States
56380LVS00003B/181-231